FICTION   Garcia-Aguilera,
GARCIAAG   Carolina.

          Bitter sugar.

WITHDRAWN

DATE			

W9-BUC-235

Bitter Sugar

LUPE SOLANO MYSTERIES
by CAROLINA GARCIA-AGUILERA

BLOODY WATERS

BLOODY SHAME

BLOODY SECRETS

A MIRACLE IN PARADISE

HAVANA HEAT

CAROLINA GARCIA-AGUILERA

WILLIAM MORROW 75 YEARS OF PUBLISHING

An Imprint of HarperCollins*Publishers*

Bitter Sugar

A LUPE SOLANO MYSTERY

HarperCollins books may be purchased for educational, business, or sales promotional use. For information please write: Special Markets Department, HarperCollins Publishers Inc., 10 East 53rd Street, New York, NY 10022.

FIRST EDITION

Designed by Shubhani Sarkar

Printed on acid-free paper

Library of Congress Cataloging-in-Publication Data

Garcia-Aguilera, Carolina.
    Bitter sugar : a Lupe Solano mystery / by Carolina Garcia-Aguilera.—1st ed.
    p. cm.
    ISBN 0-380-97781-8
    1. Solano, Lupe (Fictitious character)—Fiction. 2. Women private investigators—Florida—Miami—Fiction. 3. Cuban Americans—Fiction. 4. Miami (Fla.)—Fiction.
    I. Title.

PS3557.A71124 B5 2001
813'.54—dc21
                                                                          2001030085

01 02 03 04 05 QW 10 9 8 7 6 5 4 3 2 1

Finally, and with integrity
Cuba breaks the hangman's noose
which oppressed her
And haughtily shakes her free head!
JOSÉ MARTÍ

I personally have come to feel that nationalization is, at best, a cumbersome instrument. It does not seem to make the state any stronger, yet it enfeebles private enterprise. Even more importantly, any attempt at wholesale nationalization would obviously hamper the principal point of our economic platform— industrialization at the fastest possible rate. For this purpose, foreign investments will always be welcome and secure here.

—Fidel Castro,
Coronet magazine, February 1958

Within eighteen months of Castro's taking power in Cuba, 90 percent of Cuban industry had been nationalized, without compensation to the rightful owners. On May 17, 1959, the Agrarian Reform Law expropriated farmlands over one thousand acres, and forbade foreign land ownership.

ACKNOWLEDGMENTS

I WOULD LIKE TO THANK MY EDITOR, JENNIFER
Sawyer Fisher, for her patience and understanding, and,
of course, her superb editing skills. Quinton Skinner
deserves my gratitude not only for his ability to perfectly
channel Lupe, but for his friendship and support throughout the years.

It was necessary to conduct an enormous amount of
research to be able to write a book such as this. Although
my father, Carlos Garcia-Beltran, descended from generations of sugar growers, passed away more than fifteen
years ago, he instilled in me a love and respect for the
business. I hope I honor his memory by writing this book.
To my father's friends and colleagues who patiently
explained to me the different aspects of sugar growing, I
thank you for your knowledge and expertise. I am indebted
to Dr. Max Castro for his insight into all matters relating
to Cuba. To the gang on South Beach, in particular August,
Parzham, David, and Andrew, *gracias* for your friendship,
and support. To Adrienne, thank you for assuming the
role of my unofficial publicist, and for the many wonderful evenings at your house.

As always, I owe a debt I can never repay to my family.
My husband, Robert K. Hamshaw, in his own quiet, unas-

suming way, is responsible for a great deal of my success. My mother, Lourdes Aguilera de Garcia, has stood by me through thick and thin, although I'm sure I still, even now, astound her on occasion. My sister, Sara O'Connell, and my brother, Carlos A. Garcia, have been unfailingly supportive of me, and I thank them for that. My nephew, Richard O'Connell, is special to me in ways that I cannot properly express.

But it is to my daughters, Sarita, Antonia, and Gabby, that I am most grateful. Thank you for all the book fairs, conferences, speeches, tours, interviews, etc., that you have accompanied me to, although I'm sure you'd rather be someplace else (except for the trips to L.A.). I realize it's not easy having me for a mother, and you three handle it beautifully. Most of all, thank you for being the inspiration for me to write. I want to leave a legacy to you that you can be proud of. If I've succeeded, I'm satisfied.

Sarita, Antonia, and Gabby, you make me want to wake up in the morning, and, at the end of the day, that's a priceless gift you, my daughters, have given me.

¡Gracias! ¡Gracias! ¡Gracias!

"LUPE, CAN I SPEAK WITH YOU FOR A MINUTE?"

I started at the sound of Papi's voice calling out to me. I was sitting alone at one of the tables on the terrace behind our house, enjoying a quiet breakfast and reading the newspaper. I had just closed my eyes to enjoy the early-morning breeze wafting over me from Biscayne Bay.

"Papi!" I called back to him in surprise. Papi usually left for his office at the crack of dawn, and I'd assumed he had gone before I got up. I folded the *Miami Herald* and rose to greet him.

"*Buenos días,* Lupe," Papi said.

"Care for some *café con leche*?" I tempted him. "Aida made it particularly strong this morning."

That was an understatement. I half expected the bottom of my cup to suddenly give out. I watched Papi struggle for a moment over whether or not he should accept my offer—his cardiologist had told him not to drink so much coffee. That advice might be fine for some, but as far as I was concerned, it didn't apply to Cubans. Coffee brings us so much pleasure that it was inconceivable to me that it could really do us any harm.

"Osvaldo," I called out. I figured I'd make it easy on Papi and take the decision out of his hands. "Would you please bring Papi a *café con leche*?"

"*Gracias*, Lupe," Papi said with a sly little smile.

"Here, sit, Papi." I patted the cushioned seat of the chair next to mine. "What a beautiful morning, no?"

"*Sí, hija*. It is very nice." Papi took off his glasses, pulled a spotless handkerchief out of his pocket, and began wiping the lenses clean. As usual, he was wearing a white *guayabera*, the long-sleeved linen shirt favored by most Cuban men. I could almost hear it crinkle as Papi leaned back in his chair; Aida starched Papi's shirts so stiffly that they could stand up in the closet themselves, without the benefit of coat hangers.

Papi let his gaze wander off over the water, and for a second I had an impulse to ask him if there was something wrong. But then Osvaldo appeared carrying a silver tray with an oversized white porcelain saucer and cup filled to the brim with steaming *café con leche*. Osvaldo glared at me as he placed the tray gently in front of Papi.

"*Gracias*, Osvaldo," Papi said, looking at the cup of coffee with undisguised pleasure.

I looked up and caught another dagger from Osvaldo. I knew how much Osvaldo wanted to keep my father around as long as possible, and he felt that by openly encouraging Papi to have coffee, I was cutting short my father's life. Osvaldo had suffered an irreplaceable loss when Mami died, and I knew he didn't want to endure such an emotional blow again. I could understand his strong feelings on the matter—when you're more than eighty years old, you don't want to keep burying loved ones who are younger than you.

The thing was, I wanted Papi to live a long life as much as anyone, and I felt every bit as strongly as Osvaldo about it. But I also knew that Papi loved life's little pleasures the same way I did. A cup of good coffee, an occasional cigar,

Bitter Sugar

a glass of scotch—for Papi these things in moderation made life worth living. Being a total sensualist, I understood completely.

I gave Osvaldo my most charming smile. I saw his eyes soften a bit, not much, but enough for me to know that I had been temporarily forgiven until my next transgression. Osvaldo had been close to me for all of my twenty-eight years, so he knew about my basic disregard for most of life's rules.

Papi blew into his coffee cup before taking his first sip. His breath moved the salt-and-pepper of his mustache. I didn't like the preoccupied look on his face. I was sure now that something was troubling him. But I knew better than to pressure him when he was like this.

We sat together in comfortable silence, watching the sunlight brighten on the waters and refract into shining crescents. A few pelicans were perched on the channel markers, warming up and checking out the minnows skimming the water's surface.

My strategy proved to be the right one. After about a minute of quiet, Papi cleared his throat and shifted in his chair.

"Lupe, you know my friend Ramón," he said.

"Of course I know Tío Ramón." I referred to Papi's childhood schoolmate with the honorific conferred upon close friends who, although not related by blood, were considered as close as family.

"Well, Ramón has become involved in a situation that has turned out to be quite complicated." Papi was choosing his words carefully and looking down into his folded hands as he spoke. And from his concerned tone of voice, I knew that in this case "complicated" did not mean good things for Tío Ramón.

"I'm sorry to hear that, Papi," I said. "What's the problem?"

Papi straightened up, took a sip of his *café con leche*, and looked away from me out to the bay. It was obvious that he was hesitant about bringing up the subject of his good friend to me, and I supposed his sudden interest in what was going on in Biscayne Bay wasn't entirely unexpected. I looked out there as well, just in time to see a pelican flying low. The bird flew gracefully and easily over the waves, and I watched him open his beak, drop down, and envelop one of the fish swimming dangerously close to the surface of the water.

"You know Ramón's family was in the sugar business in Cuba, right?" Papi finally asked, as though there had been no break in our conversation.

I had to think for a second before I answered.

"They had some mills and refineries, didn't they?" I asked.

"Some!" Papi burst out laughing. "They had five. And they were some of the largest and best managed in Cuba. There were three in Oriente, and two in Camagüey."

I had a vague knowledge of Tío Ramón's family's business, but not enough to contribute anything to what Papi had told me.

Papi suddenly stopped chuckling and looked me straight in the eye. I stiffened in my chair. I hadn't seen that look from Papi since I was a sophomore in high school; I'd tried to lie my way out of explaining why Osvaldo had found me nearly impaled on the branches of the royal palm tree outside my bedroom window at four o'clock in the morning on a school night.

"Lupe, Ramón needs help." Papi sighed; I could see how hard this was for him. "I told him to call you."

I almost dropped my cup of *café con leche*. Never in the eight years I'd worked as a private investigator had Papi sent me a referral. And now he was asking me to help one of his oldest and dearest friends—his best friend, really. I was torn. I was proud that Papi entrusted me with Ramón's problem, but I also was terrified over the possible ramifications if I screwed up.

"Sure, no problem," I said somberly. "I hope I can help him."

"*Gracias,*" Papi whispered.

"*Gracias,* Papi, for having Tío Ramón contact me."

I was truly humbled that my father had paid me the compliment of his confidence and trust. I always knew Papi was proud of me, but I had thought his pride was the usual sort that parents felt for their children's accomplishments. It wasn't until that moment, though, that I realized Papi thought I was good at what I did.

Papi stood up, leaned over and kissed my cheek. For all his years, he moved like a man twenty years younger.

"You should get a call from him this morning," Papi said, fixing me with a warm look.

He waved good-bye and went inside, leaving me and the pelicans to digest our breakfasts.

2

I PARKED MY MERCEDES AND WALKED SLOWLY along the path leading to the cottage that housed Solano Investigations. As I neared the front door, I could hear the distinct sound of pots and pans banging through the open window. I groaned. This meant that Leonardo—my cousin/spiritual adviser/office manager/overseer of my personal and professional life—was in the kitchen concocting something. No doubt it was a panacea to enhance the quality of life for those of us he considered less spiritually developed—the walking wounded of the world.

I was more than a little irritated as I opened the front door and walked into the reception area. It hadn't been that long since Leo had almost gotten us raided by the DEA. He had been mixing marijuana into a pulp created from the fruit of the avocado tree growing in our backyard, claiming that the resulting potion would enhance anyone's sex life. I secretly admired his entrepreneurial spirit—he'd mixed up a ton of the stuff, and was even thinking of calling it *Avojuana*. But not knowing how best to get through to my cousin that he was sitting on a stash that could land us both in prison, one night I ordered him to dig a hole in the garden and bury it there after dark. I hated to admit it, but the grass that had grown over the filled-in hole was remarkably green, and definitely more lush than the rest of the yard—which comprised mostly sorry-looking weeds. Maybe Leonardo had been on to something—not to mention *on something*—but it wasn't worth determining the efficacy of his product only to spend some time away courtesy of the federal government.

"Leo," I called out. *"¡Buenos días!"*

"Hi, Lupe," my cousin called out from the kitchen. "Come in here. I want to show you something."

I tried to hide my reluctance as I put my purse down on the sofa across from Leonardo's desk and went into the kitchen. I blinked when I saw my cousin standing over the stove wearing a white chef's hat on his head, along with a gingham blue-and-white-checked apron with three-tiered flounces at the hem. He looked like a midwestern housewife on acid.

"What're you cooking?" I asked. "I smell crème brûlée."

White spatulas in each hand, Leonardo gave me an excited look. "I think I've discovered the cure for wrinkles," he said with an attempt at gravity that barely disguised his unhinged glee.

I peered inside a pan filled with a dark brown liquid that was bubbling away on the stove top. Now that I was closer, the fumes smelled kind of weird—like some kind of nutty aroma mixed with scalded milk. As usual, I had no earthly idea what my cousin was talking about. I couldn't imagine putting that stuff on my skin—or worse, ingesting it—without suffering serious repercussions.

Fortunately the telephone rang. Leonardo rested the spatulas on the countertop, lowered the heat on the stove, sauntered out of the kitchen to his desk, and sat down calmly, answering on the sixth ring. I gave thanks to God and the Virgin that video telephones hadn't expanded into everyday use—if anyone saw whom they were dealing with when they called Solano Investigations, we would have been out of business a long time ago.

"It's for you," Leo said, putting a hand over the mouthpiece.

"Who is it?"

"Tío Ramón."

I rushed into my office to take the call. Papi hadn't been kidding. Ramón was calling first thing in the morning.

"Tío Ramón," I said as I picked up the phone. *"Buenos días. ¿Cómo estás?"*

"Ay, Lupe, my child." Tío Ramón sighed. I was shocked by how old and tired he sounded. Tío Ramón was usually in good spirits, with a sort of manly energy that came through even over the telephone. "I am not too well. Not too well at all."

"Papi said there was something you wished to speak with me about," I said as gently as I could.

"Ay, Lupe. Sí." Ramón almost moaned in response. "I hope that perhaps you can help me." He took such a deep breath that I was worried he was going to choke on it. "Your papi said that's what you do. You help people with their problems."

Tío Ramón was making me sound like Dr. Ruth, Judge Judy, Dr. Joyce Brothers, and Merlin the Magician all rolled into one.

"I try to help people, Tío Ramón," I said delicately. "I think we should meet in person so we can talk about what's troubling you."

"Sí, you're right." Tío Ramón spoke in such a soft, hushed voice that I had trouble hearing him. "What time should I expect you today, Lupe?"

It took me a couple of seconds to realize that I was going to be conducting this interview at Ramón's home rather than at my office. I really shouldn't have been at all surprised. Tío Ramón was an old-guard Cuban. People went to him, and not vice versa—even if he was the one asking for help. Our age and gender difference also made it a foregone conclusion that I would be the one going to see him.

I glanced at my schedule for the day. All I had planned was writing up some cases I had recently closed so that Leonardo could calculate hours for billing and send out invoices to our clients. He had been after me for a couple of weeks to get this paperwork done.

"Would two o'clock be convenient?" I asked.

"Two o'clock would be fine, Lupe," Tío Ramón said. "I'll be expecting you then."

I heard the soft click on the line that indicated Tío Ramón had terminated our conversation. I had known and loved Tío Ramón all my life. His one characteristic that never changed was an expectation that his authority was unquestioned.

I hung up the phone and sat down behind my desk. I looked out the window at the avocado tree in the yard and saw that the family of parrots who lived in it had embarked on a new architectural project. They were using twigs, leaves, and small branches to make a structure that resembled the Leaning Tower of Pisa. They had already made elaborate edifices that, to me, looked like the Eiffel Tower and the Roman Colosseum. A couple of months ago I'd brought a book on European architecture to the office, and gotten out my camera prepared to take pictures for comparison. Then I stopped myself. I didn't want to end up like some Idaho potato farmer who grows spuds that he swears look like all the former presidents.

The conversation with Tío Ramón echoed in my mind. I had never heard him sound so worried, so down. And I had known him as long as I could remember. He and Papi met when they were six years old, in the first grade. They had both received the finest education the Jesuits could provide, first at Belén in Havana, then later at Georgetown in Washington, D.C. Each had been best man at the other's wedding and, later on, godfather to the other's eldest child. Their lives had been intertwined for more than six decades.

It seemed no one today had enough time to dedicate to one's friends, resulting in a sorry state for most relationships—so it was hard for me to imagine enjoying such a long-lasting friendship as that which Papi and Tío Ramón enjoyed. Thinking about it, I was hit hard by the realization that my own life was sorely lacking in that department. The hours I spent working, with my family at home, and with the men in my life, left little time to dedicate to cultivating my friendships with women.

Actually, I did have a best friend once, Margarita. But she had died in a car accident a few years back. Maybe the horrible experience of losing her had kept me from nurturing another close friend. No one could take Margarita's place for me. And if someone did, I was afraid of losing that person suddenly in a similar wrenching, violent fashion.

Damn it, I'd thought I was past crying over losing her. But there I was. I reached into my desk and took out a tissue to dry my eyes and blow my nose. I couldn't control the deep sobs that were pulsing inside my chest.

A few minutes passed, and I got up. I forced myself to think about my day ahead—first the paperwork on my desk, then my afternoon meeting with Tío Ramón.

I opened up the first case file. Leonardo would never forgive me if I didn't get the cases squared away. He had moved on from his dream of an ass-reduction machine to another device; this one claimed to eliminate love handles while sculpting the abdomen and legs into a replica of Michelangelo's *David*. And the cure for wrinkles! What next?

Who was I to stand in the way of my cousin's aspirations?

3

AT PRECISELY ONE-THIRTY I LEFT THE OFFICE TO
meet with my new client. Tío Ramón and Tía Alina lived
on Key Biscayne, which was barely twenty minutes away
from Coconut Grove and Solano Investigations, but I
thought it would be a good idea to allow myself some extra
leeway. Miami traffic was unpredictable to say the least,
and it was impossible to count on arriving anywhere at a
particular time. Not only were the avenues and streets
perpetually torn up with never-ending construction projects, but the drivers who clogged the roadways were
enough to inspire unmitigated fear and terror.

A few years ago I was pulled over for speeding and was
unable to sweet-talk my way out of the ticket—unfortunately the officer who stopped me was a woman and was
immune to my entreaties. As a result, I had to attend driving school to avoid getting points against my license. The
classes were four hours long, held at night in a high school
classroom in southern Dade County. The experience
shook me to the core. For months afterward I suffered
nightmares about the fellow motorists I saw in that class,
knowing that each of them was out there somewhere
behind the wheel.

I still remember the scene in the parking lot after

class. I don't know who scared me the most. There were
the teenage boys peeling out of the lot, laying burnt rubber on the asphalt, hip-hop music blaring from their hot
rods. There were the society matrons checking out their
makeup in their rearview mirrors, liberally applying lip-
stick as they cut slow arcs across the painted dividing
lines. Maybe it was the businessmen conducting business
on their cell phones, making notes on a pad and steering
with their elbows. Or the elderly ladies slunk down so low
in their seats that they could see out only through the
space between their dashboards and the top of their steering wheels. Not to mention the families in their thirties,
with multiple children in the backseat of their minivans,
constantly turning around to wipe crying faces and blow
little noses.

And this didn't even include the tourists—they didn't
have to go to driving school for their crimes, so they
weren't eligible for the list. If you included them, you
added strong contenders for the title of most nightmarish
driver.

The gods must have taken mercy on me this afternoon, though. The roads were relatively clear and the
traffic was light. I made good time to Key Biscayne.

Tío Ramón and Tía Alina lived in a palatial home on
Harbor Drive, the curving road that hugs the bay side of
the key. They had lived on the key since they first arrived
in Miami in the early sixties, but not in the same house.
They had bought their first place for a few thousand dollars. They lived in what was called a Mackle house, named
for the developers who built them. It was a modest three-
bedroom, two-bathroom place on one of the key's interior streets. Now those same houses were selling for up to
a million dollars apiece, and the value of other homes on

the island had gone up proportionately as well. The place where Tío Ramón and Tía Alina now lived was easily worth more than five million. Life in exile hadn't been all hardship for the couple and their three children.

I took in the view of the bay as I neared the key. The place was alive with activity: groups of young mothers with their children splashing about in the shallow waters, young guys throwing Frisbees to their dogs, snorkelers paddling around facedown observing the sea floor, and others just treading water in the gentle waves. I let my eye linger on a group of windsurfers, their brightly colored sails pointed out to sea.

It wasn't easy for me not to exceed the strictly enforced forty-five-mile-an-hour speed limit, but I compensated by enjoying the sunshine and the view. It was only seven miles from the tollbooth to the key entrance, but on the crest of the expansion bridge with the waters stretching out as far as I could see, I always felt that Miami seemed much farther away.

When I was on the key, I turned right from Crandon Boulevard onto Harbor Drive. The speed limit there was a measly thirty miles per hour, so I had plenty of time to think about Tío Ramón and wonder what he might possibly want with me. I wasn't too knowledgeable about his Miami business; I only recalled that it had something to do with insurance. I did know that growing up in Cuba, Ramón had been the second son of the Suarez family's patriarch, and that he had been groomed to eventually manage the family's sugar mills. But fate in the person of Fidel Castro had intervened, and the mills were confiscated by the Cuban government.

It had been at least a couple of years since I'd last visited the Suarez home, and I had to slow the Mercedes to make sure I didn't inadvertently pass it. I had almost reached the end of Harbor Drive when I spotted the place; it was hidden from the road by landscaping so lush and thick that it might have come from a tropical jungle. I turned right, into the driveway. I was a little worried that some out-of-control exotic plant might devour my Mercedes while I was inside, but I went ahead and parked under what looked like a banyan tree. I muttered a quick prayer for the car's safety and got out.

The front door was so massive that it must have taken half a Honduran forest to construct it. Strangely, I didn't remember the door from my previous visits—it must have been a new addition. I paused a moment before ringing the doorbell—actually, it was more like a gong than a simple little chime—so that I could have a quick look around.

Things were different, I was sure of it. It had only been two years, maybe three, since my last visit, but it seemed to me that nearly everything had changed save for the actual structure of the house. The portico over the porch was new, the house's facade had been renovated, the windows had been redone, and the landscaping had been totally overhauled, down to the stone paths and masonry that ringed two sides of the property. Papi was in the construction business, so I was well aware of the cost of such grand-scale projects. The Suarez family was definitely doing very well.

Even though I still hadn't rung the doorbell, the door opened anyway. A young woman in a black dress with a frilly white organdy apron greeted me and quietly beckoned me to enter. As I stepped over the threshold I looked around the foyer; in a glance I noticed that Tío Ramón had installed an elaborate security system, with top-of-the-line surveillance cameras. The system had been set up recently—there was a patch of chipped plaster and exposed wiring that needed to be touched up and hidden. I wondered if this new development had anything to do with the "complication" that Papi had first brought to my attention.

I followed the maid through the house; the rooms were elegantly decorated, and this side of the house featured a uniformly breathtaking view of Biscayne Bay. I would have liked to have taken a better look around, but she was leading me at such a fast clip that I had to hurry to keep up. Obviously the insurance business had paid off well for Tío Ramón. I saw several paintings by Cuban masters—Wilfredo Lam, Amelia Pelaes, Portocarrera—prominently displayed on fabric-covered walls.

It was only when we reached a room at the back of the house that my guide stopped and knocked softly on an intricately carved wooden door.

"Come in," I heard Tío Ramón call out in his familiar deep voice.

The maid opened the door and stepped aside for me to enter. I saw Tío Ramón seated on a red leather easy chair, the *Wall Street Journal* unfolded on his lap. As soon as he saw me, he took off his reading glasses and stood up to greet me.

"Lupe," he said warmly.

Because of the way he had sounded on the phone, I had prepared myself for a marked deterioration in his appearance, but I was relieved to see that Tío Ramón looked much the same as when I'd last seen him. He was stocky, with wavy salt-and-pepper hair cropped close at the temples. I began to relax when I saw the light in his dark eyes, thinking that perhaps the situation wasn't as dire as it had sounded that morning.

"It's been far too long," Tío Ramón said, kissing my cheek. He stepped back to inspect me, his piercing black eyes seeming to miss nothing. I was pleased that I had dressed with appropriate conservatism that day, in a black cotton T-shirt and a khaki skirt that was a bit snug but which was of an acceptable length. Cuban men of Tío Ramón's generation looked disapprovingly at what they considered inappropriate modes of dress for young women. I basically thought they were full of it, but I was willing to comply at certain times out of respect.

"It's good to see you, Tío Ramón," I replied. He was dressed in a *guayabera* just like the one Papi had worn that morning, along with navy blue slacks. I could detect a faint odor of tobacco smoke on him, which I knew meant he had violated Tía Alina's strict prohibition against smoking cigars.

"Please, child, let's sit." Tío Ramón steered me toward one of a pair of armchairs next to the window. "Can I offer you anything to drink? Are you hungry?"

"No, thank you, Tío Ramón," I said. I made myself comfortable in the chair. My curiosity was intensifying by the second; although I was relieved he looked all right, I still remembered the way Tío Ramón had sounded over the phone that morning.

He sat down across from me and smiled. "So, Lupe," he said. "Tell me. How is your papi?"

"Very well," I replied.

Then Tío Ramón went down the list. He asked about everyone in the family, moving on to my sisters and my nieces and ending up with Osvaldo and Aida. This was pretty interesting, I thought—since I knew that he and Papi talked at least once a week and kept each other up-to-date on their families. This line of questioning could have been traditional manners and courtliness. It could also have been a way of postponing coming to the point.

Finally he paused. He folded his arms and rested his chin in his hands. "Lupe, did your father tell you anything about the little complication that I have found myself involved in?"

"No, Tío Ramón," I said. "He didn't give me any information."

Tío Ramón nodded, seeming distracted. For the first time since I'd arrived, I thought I saw something resembling fear in his eyes—with a hint of sadness. It was quite disconcerting, and I was shocked for an instant. I had never seen Tío Ramón exhibit such emotions.

He clapped his hands together; I jumped slightly in my chair.

"Do you know much about what is happening to private property in Cuba?" Tío Ramón asked me.

"I didn't think there *was* private property in Cuba," I replied. "I thought the government essentially owned everything."

Tío Ramón lit up with pride. "Precisely!" He beamed at me as though I was a prize student who had come up with a brilliant response to a difficult question. "And that is why I asked you to come see me today."

"I see." I thought for a moment about what he had just said. "But, Tío Ramón, what exactly do you mean?"

As soon as the words were out of my mouth, I saw Tío Ramón's face fall. I hated to disappoint him, but he wasn't giving me much to go on.

He looked at me long and hard, and then stood up. One hand went into his pocket, searching for something. Then, key chain in hand, he went over to his big wooden desk, bent down, and unlocked the bottom drawer. He rummaged around and then stood up. When I saw him reappear over the desktop, there was a huge cigar in his mouth.

"Ahhhh!" Tío Ramón said, a groan of pure enjoyment as he lit up the *puro* and breathed in deep. He took a seat in his chair, and in no time the sweet aroma of smoke wafted toward me. I always loved the smell of a really good cigar, so I had no problem with Tío Ramón's secondhand smoke. One could do worse than to puff vicariously on a Montecristo Numero Uno.

"You don't mind?" he asked me, holding the cigar aloft.

"Of course not, Tío Ramón," I said.

I tried not to think of Tía Alina's disapproving face as I watched Tío Ramón enjoy his cigar. Rules are made to be broken on certain occasions, and I could see that discussing the gravity of his "complication" was a rulebreaker for Tío Ramón.

I cleared my throat quietly and leaned forward. I was apprehensive about taking control of the meeting, but I was anxious to address my real reason for being there.

"The thing you mentioned," I said politely. "About private property. Could you please tell me more about your situation?"

Tío Ramón just puffed away for almost a full minute, apparently trying to figure out what to say. I could almost hear the wheels clicking in his head, and this really worried me. This was not the Tío Ramón I had known all my life, a man who always said what was on his mind.

"You know, Lupe, that in Cuba the Suarez-Mendez family was in the sugar business?"

I nodded. "You owned five mills and refineries."

Tío Ramón's eyes blazed with warmth. "Yes, in Oriente and Camagüey. We owned them for almost two hundred years, since 1789. Of course, they were confiscated by the Castro government in 1960."

He shook his head sadly. I hoped it was the cigar smoke that was making his eyes now glisten.

"I've kept track of what has happened to our mills since they were taken from us," Tío Ramón continued. "The ones in Oriente—Santa Tomasa, Santa Teresa, and Milagos—those are still in operation. The ones in Camagüey—Angeles and San Jeronimo—are not. They have been dismantled. And, of course, the ones that remain have changed in name. For example, they have become Che Guevara and Revolución: names that sound like the garbage they describe."

Tío Ramón almost spat out his words. Although his tone of voice was calm, he puffed almost incessantly on his cigar. A cloud of smoke hung low over most of the room.

I sat quietly for a moment, realizing how painful it must be for Tío Ramón to discuss the state of his family's mills. I didn't know much about the sugar business in Cuba, and this seemed like a reasonable time to find out more.

"How many mills were there in Cuba when Castro took power?" I asked.

"In 1958 there were one hundred and sixty-one sugar mills in Cuba," Tío Ramón said, his voice slow and flat, looking straight into my eyes. This information was obviously embedded in his consciousness. "Of those, thirteen have been dismantled. Eight new mills have also been formed. That leaves a hundred and fifty-six remaining in Cuba."

"And are they all fully operational?" I asked. I vaguely remembered hearing once about the Cuban sugar harvest, and how grim it had been for the country when production didn't meet projections.

"No," Tío Ramón said. "The new mills were created only because the Soviet Union was subsidizing the Cuban economy. That assistance is obviously a thing of the past. After the Soviets withdrew their aid, at least thirty sugar mills fell out of operation."

"I see."

Tío Ramón took another puff on his cigar. "But this is not what I asked you here to speak about," he said. "I want to use your expertise as a private investigator to uncover some information for me."

"Of course," I answered. "If there's anything I can do to help you, please know that you can count on me."

Tío Ramón nodded gravely. "*Gracias*. You're a good girl, Lupe. I know I shouldn't say this, but you were your mother's favorite."

I didn't know how to react, so I remained motionless and quiet. But my heart was beating hard because of what Tío Ramón had just said. I had always thought of myself as Mami's favorite, but I had convinced myself that each child secretly thinks of herself as the primary recipient of her parents' love and affection. Now Tío Ramón had shared this intimate secret with me. It made me wonder what other surprises he might have for me that afternoon.

Tío Ramón continued talking as though he had told me nothing out of the ordinary.

"You know that I had a brother, Julian," he said.

"Of course," I told him. "Julian passed away five years ago."

Tío Ramón nodded. "Julian was a widower when he died. But perhaps you remember that he had a son—

Alexander. Just the one child, my nephew Alexander, who now lives in New York."

"I've met him, Tío Ramón," I said. I vaguely recalled being introduced to a man my age at some social function—come to think of it, I thought it might have been my sister Fatima's ill-fated wedding reception. My memory of Alexander was that he hadn't been very impressive in any way, although I recalled that he seemed ill at ease in that setting. I was beginning to wonder about Tío Ramón's mental sharpness—so far he had brought up Cuba's sugar industry, then Mami, and now his family tree. What I didn't follow was how these subjects could possibly be connected.

"I really haven't had much contact with Alexander since Julian died," Tío Ramón said meditatively, inspecting the burning tip of his cigar. "Until recently."

A cold, hard look entered his eyes, startling me. Tío Ramón took a puff. The mushroom cloud hanging over us reminded me of the pictures I'd once seen of Hiroshima.

"You're aware that the Cuban government has been selling property to foreigners, aren't you, Lupe?"

"Sí," I told him. "Papi says the Spanish are buying up most of the properties—he says that the Spanish now own so much of Cuba that we're reverting back to being a colony."

"Your papi is right, child." Tío Ramón shook his head. "Well, that brings me to the reason I asked you to come meet with me today."

Finally. I was gripping the arms of my chair with anticipation.

"Some of the individuals and corporations buying up properties don't care that these properties were confiscated by the Cuban government without compensation," Tío Ramón explained. "But there are others who don't

care to buy stolen properties—especially since they understand that Castro is getting old and that the system won't
survive much longer in its present form. They want to
obtain a clear title from the rightful owners, documenta-
tion stating that they obtained the properties in a legal
manner."

"But how can that happen?" I asked. "If the properties
were confiscated by the Cuban government, doesn't that
make the government the owner?"

"Yes, that's true, but it only has physical ownership,"
Tío Ramón said softly. "It is not the legal and rightful
owner. Remember, Lupe, after Castro goes, no one
knows what's going to become of property confiscated by
his government."

"So these investors are basically covering their behinds—
pardon the expression," I said. I thought for a moment.
There were so many questions. "Then who gets the money
from the sale of the properties? How does the Cuban government deal with that? And what about valuation? How
are prices set in a society in which one single entity owns
essentially everything?"

"I always knew you were sharp, Lupe," Tío Ramón
said with an approving smile. "Allow me to describe my
situation."

"Please," I said.

"You know about my family's five mills." Tío Ramón
stared at me so intently that he might have drilled holes in
my skin. "Well, I received a call from Alexander last week.
It was the first time I've heard from him since my brother
died—except for calls asking me for money, that is."

Tío Ramón waved his hand in the air between us, as
though erasing bad memories. I noticed that his demeanor
changed when he discussed his nephew.

"Anyway, Alexander called to tell me that he'd received

a letter addressed to his father. It was from a lawyer in Madrid who represents some clients interested in investing in Cuba. He wanted to discuss the purchase of the land and holdings from my family's two mills in Camagüey."

"I see."

Tío Ramón nodded as if I had said something very significant. He puffed on his cigar so intently that the tip glowed red like a traffic light. That Montecristo was a perfect barometer of how distressed Tío Ramón felt at any given moment.

"According to the letter, the lawyer had conducted a title search," Tío Ramón said. "He discovered that Julian and I were joint owners of the mills. He sent the letter first to Julian, since he was the older of the two of us."

"So this lawyer has clients who want to buy the land and what's left from the defunct mills," I said. "For how much? How would he know how much they're worth?"

As soon as the words escaped my mouth, I realized from Tío Ramón's expression that I was asking the wrong question. What needed to be answered was whether he wanted to part with property that had been in his family for almost two hundred years.

Tío Ramón pondered what I had just asked. He reached into the pocket of his *guayabera*, pulled out a sheet of paper, and held it out for me.

"Here," he said. "Alexander faxed me a copy of the lawyer's letter. Read it for yourself."

I unfolded the paper and began reading. The situation was just as Tío Ramón had portrayed it. To begin with, it was obvious that the attorney had no idea that Julian had passed away. What Tío Ramón hadn't mentioned was that a valuation of the properties had already been made—and that the assessor had placed their worth at thirty-five million dollars. The lawyer's clients were offering ten cents on the dollar in exchange for a clear title. The math was easy. Three and a half million, right now, money in the bank, and all the Suarez family had to do was give up all future claim on the properties.

"Interesting, isn't it?" Tío Ramón asked me.

"What does Alexander want to do?" I suspected I knew the answer already, based on the fact that he had been hitting up Tío Ramón for cash since his father's death.

"Oh, Lupe, please," Tío Ramón said derisively. "In Alexander's mind, the money is already in his checking account." He stabbed at the air with his cigar so sharply that it left a trail of smoke.

"That figures."

"But he needs my agreement before he can take the lawyer up on the offer," Tío Ramón said, holding the cigar in the air. "Alexander figured I would jump at the chance to make a quick buck. That's why he came to me with the offer. In truth, I wouldn't put it past my nephew to try forging my signature on the document. It's sad, that's what it is. When I think of how honorable a man Julian was."

I tried to steer the conversation away from the past. "So if you agreed to this proposal, Alexander's share would be $1.75 million, right?"

Not a bad chunk of change, I thought.

"That's right," Tío Ramón agreed. "If I were to agree. And that is a very big 'if,' Lupe."

"And he can't sell without you, right?" I asked. "But you don't want to sell, do you, Tío Ramón?"

"No, I don't."

"That's what I thought."

"I'm fortunate enough that I don't need the money,

Lupe," Tío Ramón said. "Besides, the land has been in my family for centuries. Fidel Castro has been in power for only forty years. He will die. That is the one thing the old bastard cannot control!"

Tío Ramón permitted himself a half-smile. This sudden rage at Castro was hardly surprising to me. It's the daily fare for life as a Cuban exile.

"*Ay*, Lupe, child." A dreamy look came into Tío Ramón's eyes. "You don't know much about how important sugar was to Cuba, do you?"

"I'm sorry, I don't." I decided to humor Papi's old friend. It was clear he needed to talk. "Tell me about it."

Tío Ramón puffed on his cigar and looked out over the water. I knew he was ninety miles away, in his *patria*. "In Cuba, there's a saying: *'Sin azúcar, no hay país.'* You know what that means, Lupe: without sugar, there is no country. And that's the way it's been in Cuba for hundreds of years."

I silently waited for him to continue. Watching him, I could see how he might have been as a young man—optimistic, confident, and passionate about the crop that had been responsible for his family's livelihood for generations.

"You know, Lupe"—Tío Ramón turned from the waters to look at me—"the sugar you buy at the grocery store, in the paper sacks. Do you know how it got there?"

I shook my head. Apparently I was in for a lesson on the growing, harvesting, and refining of sugar.

"Sugarcane is a type of grass, and it can grow up to twenty feet high, but it's cut when it's just over seven feet. It's very inexpensive to grow, because one plant will regenerate itself for ten years. After that time, the top of the cane is planted in the soil, and a new plant grows from that. The *zafra*, the time of year during which sugar is harvested, lasts for six months during the winter and spring."

I thought about what little I knew about the subject. "The harvesting is hard work, isn't it?" I said.

"It's backbreaking and dangerous," Tío Ramón declared. "The sugarcane is very fibrous and can't be cut easily. It has to be whacked with a machete, and accidents happen. Bad accidents."

"Can't machines do the work?" I asked.

"Sometimes, but mostly it's still harvested by hand," Tío Ramón explained. "Not much has really changed in the hundreds of years of sugar growing in Cuba. Machines are used, but the predominance of harvesting is by hand. You see, if the cane is cut too low, the plant dies. Cut too high, the sugar isn't right.

"The machinery being used in Cuba has been there for decades. It's American-made, and because of the embargo parts cannot be replaced. So workers cut by hand, moving down the fields in lines, whacking the cane from the stalk, then removing the leaves and laying it down in the field. Another worker comes along with an ox-driven cart to pick up the cut cane. Then the cane is taken to the mills as quickly as possible—otherwise the juice begins to leak from it, and the fermentation process begins ahead of time."

Tío Ramón seemed both faraway and very alive as he spoke.

"The cane is crushed at the mill," he continued. "The pulp becomes what is called *bagasse*. There are many uses for *bagasse*, from fuel to building supplies to rope. The liquid that is extracted from the cane—the *guarapo*—is mixed with lime to make it as pure as possible. After that it's cooked several times until it begins to crystallize. That mixture is then treated in different ways, depending on how it's going to be used. The raw sugar, the brown sugar, can be processed further until it's pure enough to be sold as refined sugar. And that's what you buy at the Publix grocery store, Lupe."

Tío Ramón glanced away, back over the waters. For a moment he had been back in Cuba, in the pride of his family business. Now he had to come back to reality, and his sadness was palpable. He caught himself, forcing himself to attend to the matters at hand.

"I don't know what will happen in Cuba after he goes," Tío Ramón allowed. "But I'm willing to gamble that things will change. I don't know if we'll get the mills back. No one knows what will happen. But I know I'm not going to sell them to foreigners who are offering me ten cents on the dollar."

"I wonder how they arrived at this figure of thirty-five million," I mused. "The letter doesn't say. And who are the buyers, anyway?"

"That's where you come in, Lupe." Tío Ramón leaned back. "I want you to get to the bottom of this."

"Tío Ramón." I sighed. I hated to admit there were actually some things I couldn't do. "I have to tell you—I have no idea how to go about this. I'm a private investigator. I investigate civil and criminal cases—situations that happen here in the United States. I'm not involved in international business matters."

Well, a couple of times I had gotten involved in matters on Cuban soil. But no one was supposed to know about *that*.

Tío Ramón thought for a minute. "Well, Lupe, there is a national angle to this," he said, pausing for effect.

"And what would that be?"

"Alexander has vanished. He's been missing for four full days."

Hmm. Maybe there was something I could do, after all.

4

MY CELL PHONE WENT OFF AS ALVARO AND I FIN-
ished our steaks at Smith & Wollensky's restaurant on
Miami Beach. We were just about to tackle the last of our
home-fried potatoes.

I cursed because I had forgotten to turn the damned
thing off. But now it embarked energetically on the third
stanza of the Cuban national anthem—which I had pro-
grammed it to play instead of a boring ring—and it was
impossible to ignore. I glanced down at the caller ID and
saw the number began with a 361 exchange. That meant
the call was coming from Key Biscayne. I thought I recognized the number as Tío Ramón's. My heart beat a little
faster, but I told myself to keep calm. After all, I had just
left him a few hours before. How much of an emergency
could have developed in such a short time?

"Alvaro, I'm sorry, but I have to take this one," I said a
bit sheepishly.

I looked across the table at him and reflected yet again
how handsome he was with his big brown eyes, his dark
brown hair that always seemed to need a trim, and his ever-
present two-day beard. He was so calm, so at ease with himself and his body—no one would ever suspect that this was a
man who received daily death threats on his E-mail.

Alvaro and I had been together for about a year. He knew I would never interrupt a meal—especially at the crucial juncture when dessert was about to be ordered—to take just any phone call. He simply shrugged and took a long swallow of wine, shifting to direct his gaze out over the water. I interpreted his reaction to mean that he wasn't overjoyed, but that he wasn't going to make things difficult for me. I resolved to make it up to him later.

I pressed the button to take the call and turned my face downward, trying to carve out a bit of privacy in the restaurant. We were seated at one of the outdoor tables on the walkway next to the embankment that ran along the canal leading out to sea, but I knew that the sound of my voice would carry. I tried to speak softly—I've always thought there was nothing more obnoxious than people who talked on their cell phones as though they were the only people around. Anyway, I also didn't want strangers to hear the content of a conversation that pertained to a case I was working.

"Lupe! Is that you, Lupe?" asked a woman's breathless, agitated voice. "This is Tía Alina!"

What the hell. Something was wrong.

"Yes, Tía Alina. I'm here."

"Oh, it's Tío Ramón!" Tía Alina was so worked up that, as she started speaking, it was impossible for me to understand her. Just at that same moment a monstrous freighter headed out of the canal, pulled to sea by six tugboats.

"What's that?" I asked.

"He's in terrible trouble!" she yelled. "He needs help!"

"Tía Alina, please," I said. "Slow down and explain."

"You know Alexander? Julian's son?" She was still yelling in my ear, as though that would make me understand her better. I put my hand over my free ear. I glanced around to see if anyone had noticed, but they were all too engrossed in their own meals or the scenery. Mercifully, no one was paying attention to me.

I looked up and noticed Alvaro refilling my wineglass. It was a very fine Château Gloria. I took a sip. Tía Alina was still incoherent, and the freighter and the tugboats were making such a racket that I couldn't understand a thing. I wondered vaguely whether I could write off this meal—after all, I was discussing business matters, wasn't I? But no, there would be no way. Consummate gentleman that he was, Alvaro would never allow me to pay.

Finally the noise died down a little on the canal. I listened hard to Tía Alina and made out three words: *disaster, lawyer,* and *jail.*

Ay, Dios mío.

"Tía Alina! Please slow down!" I ordered her. "Tell me again, slowly this time. What happened? Start at the beginning."

"Alexander is dead! He's been murdered! And the police have arrested your tío Ramón!"

Tía Alina was still almost hysterical, but at least she had calmed down enough that I could put the phone against my ear without hearing an echo.

"Tío Ramón has been arrested?" I asked. I couldn't understand. Only a few hours ago Tío Ramón had told me about Alexander's disappearance and retained me to locate him.

"Oh, Lupe. The police are saying that Ramón killed Alexander. Ramón called me from jail. He told me to call you right away, that you would know what to do."

Tía Alina moaned softly. "Take a deep breath," I said.

"Ramón said he couldn't talk any longer. That he had

no time left, or something like that. It was so hard to hear him! He just kept telling me to call you, and that you would take care of everything. He said you would know what to do."

I took a long sip of my wine. "Of course," I said. "I'll take care of it."

I had no idea where Tío Ramón's confidence in me had come from, but I knew I couldn't let Papi's old friend down. For the moment, I knew there would be no use trying to get more details from Tía Alina.

"Tía Alina, are you alone?" I asked. I tried to think of her children's names, to ask if she had called them.

"Sí, only Teresa is in Miami at the moment," she replied. "She's coming over right away. Carlos is in New York and Sofia is in the Bahamas, on spring vacation with her son."

Tía Alina began to sob quietly. "Listen, don't worry," I told her. "I know it's difficult, but please try. I'll call you as soon as I have any information."

I reassured her once more, then hung up the phone. In his discreet way Alvaro had been following the conversation; knowing our time left at Smith & Wollensky's was limited, he'd ordered the chocolate mousse cake, two double espressos, and the check. All arrived at the same time.

"Trouble," he said in a sympathetic voice. It was Alvaro's way of offering me advice or sympathy, whichever I might need.

Alvaro Mendoza knew all about trouble. He was one of the few Cuban exiles in Miami willing to go against the hard-line politics of Cuban—United States relations. He was on the hit list of almost every Spanish-language radio talk show in South Florida. As an immigration lawyer, Alvaro believed in the U.S. Constitution—particularly in terms of freedom of speech. For him, that meant expressing a desire to open dialogue between Cubans living in exile and Cubans on the island, as a means of resolving the gulf between the two. He felt that the policies of the past forty years hadn't worked, and were unlikely to do so now. For making his views publicly known, he had incurred the wrath of thousands of angry exiles.

"Gracias," I said. I took a big bite of the chocolate cake and followed it with some red wine. There was surprisingly little left in our second bottle of the evening.

"Care to talk?" he asked.

"For now, I'd rather just concentrate on this." I motioned at the cake and espresso. "And I'm sorry, but I have to go work now. My client is in jail. And I have to come up with a way to get him out."

A cloud passed over Alvaro's face. The implication of what I was saying was sinking in. We both knew who I was talking about.

Tommy MacDonald.

5

ALVARO AND I MADE IT BACK FROM SOUTH BEACH
to the Grove in record time. I had left the Mercedes in the
Grove when Alvaro drove us to dinner. As soon as I pulled
away from the curb, I picked up my cell phone and
punched in number five on the speed dial.

"Tommy?" I said when he picked up.

"Hi, Lupe." Obviously Tommy was screening calls
using his caller ID—fortunately I rated a pickup, and I was
inordinately grateful to get him on the line instead of his
voice mail.

"I need your help," I said to him.

"What's up?" he said.

A year ago, Tommy wouldn't have asked me that question. He would have simply invited me over, and things
would have proceeded from there. But now that I was
involved with Alvaro, Tommy was acting like a complete
gentleman—contradicting his public image. Still, I knew
that I had an unspoken invitation should I ever decide to
change my mind. I had only done so on a couple of previous occasions, certainly not often enough to constitute a
real pattern of transgression. And both of those times had
happened after Alvaro and I had had a fight, so they tech-
nically didn't count against me. At least, that's what I was

telling myself. Besides, as Tommy was a dear friend, a love I had known for many years, I wasn't breaking any new ground on the occasions I slipped back into my old ways.

"Let me guess," Tommy said. "You're on your way over to pick me up so we can bail one of your clients out of jail."

He chuckled when I said nothing in return. He knew me too well.

"Tell me where you are," Tommy said. "And how long I have to get ready."

"You're a real prince, Tommy," I told him. "I mean that."

Tommy chuckled again. "Who fucked up?" he asked me. "And how badly?"

I gave Tommy my present location, then a quick rundown of what Tía Alina had told me. It wasn't much, but it was enough for us to know where to begin. On the way back from Smith & Wollensky's I'd made a quick call and confirmed that Tío Ramón was being held at the Dade County Jail.

Tommy was waiting downstairs in the lobby of his Brickell Avenue building when I pulled into the driveway. I slowed to a stop and observed him through the floor-to-ceiling glass as he spotted me and came my way. In spite of the late hour, Tommy was, as usual, impeccably turned out. Tonight's selection was a double-breasted navy blue suit with a light pink, almost lilac-colored shirt. He looked like a male model who had just stepped out of *GQ*, and not like the top criminal defense attorney in Dade County on his way to interview a client in jail.

As Tommy reached for the door handle, I noticed that he was wearing the gold cuff links I'd given him a few years ago. I wondered whether he'd worn them tonight for my benefit.

"Ah, Lupe," Tommy said with a sort of amused sigh as he slid across the passenger seat to kiss me. "It's good to see you, even if the circumstances suck."

I returned his kiss. Anyone watching would have thought we were a couple heading out for a night on the town instead of a grim trip to the Dade County Jail. Tommy and I enjoyed a relationship based on affection, trust, and professional respect. It was a complicated arrangement that I generally chose not to analyze too much—maybe I was afraid of killing the magic.

I knew that, in his private thoughts, Tommy had wondered what would happen if we were to establish some sort of permanent relationship. I'd certainly wondered. I didn't know much about Tommy's love life, and I didn't want to. We operated in a "don't ask, don't tell" sort of vacuum that always worked for us.

My relationship with Alvaro, it almost goes without saying, was completely different. We had known each other nearly all our lives. Our families were friends, and we grew up a few blocks from each other. It was only in the last year, though, that we had begun seeing each other and gotten "serious." We didn't talk about it much, but I knew the unspoken assumption was that we were in a mutually exclusive arrangement.

It wasn't easy for me. Alvaro and I had had a serious blowup the year before over my actions on a case. We had worked our way through it, though, and now I thought we were back on track. But here was Tommy, sitting a foot away from me. I could smell his aftershave in the close quarters of the car.

"Where did you go to dinner?" Tommy asked, oblivious to the thoughts whirling in my head. He took in my black leather skirt and wine-red wraparound body-hugging top. It wasn't the kind of outfit I normally wore to the office. I knew I should have gone home and changed, but I didn't want to waste time. I was familiar with the Dade County Jail, and I didn't want to leave Tío Ramón there a minute longer than I had to.

"Smith & Wollensky," I said, without elaborating any further.

Tommy nodded approvingly. "Great home fries," he said in a neutral voice.

"That's true," I said, keeping my eyes on the road.

For about fifteen seconds I could feel Tommy's eyes on my face, inspecting me and looking for something. Then he seemed to shrug and shift gears. He opened his briefcase, got out a yellow legal pad, and unscrewed the top of his gold Cross pen.

"Okay," he said. "Clue me in."

I had already told Tommy about Tío Ramón's arrest; now I was able to fill in the background—including the friendship between the Suarez family and my own, then the events of my meeting with Tío Ramón that afternoon in Key Biscayne. Tommy said nothing, but he scribbled furiously.

At that time of night the drive between Brickell Avenue and the county jail took only about fifteen minutes. Tonight I-95 was eerily empty, almost deserted. I moved into the left lane and got off at Exit 6, the Jackson Memorial Hospital ramp. Once off the interstate I headed west until I reached Twelfth Avenue, where I hung a right.

The jail was part of a locus of buildings that included not only Jackson Memorial but also Cedars of Lebanon Hospital and the Veterans Administration Hospital. There was always plenty of pedestrian and vehicular traffic day and night. In addition to the jail there was also the

Justice Building and the State Attorney's Office, which added to the twenty-four-hour logjam.

I drove by the jail in a quixotic hope that a parking space might miraculously appear. It wasn't my lucky night; the street parking was all full. But on my third pass, I managed to snag a place just as a banged-up Toyota of indiscernible color and vintage was pulling out. We weren't far from the jail, and I parked the Mercedes snugly between two long white vans bearing the green-and-white shields of the Corrections and Rehabilitation Department on their doors. I hoped that would afford us some protection, and that the Mercedes would be in the same condition as it was now when we returned for it. I patted it on the hood after locking up, as a gesture of good luck and potential farewell.

There were a lot of law-enforcement types milling around, mostly corrections officers smoking a quick cigarette on their break. At the pay phones on either side of the jail were a hodgepodge of suspicious-looking individuals hanging around. The sign over the phones told visitors that by dialing 547-7379 they could gain information on inmates; the sign was cemented to the wall and intact, no mean feat considering the determination and creativity of the various felons who walked by it every day. I hoped the Mercedes would prove as resilient.

Tommy and I moved quickly for the door. I suppressed a shiver when I read the sign identifying the place as the Pretrial Detention Center. Part of me wanted to grab Tommy by the arm and tell him that my tío Ramón didn't belong there. Of course, that wouldn't mean much to Tommy. According to him, none of his clients belonged in jail.

Inside we walked to the booth where a bulldog corrections officer was sitting, then we filled out a request form. We handed over our driver's licenses, as well as Tommy's Florida bar card and my PI license. The officer kept them all; in case we got into any trouble inside, they could notify our next of kin. It might have been a precaution in case we tried to spring our prisoner, or else it might have been a way of identifying us if we were maimed or killed inside. These weren't cheery thoughts, but then Dade County Jail was anything but cheerful and reassuring.

Unlike Proust's madeleines, the smell of the jail evoked not-so-fond memories of all the times I had been there before. It was an odor unlike any other in the world, a mixture of sweat, funk, musk, hopelessness, and fear— along with cheap industrial-grade disinfectant. All prisons and jails have such a distinctive scent, and Dade County's was about the worst I'd ever come across. It had a life of its own, and it stuck to hair and clothes. I knew I would be scrubbing myself for a long time after I got home that night, and that my outfit was heading straight for the dry cleaners.

I slid the visitor's form back through the two-inch slot to the corrections officer perched behind thick bullet-proof glass. He accepted it without saying anything or looking at me, and Tommy and I sat down in green vinyl chairs facing the booth. We had both learned from experience that there was no way to predict how long we would have to wait.

It had been a couple of months since I'd been in the jail, and I let my eyes wander. I saw a sign that I didn't remember from before, to the left of the corrections officer's booth. It read: "No open toe shoes front and back." I looked down at my favorite five-inch fuck-me fire-engine-red stilettos. Well, at least I wasn't breaking *that* rule. There was another, more familiar sign gathering dust that read: "You are now entering the Dade County Jail. It is a crime to bring in articles such as weapons, narcotics, explosives, uncensored letters, etc." As always, I wondered what the "etc." might mean, but I knew better than to ask.

What a room. The chairs lined up along the back wall illustrated nasty shades of vomit green, electric blue, and indeterminate orange. The floor was covered in dirty, worn brown linoleum, and had been badly patched so often that parts of it resembled the splotches of a Rorschach test. The two columns in the center of the room looked as though they were barely able to support the ceiling.

On the wall, next to the announcement detailing visiting hours, was a list of Miami Dade Surety Agencies—bail bondsmen—ensconced in a very large frame. I counted them. Sixty-three. The last time I was waiting to see a client, there had been sixty-four. I wondered what happened to the one who dropped off the list. He was probably inside, keeping his old clients company.

I glanced over at Tommy. He was in his Zen-master mode, looking at nothing, there but not there. He was a real wonder in his ability to remain calm and content amid the worst conditions. As we sat there, people kept streaming in and out of the reception area—corrections officers talking and joking with one another, families gathering in clusters to argue, cry, or just look stunned. And, of course, there were the individuals with the bored "here we go again" look on their faces.

I jumped every time the steel gates opened and closed—either admitting or releasing someone from the cavernous room on the other side. The place was like this all the time—always hopping. The concept of orderly time and keeping regular hours didn't mean much in Miami, an attitude that carried over to the county jail.

I listened closely. Through the din of activity I could hear Tommy humming something to himself, soft and low. I couldn't place the tune. I knew how much Tommy hated visiting the jail; he'd much rather see his clients after they were bonded out, in his office, drinking Cuban coffee and maybe even lighting up a Montecristo Número Uno.

"We've gotta get out of this place," Tommy sang softly to himself. "If it's the last thing we ever do."

Suddenly the loudspeaker crackled and our names were called. Tommy sprang to life and unfolded his long body with an approximation of enthusiasm. We walked together toward the booth, ready to go through the steel doors to meet with Tío Ramón.

Tommy was still singing and humming to himself. I felt like telling him to stop, but his choice of song was just too appropriate.

6

TÍO RAMÓN WAS BEING KEPT IN A CELL ON THE
sixth floor. Once inside the gate, we turned left and
pressed the button for the first elevator. Tío Ramón
wasn't considered a high escape risk, nor was he violent or
a known police informant, so he was being kept with the
general prison population—and wouldn't have to wear a
distinguishing bright orange uniform.

Visitors weren't allowed to bring anything into the
jail, so we'd left Tommy's briefcase and my purse downstairs. I was familiar with operating procedures at the jail,
but I still felt naked without my bag. My Beretta was locked
safe and sound in the trunk of my Mercedes. There was no
point in looking for trouble by bringing it inside, even
though I was licensed to carry it.

When we arrived on the sixth floor, we approached the
corrections officer's booth and gave Tío Ramón's name. I
knew we wouldn't have to wait long, since prisoners were
kept right on the same floor, in cells located at the end of
the corridor. Tommy and I stared into space while the
officer mumbled into his telephone. A trustee dressed in a
white uniform soon approached and escorted us to an
interview room at the end of the corridor. Tommy and I
went into the stark, claustrophobically small space.

I shuddered involuntarily when the trustee slammed the door loudly and authoritatively behind us. Tommy and I sat down on hard wooden chairs placed around a table that had last seen a good day at some point in the mid-seventies. Mercifully, we didn't have to wait long.

Tío Ramón came into the room looking nothing like the proud and dapper man I'd seen earlier. I tried to give him an impression of solidity and competence, although inwardly I was shocked and dismayed by his appearance. Prisoners were allowed to wear their own clothes until their arraignment. Tío Ramón's *guayabera* was wrinkled and stained, and his once-immaculate slacks looked as though they had been stomped on. His hair was sweaty and disheveled, and a five o'clock beard shadowed his face. It wasn't a pretty sight—but then, I had never known anyone to leave the Dade County Jail looking better than when he had gone in.

"Thank you for coming, Lupe," Tío Ramón said gratefully after he sat down. He wearily looked over at Tommy.

"This is Thomas MacDonald, a criminal defense attorney whom I've worked with for several years," I explained. "He's going to work to get you out of here as soon as possible."

Tío Ramón looked around the room as though unable to believe that he was actually in such a place. "Thank you for helping me," he said to Tommy. I was gratified to see that Ramón had lost none of his courtly manners.

"I can't promise you anything beyond the fact that I'll try my best to get you home," Tommy said, his stock answer, which I'd heard many times before. "Now, tell me what happened earlier today."

Tío Ramón gave a little shrug; he seemed resigned to the necessity of revisiting an unpleasant chain of events.

"Remember I told you my nephew Alexander had disappeared?" he asked me. "Well, a few hours after you left I
received a call from him. He said he was in Miami and that
he wanted to speak with me."

Tío Ramón's voice had dropped into a dull mono-
tone. Beyond the door, there was the sound of steel
doors opening and shutting. It made me think of all the
miserable humanity inside these walls. The room was
getting hot, and I was starting to sweat. I glanced over at
Tommy and saw him tug at the neck of his shirt.

"And what happened next?" Tommy prodded gently.

Tío Ramón's eyes widened. "It was all so strange. Alexander asked me to meet him in a hotel room."

"Why was that strange?" I asked. "Didn't he want to speak
with you about selling the mills? Maybe he was just following up on his initial contact with you."

"That's not what was so strange, Lupe." Tío Ramón
sighed. "It was the place where he wanted to meet that gave
me pause."

The older gentleman took a deep breath; he suddenly
seemed discomfited, and I exchanged a glance with Tommy.
I wondered what could embarrass a man sitting in the
Dade County Jail charged with murder.

"Alexander was staying at a hotel in Little Havana, on
Eighth Street," Tío Ramón told us. He went on to give us
the place's exact location, and Tommy and I were instantly
clued into the source of Ramón's mortification. It was a
hot sheet hotel that Ramón was describing, the type of
place that charges by the hour and typically was the home
for various illicit trysts.

"So why there?" I asked. "Why not a regular hotel?"

"Alexander was being very mysterious," said Tío Ramón.
"He said he didn't want anyone to know where he was. No

one would think to look for him in such a place, he
explained, and he hadn't needed to show any identifica-
tion when he checked in. He paid in cash."

"What was the place called?" Tommy asked.

Ramón looked down. "The Ecstasy Hotel," he said,
barely able to utter the name. I had trouble picturing him
entering one of those places. More than once, I'd had to
follow a client's cheating spouse to a hot sheet hotel. And
I'd actually been to the Ecstasy, on a surveillance of a
woman suspected of having an affair with the family land-
scaper. The husband was sure the gardener had been
planting seeds in places other than the soil. He'd confronted the wife, who told him he was crazy—no surprise
there. I was retained to prove otherwise, which I did. I
remembered a lot about the Ecstasy, down to the depress-
ing cheap floral-scented disinfectant that hovered over the
place like a cloud of radioactive fallout.

For a man of Tío Ramón's stature and station to go to
such a place must have been completely bewildering. Not
that Cubans were prudes—in pre-Castro Havana there had
been a popular house of ill repute called La Casa de las
Naciones (the House of Nations), in which ladies from
various countries reportedly entertained male guests in
the particular style of their homeland.

"So you arrived at the hotel," Tommy interjected. The
time for worrying about Ramón's sensibilities was over.
There was a dead man to be accounted for.

Tío Ramón pondered for a moment. "Alexander had
told me that he was staying in Room 7, at the corner of the
building. I was supposed to park my car on the street and
walk into the courtyard, then turn left. He said he would
be looking for me."

"Why did you go?" Tommy asked in a cold voice.

"I was curious," Ramón admitted. "I thought my nephew might be in trouble. And I wanted to settle the damned matter of the plantations."

I remembered the layout of the Ecstasy. There were ficus trees planted all around the place, to create privacy.

"When I got there it was just as Alexander had said," Tío Ramón continued. "I went to the courtyard, turned left, and started looking for Room 7. And then . . . I can't believe all this. What a nightmare!"

Tommy and I looked at each other. We knew this was a delicate point in the interview. And we both also knew we had no idea whether our client had in fact murdered his nephew, or whether he was a man unfairly accused. Tommy gave me a little nod, telling me to take the ball and run with it.

"Please go on," I said in a kind voice.

"I found Room 7," Ramón said, his forehead beaded with moisture. "I just stood there in front of the door. Alexander said he would be looking for me, so I waited for a minute. I didn't like standing in that corridor, in plain view, but I didn't want to attract even more attention by knocking. I thought maybe he was on the telephone, or in the bathroom."

Tommy took a handkerchief from his breast pocket and handed it to Tío Ramón. I took my own out of my pocket and dabbed the cloth over my own forehead in as ladylike a manner as possible. The heat was getting stifling. I caught a faint trace of Tommy's cologne, Vetiver, which made me feel unaccountably better.

"I must have waited two or three minutes without any sign from Alexander," Ramón said. "So I began knocking. I knocked quite hard, and I knew he would have heard me if he was inside. I didn't know what to do, but I wasn't going to stand out in the hallway much longer."

"What was going through your mind at that point?" Tommy asked.

Tío Ramón met Tommy's eyes, then my own. "I didn't know what to think. Alexander had been behaving strangely. I started to convince myself that something was wrong. I put my hand on the doorknob and turned it. It was unlocked, so I opened it a little bit and called out Alexander's name."

I waited a moment before prodding him. "And what did you find inside?"

Tío Ramón rubbed his eyes very roughly, as though trying to eliminate the memory of what he'd seen.

"The room was empty. I kept calling out Alexander's name." Tío Ramón took a deep breath. "The bathroom door was partly open, so I pushed it a bit. And that's when I saw red on the floors and walls inside." Ramón shifted in his chair so hard that it scratched against the floor. "It was blood, of course. But in that first moment I don't think I recognized that fact."

"And what next?" Tommy said, his voice quiet.

"The blood led me to the shower stall. The curtain was closed. I didn't know what to do, but I had to look. So I pulled the plastic curtain to one side. Alexander was lying in there, on the floor of the shower, in a very strange position. And . . . and . . . there was a knife sticking out of his chest."

I looked down at the table. Next to me, Tommy calmly waited for what was coming next.

"He was just lying there, and I reached for the knife. I tried to pull it out of Alexander's chest." Tío Ramón's voice shifted, and he was pleading with us to understand. "Of course, I know now that this was a very stupid thing to do. But in that moment it seemed right."

I was sweating, and Tío Ramón was sweating. I glanced

over at Tommy and saw that he, too, had a ring of perspiration around his neck. It was a frivolous thought, but I realized that it *must* have been hot in that interview room. Tommy never broke a sweat, not even in the days when we would spend the entire night making love.

"The knife was stuck tight in his chest, between his ribs," Ramón continued. "So it didn't come out when I pulled at it. You see, I wasn't sure that Alexander was really dead. I mean, I've never seen a man with a knife sticking out of his chest. I was convinced that he had a chance, if I could just get that knife out of him."

"I see," Tommy said.

"I know, I know." Ramón exhaled sharply. "So I put my foot on him and yanked it out. And it came out, all right. With blood all over my face and arms." He looked down at his *guayabera*. "I don't know how my clothes were spared."

My mind was racing, and I knew Tommy's was, as well. We were both envisioning the nightmare scenario of Alexander in the shower, the bloody bathroom, Ramón's struggle with the knife.

"So then you had the knife in your hand?" Tommy asked.

"I shook Alexander, hoping to revive him," Ramón said. "But I only made it worse, because he started bleeding everywhere. I tried to call for help, but I couldn't work the phone in the room. My cell phone was in my car, so I went out to call 911. But as soon as I opened up the door, there was a woman standing there. She started screaming."

"Because of all the blood," said Tommy.

Tío Ramón nodded. "And I still had the knife in my hand. It was the cleaning lady. I guess I frightened her, looking the way I did. Blood was dripping from my hair, but my clothes were spared. Strange, no?"

Tío Ramón asked this question as a child might. It was strange but not impossible. And it was quite a picture. A maid at the Ecstasy was trained to look the other way—and might want to lie low, depending on her immigration status. But there was no staying cool when suddenly confronted with a man trailing blood, spattered with it, a knife in his hand and a look of panic on his face.

"A security guard came right away," Ramón said. "He had a gun—more like a sawed-off shotgun. He was waving it around, yelling at the maid to stop screaming. Finally he pointed it at me and called the police on his cell phone. I was trying to tell him that Alexander needed an ambulance, but he pointed the gun at me and told me to shut up."

Tío Ramón's eyes were dry, which was why I was surprised when his body shook with a sobbing that he was desperately trying to suppress. It was heartbreaking. Dirty, disheveled, and broken, he started gasping for air. I remembered all the times I had seen him happy, self-confident, and surrounded by family and friends.

"What happened when the police arrived?" Tommy asked, respectfully overlooking the older man's condition.

"They took one look at me and put on the handcuffs," Tío Ramón said quietly. "I tried to explain how I found Alexander, and how I had nothing to do with his death, but they told me to save it for my lawyer."

Ramón looked over at me and shook his head with apparent wonder. "You know, Lupe, it's just like they show it on TV. The police read you your rights, you have the right to remain silent . . ."

"Mr. Suarez," Tommy interrupted gently. "The first thing I'm going to do in your case is get you bonded out tomorrow morning."

Tommy went on to discuss the procedural particulars—how an arrested individual in Dade County has to be arraigned and brought before a judge within twenty-four hours. Tommy estimated Ramón's bail, and the two men discussed financial matters while I tried to look through the sweat and fear and see Tío Ramón as he once was.

When it was over I gave Tío Ramón a hug. I tried not to flinch at the way he smelled. My heart was heavy as he was taken away and led back to his cell. My only consolation was that Tommy would make sure that Tío Ramón was free in a few hours.

Tommy would handle the legal aspects of the case. And I knew he would do a great job.

I was going to have to focus on my end of things. Which was dealing with the question of who killed Alexander, and why.

7

THE MENTAL IMAGE OF TÍO RAMÓN IN JAIL haunted me through the night. I didn't sleep much, and when I did I had nightmares in which Tío Ramón's and Papi's faces became interchangeable. I was determined to begin the investigation right away, and decided not to tell Papi about his old friend's plight at least until Tío Ramón was out of jail. Papi's health was good—a situation I didn't want to jeopardize by putting him through the stress of learning that Tío Ramón was locked in a cell.

Dawn found me puttering around the kitchen, trying to fix breakfast in a haze of sleep deprivation. I must have made more noise than I thought in my search for the espresso maker and a saucepan in which to heat up milk, because it wasn't long before I was no longer alone in the kitchen.

Aida had a sixth sense that told her whenever someone was invading her turf; she came into the kitchen with a stern look, eager to see who was there without her permission. I almost didn't recognize her in her nightgown and bathrobe, with pink fuzzy slippers on her feet and pink curlers in her hair. It had been years since I'd seen her wearing anything other than her white uniform and tennis shoes, her hair always perfectly coifed. I tried not to show my surprise.

"Lupe, child," Aida said, her hands on her hips. "What on earth are you trying to do?"

I guess the sight of me in the kitchen trying to fix my own breakfast was almost too much for Aida to handle. The kitchen was definitely not my regular stomping grounds.

"Uh . . . making breakfast?" I said, treading softly.

"Why did you not wake me up?" Aida said in the same tone she might have used to shoo baby ducklings from the back doorstep. "You don't know anything about cooking!"

"I'm sorry," I said, kissing her cheek on the way out. "I'll never come in here without you again. I promise."

Aida started scurrying around opening the kitchen cupboards, gathering the pots and pans to assemble my breakfast. I wasn't sure she had heard me; her hearing wasn't what it used to be. Aida and Osvaldo were so active and spry that it was easy to forget they were both more than eighty years old. It was unbearable for me to contemplate a time in the future in which they would no longer be around.

I had been effectively evicted from the kitchen, so I went outside to the terrace. The sun was just coming up, bathing the Miami skyline in a rosy glow. Often I was just going to bed at this hour, after arriving home with a fair amount of alcohol in my system. I never really appreciated the beauty of the dawn. I was in wonder at its crisp magnificence, but not enough to change my habits and become an early riser. My kind of nine-to-five starts at nine in the evening and ends at five in the morning.

The pelicans appeared and swooped low over the waters of Biscayne Bay, planning their own breakfast just as Osvaldo came out to the terrace with mine. In his arms was a silver tray loaded up with a pot of *café con leche,* and a basket filled with slices of Cuban bread dripping with butter. As the smell of the coffee and bread hit my nose, I felt a moment in which life was perfect.

I unfolded the morning's *Miami Herald* and carefully read through the Metro section, dreading what I might find. Thankfully, there was no mention of the murder at the Ecstasy Hotel. Given Tío Ramón's position in the community, not to mention the lurid circumstances of Alexander's death, it would make a good story. I hoped Channel 7—"If it bleeds, it leads"—wouldn't get hold of the story. I had reason to hope. Crime and murder were everyday events in Miami, and more sensational stories might distract the media's attention.

The morning was so cool and pleasant that I was reluctant to get out of my chair and officially start the day. It was possible to pretend for a bit longer that the scorching heat of the day wasn't on its way. But I had things to do, so I folded the paper for Papi to read when he got up. I stopped off in the kitchen to thank Aida and Osvaldo for breakfast; Aida had found time to change into her uniform and take the curlers out of her hair. It was a reassuring sight. She had looked too fragile and frail in her nightclothes.

"So where are you going today?" Osvaldo asked, rinsing out the coffee urn.

"I'm on a new case," I said.

"Something exciting?" the old man asked.

I paused a second. "I hope not," I said. "I hope it's as exciting as it's going to get."

This was, I knew, a hope that almost invariably would not come true. Not in Miami. Not with murder.

IT HAD BEEN A FEW YEARS SINCE I'D VISITED THE ECSTASY Hotel on Eighth Street, but I found that almost nothing had changed. I parked outside on the street, possibly in the same spot that Tío Ramón had used. To begin the formal investigation I needed the "A" form, the arrest record, and the court file, but I wanted a picture in my mind of what might have happened.

I walked into the courtyard and turned left, just as Tío Ramón had done the day before. At this time of the morning there were no cars in the parking lot outside—no surprise, since hot sheet hotels didn't do much early-morning business, when their patrons were at home with their spouses, families, or significant others.

The Ecstasy's physical layout was pretty straightforward, like a regular motel, with rows of rooms side by side facing out toward the parking lot. Wide walkways and latticed outer walls gave the feeling of a corridor, almost as though one was indoors—except for the heat, which was already starting to build. An out-of-town visitor might even think it was a regular motel—until he saw the signs advertising the prices of the rooms by the hour, with a three-hour minimum, and with cash as the only acceptable form of payment. I was willing to bet the Ecstasy didn't have a hookup with American Airlines to issue frequent-flyer miles for patrons or rewards for repeat visits. Another marked difference was the fact that most hotels didn't sell small bottles of liquor and wine on racks at the front desk.

Yellow-and-black crime-scene tape sealed off Room 7's door, as I knew it would, to preserve the integrity of the area. It had been less than twenty-four hours since Alexander Suarez's body was found by his uncle. It was possible that the police techs might come back to the room for a follow-up sweep.

I stood there in the courtyard, looking at Room 7's

door, when I heard the soft whir of a car's engine behind me. I knew that privacy and discretion were paramount in a place like this, so I was reluctant to turn around and see who had arrived. I stood still, hoping whoever it was wouldn't recognize me. I didn't want to have to explain what I was doing at the Ecstasy Hotel at eight o'clock in the morning.

"Lupe!" a familiar voice called out. So much for anonymity. "I should have known you'd be close by if there was a dead body found."

"Detective Anderson," I said, trying to sound pleasant. I knew what he meant. Every time Anderson and I ran into each other, someone was either dead or would soon be dead. He had, at times, made me think that I was some kind of angel of death.

I represented a lot of work for Anderson in his capacity as homicide detective for the city of Miami. Still, we got along reasonably well. We respected each other and, as yet, hadn't betrayed one another. In Miami, it said a lot for an Anglo man and a Latina to have such a good professional relationship.

"I heard that Tommy MacDonald was the attorney on the Suarez case," Anderson said. He got out of his official city-issued dishwater brown sedan and straightened his tie. "I should have known you'd be on board as the PI."

I saw that the three or four months since I'd last seen Detective Anderson had failed to change him at all. He was still wearing the same outfit he always wore: a khaki poplin suit, a white shirt, and an undistinguished tie that might have been a Christmas gift from a seven-year-old niece. All he needed was a rumpled raincoat to look like a WASP version of Columbo.

"Ramón Suarez is a friend of my father. A good

friend." This was my way of putting Anderson on notice that the case was personal for me. "Are you working this one?"

Anderson nodded. Of course he was. I suspected that Detective Anderson had no personal life whatsoever, and I didn't think that he sank to satisfying his sexual urges at the Ecstasy Hotel at eight in the morning.

He looked around the empty parking lot. "Yup. This one's mine."

I was actually pleased to hear it. Anderson might have been stiff as a board, but he was helpful; he knew that it was to both our advantage to cooperate. I was a little intrigued by him. He revealed nothing about himself, while at the same time gave the impression that he missed nothing about others.

"Any suspects?" I teased him, knowing full well the details of the case so far.

"Only one, Lupe." Anderson fixed his watery blue eyes on mine. "Your father's friend."

"We'll see what we find," I said.

Anderson started walking toward Room 7; his body language indicated that I wasn't invited to follow.

"It doesn't look good for Ramón Suarez," he said. "Not good at all, Lupe."

8

I LEFT THE ECSTASY AND HEADED FOR THE OFFICE. Given the apparent case against Tío Ramón, I had to get busy. I was confident that Tommy would be able to bail out his client—Ramón had no priors, and he was a respected member of the community. I knew the prosecutor would object—that's his job—but Tío Ramón would almost surely be out of jail and on his way home to Key Biscayne as soon as the court paperwork was completed.

Until then, though, I would have to work the case without having a chance to speak with him. I was eager to interview Tío Ramón again, although I had no idea how much additional information I could get from him. The more I thought about it, the more I realized that I had been handed a lucky break when Detective Anderson was assigned to the case. He would keep me informed as well as he could on the developing police investigation.

When I pulled into the cottage's driveway I saw that Leonardo hadn't yet arrived at the office. This was no surprise, since it wasn't quite nine yet. And it had been a full moon the evening before, which always meant that Leo had a late night in store.

For the past few months, Leonardo had gotten involved with a group of Latinas who worshiped the moon; as far as

I could discern, they seemed to feel that the moon goddess had power over their body weight. Leonardo had tried to explain the preposterous concept, that it had to do with the tides and women's monthly cycles. I had tried to point out that, as a biological male, he had nothing to do with monthly cycles. Leonardo, as usual, had wanted no part of logic. He was becoming so touchy that he was developing classic PMS symptoms, so I let the matter drop.

I didn't have the courage to ask precisely what it was Leo and the women did on the night of a full moon. I only prayed that it didn't involve any banned controlled substances. In light of things that had happened in the past, I didn't want to know any more information than I absolutely needed. I had enough problems just then.

Crack detective that I was, I had seen no difference in Leo's physique, a fact that I wasn't about to mention to him. I knew that, since it was the morning after a full moon, he was going to arrive late to work—and looking like the morning after the night before. I parked in my usual spot under the frangipani tree, knowing well that Osvaldo would give me a hard time later about the sap damage on the Mercedes' paint job. It was the only shade in the driveway, so I had to park there or face getting into a steel oven when I wanted to drive someplace.

I unlocked the cottage, turned off the security lights and the alarm, checked out the number of messages on the answering machine—six—then went into my office. As much as I loved Leo, I really enjoyed the time I spent in the office alone before he arrived. I took a moment to look out at the parrots in the avocado tree. They were never early birds, and they were just beginning to stir. Their feathers ruffled in the breeze, catching the soft morning light filtering through the tree's leaves.

I was tempted to make a *café con leche*, but the one Aida made for me had had the effect of rocket fuel already. I sat down and pulled out the Suarez file I had begun yesterday after returning from Tío Ramón's house. I skimmed it quickly, because there wasn't much there. Just a few notes and the letter from the lawyer in Madrid offering to buy the mills in Camagüey.

Alexander's murder certainly changed the focus of my investigation. My priority had been to locate Ramón's nephew to ask him some questions. Well, he'd been found. And he was in no condition to shed any light on the situation.

One thing I knew. Whatever Alexander had wanted to speak with Tío Ramón about at the Ecstasy Hotel, it had led to his murder.

I drew a line on a blank sheet of paper to indicate the date that the Spanish lawyer had sent his letter. Another line marked the date of Tío Ramón's murder arrest. In between, Alexander had told Ramón nothing about his decision as far as the offer to buy the mills was concerned. Between the time Ramón spoke with Alexander about the letter and the date of the murder were four days in which Alexander had been missing—at least, that's what Tío Ramón had told me.

I needed to know what happened during those four days. Alexander might have spent all that time in New York, or he might have come right away to Miami and only contacted his uncle on the fifth day. Or he might have gone someplace else entirely.

Questions. And no one to supply answers. I had only one chance of helping out Tío Ramón, and that was reconstructing the last four days in a dead man's life. *Dios mío.*

9

"LUPE!" I HEARD LEONARDO CALLING OUT FROM THE reception area. *"Buenos días, prima!"* He stuck his head in the door of my office. "How about some *café con leche*? I feel like making a really strong batch. I had a late night."

"It looks like it," I said, getting up to greet him. "*Café con leche* would be great." The hell with tachycardia. I had unpleasant tasks ahead of me.

Leo was more than my cousin; he was also my office manager and, as such, he was privy to a lot of the goings-on with my cases. I would have to bring him up to date on Tío Ramón's situation. Neither Leo nor I was related by blood to Tío Ramón, but his mother—Papi's sister—also knew the Suarez family well. The adults had all been brought up together in Cuba and still socialized as families in Miami.

Other than red eyes and a hitch in his step, Leo actually didn't look much the worse for wear after his full-moon escapade of the evening before. The rest of him, I saw as I checked him out on the way to the kitchen, was a different story. This morning's selection of attire was a burnt-orange tank top over matching bicycle pants. Both garments were so skimpy that their manufacturer must have run out of material before finishing the job. On his feet were golden Top-Siders. He looked like a big pumpkin that had gotten lost on the way to a Halloween party.

Soon the heavenly aroma of *café con leche* wafted in from the kitchen. I accepted a cup from Leo and, quickly and concisely, updated him on Tío Ramón. I left him shaking his head, trying to absorb what he had heard, and returned to my office and punched in a number on the phone.

"La señora Alina, por favor," I asked the housekeeper after identifying myself. It couldn't have been more than ten seconds before Tía Alina came on the line.

"Ay, Lupe!" Tía Alina said in an anguished voice. "What is happening? Is Ramón out of jail yet?"

"I don't know what's happening this very minute," I admitted. "But I was at the jail last night, and I saw Tío Ramón. I'll be honest with you—he's tired, confused, and upset. But he's all right. Mr. MacDonald, Tío Ramón's attorney, is at the courthouse right now. He'll get Tío Ramón out as soon as possible. It shouldn't be much longer."

"Lupe, what has happened to my manners? But first Alexander was killed, and then Ramón was accused of doing it! Ramón in jail for having killed that little . . . that little . . ."

Tía Alina groped for the right word. She muttered something underneath her breath. I wasn't sure, but I thought it was *"maricón,"* the insulting slur for a homosexual, the Spanish equivalent of the English "faggot." *Maricón* wasn't necessarily restricted to homosexuals, and was really a generally dismissive and insulting term. I was surprised to hear it from Tía Alina, a refined and cultured lady. It was obvious now that the Suarez clan had a very low opinion of Alexander.

Tía Alina paused to catch her breath. "I have not thanked you properly for your help. Ramón called earlier and told me all that you have done for us. How can we ever thank you, dear?"

"Don't worry about that, Tía Alina," I said soothingly. "Right now, I need you to do something for me."

"Anything, Lupe," Tía Alina replied, sounding relieved to be able to do something concrete. "I feel so useless sitting here at home, with nothing to do."

"I need some information about Alexander," I told her. "I need his full name, his address, telephone number, and his date of birth."

"But why?" she asked, sounding confused. For the moment I figured all her concern was for her husband. "Alexander is . . . well, you know."

"Yes, Tía Alina. He's dead. But this has to do with helping Tío Ramón. I need to trace Alexander's actions prior to his being killed."

"Just a moment while I fetch my address book." I heard a click. I'd been put on hold.

A moment later she was back on the line. "Alexander Julian Suarez," she read aloud. "He lives on West Fifty-fifth Street in New York. I don't have his date of birth written down, but I can figure it out. He was born just before New Year's—December thirtieth, I think. No, I'm sure of it. And he turned thirty last year, so he was born in 1970."

I was busy writing all of this down. "His father, Julian, he lived here in Miami, right?" I asked.

"Julian? Yes, in Coral Gables. He stayed in that house even after Esperanza died," she said. "He should have moved, but he didn't want to. Do you need information on him?"

"No, but I'm wondering about something. Did Alexander return to Miami and visit his father often?"

"Yes, all the time, especially after his mother died," said Tía Alina. Her voice dropped low and confidential. "Lupe, I don't think Alexander was doing very well, you know, financially. He was an artist, remember. Julian used to help him out quite a bit."

"So how did Alexander pay for all these visits to his father?" I asked, hoping to hear the answer I was looking for.

"Julian used to pay for all his tickets. He sent them to him." Tía Alina's voice turned disapproving. Obviously this was a practice that she did not like.

"Thank you for your help, Tía Alina," I said warmly. "I know this is a very difficult time. I'm sure Tío Ramón will be home with you before much longer. Thomas MacDonald is an excellent attorney, and Tío Ramón is in very good hands."

"*Gracias,* Lupe, for helping our family. We've never had trouble like this before. In your line of business, I guess, you know a lot more about this kind of . . . situation." Tía Alina's voice trailed off.

I knew what she meant, and I wasn't insulted. I was the only person anyone in my social world knew who worked in such a sleazy business.

"I do know a lot about it," I told her. "Although I never get used to it."

"AMERICAN AIRLINES ADVANTAGE PROGRAM. MISS STEVENS speaking. How may I help you?"

The voice on the line came out in a flat midwestern accent. I was momentarily disappointed that I hadn't been assigned a male operator. I always did better with men. Still, this was better than struggling through an automated system, where the chances were high that I would disconnect myself—as I had already done twice.

"Yes," I replied in my sweetest voice. "I'm trying to verify that miles were credited for a trip from New York to Miami this past week. It was an electronic ticket, you see." I added the last part to explain my call—a lot of people were still uncomfortable with electronic ticketing and might not believe that their miles would be automatically credited.

I knew that airlines didn't give out information about passengers' schedules—that was strictly confidential. So I had to come up with another way to find out about Alexander's movements. I knew that if he traveled as much as Tía Alina said, then he probably had a frequent-flier mileage account. Since American Airlines had the most flights to Miami from all three New York area airports that would be the logical place to begin.

"Certainly. Account number?" Miss Stevens asked solicitously. I imagined her at her keyboard, fingers poised and ready.

"I'm sorry, I don't have the account number in front of me. But I have all the other relevant details." Without waiting for Miss Stevens to reply, I rattled off Alexander's information. I was hoping that, if I showed enough information about Alexander, then I might gain access to his flight schedules.

I waited a second, holding my breath. Then I heard a clackety-clack as Miss Stevens's fingers flew over the keys.

"Yes, the trip from La Guardia to Miami was credited to Mr. Suarez's account," she said confidently.

"Which trip *was* that? We've taken so many." Again I

gave her no chance to say anything before I bulldozed on. "I'm sorry to trouble you with all these questions."

Miss Stevens started to reply when I said, "What's that? I'm so sorry. I'm a bit hard of hearing."

I hated using such a lowdown tactic, but I knew that people were sympathetic to individuals—especially customers—with afflictions.

Miss Stevens paused, seemed to think it over. "No problem," she finally said. "I'll speak a bit louder if that would help."

"Oh, thank you."

"The last trip that Mr. Suarez took was Thursday, May eighteenth."

Bingo. Today was Tuesday, May 23. So I could assume that Alexander had left New York for Miami right after speaking with his uncle about the letter from Spain. And he had spent four days in Miami before requesting his meeting with Tío Ramón. I was sure he hadn't been staying at the Ecstasy all that time—no one could, not without raising suspicions.

"Is there anything else I can help you with?" Miss Stevens yelled into my ear, making me jump. If I extended this conversation much longer, I really would be hearing-impaired.

"No, thanks. You've been very helpful." And so she had.

10

I LOOKED DOWN AT MY WATCH. SIX O'CLOCK: ONE hour to go before I planned to return to the Ecstasy. It had been a long day, and I hadn't slept much the night before. Even the parrots outside my window looked as though they were thinking about settling down for the night. I looked at them with pure envy. My mouth opened into such a wide yawn that I heard my ears click. I needed a pick-me-up if I was going to get through the rest of the evening.

I went into the kitchen. Leonardo had gone home an hour before, proclaiming that he was headed for his "Yoga for a Smaller Ass" class. I opened up the refrigerator to see what called out to me. I spotted a bottle of Morgan, a chardonnay that I loved. One glass wouldn't hurt, I decided.

I poured a healthy amount and sipped the cool wine as I walked back to my office. I set the glass on the corner of my desk and started jotting down notes on what I hoped to achieve by going to the Ecstasy.

I wanted to be there at the same time that Alexander had asked Tío Ramón to meet him the night before. It always paid to revisit the scene of the crime at the same time of day. At the Ecstasy, I wouldn't exactly be rubbing shoulders with the higher echelons of Miami society. I would probably run into hookers turning a quick trick, and some two-bit drug dealers selling quick hits to laborers who needed a taste of something strong before going home for an evening with their families. Any of them might have seen something the night before—these types tended to be regulars. The cops would be out canvassing in force soon enough, so I had to move fast.

I also wanted to speak with any Ecstasy employees who might have been on duty when Alexander was murdered. Most of all, I wanted to get to the maid who had seen Ramón coming out of Room 7 covered in blood. Maids at a hotel like that were trained to ignore the guests, but that sight would be too much for anyone to forget.

I sipped my wine. I had to tread carefully on this one, since it was part of an open police investigation. I didn't want to be charged with witness tampering or destroying evidence—both felonies. It was a fine balancing act, getting involved in a capital crime without ending up behind bars myself.

As expected, Tommy had been able to bond Tío Ramón out of jail. He had called earlier from the Justice Center saying that Tía Alina was on her way there with cash to pay the high bail that the judge had set.

And Tommy had couriered over a copy of the "A" form, Tío Ramón's arrest affidavit. I spent some time reading it carefully, trying to learn something new, but it contained the same story Ramón had told Tommy and me—albeit in dry, terse police lingo. But I got a useful name: Francia Alvarado was the maid who had seen Tío Ramón coming out of Room 7. In police terms, she had been the witness who advised them as to what had happened.

Tío Ramón was described as a Hispanic male, seventy-one years old, DOB 7/12/29, six feet tall, one hundred sixty-eight pounds, gray hair, black eyes, with no scars, tattoos, or unique physical features. Tío Ramón had "no known aliases." The arresting officer indicated that Ramón Suarez was not under the influence of alcohol or drugs at the time of his arrest. The weapon, a serrated knife, had been seized from the suspect and impounded. Ramón's address and phone number in Key Biscayne were listed, as well as his profession—"health insurance executive." He was charged with one count of murder in the second degree. The arresting officer said that he had turned over the investigation to Miami-Dade Police Department Homicide Detective Anderson, who arrested the subject at the scene and took him into custody.

It was sad to see how one person's life could be compressed into a single sheet and defined by a single suspected act. This obviously wasn't the first "A" form that I had seen, but it was the first one that dealt with someone so close to me. I told myself to shake off this feeling, that I would be doing Tío Ramón a disservice if I lost my objectivity.

When Tommy had gotten back to his office from the court he had phoned again, this time with details of the bond hearing and his impressions of the case. I told Tommy what I found out from Miss Stevens at American Airlines. Before he hung up, I also told him about my planned trip back to the Ecstasy. Tommy wished me luck, then asked if I was interested in investigating the Ecstasy's unique amenities with him. We had been adventuresome in the past, but we had yet to sample the charms of such a place. I laughed and turned him down. But I had to admit I was tempted.

I finished off the wine and reached for the phone. I wanted to speak with Alvaro before I set off, but he wasn't in his office. I left a message on his machine. I could have tried him on his cell phone, but I didn't feel like chasing him around. I would call him later.

I rinsed off my wineglass in the sink, then turned off the lights and set the alarm. One more thing—I checked inside my purse to make sure the Beretta was loaded and operational. After all, you never know.

The trip from Coconut Grove to Little Havana didn't take long, only about fifteen minutes. I drove north on Le Jeune Avenue, until Eighth Street, where I took a left and headed west. As I approached Red Road, I started looking for a side street where I could park the Mercedes. I didn't want to park in the Ecstasy courtyard where I'd attract attention by showing up in such an expensive car. I might have been exercising too much caution, but I figured I should be low-key.

Luck was with me. I found a spot on a quiet dead-end street, directly across from the Ecstasy, with a clear line of vision to the hotel. I took this to be a good omen.

I sat in the car for a while, checking things out. The area around the Ecstasy was strictly commercial: a liquor store across the street, a fast-food joint to one side, and a huge car lot on the other. It wasn't exactly a warm, romantic setting for trysts, but then it didn't have to be. The Ecstasy served a purpose, without frills or pretensions.

I decided to watch the front entrance for a half hour or so. There were no cars parked on the street alongside the wall that enclosed the Ecstasy. Nor was there anyone walking around looking for action, other than a couple of men in their forties who from their irregular pace looked like they were walking home from a bar.

I opened up the glove compartment and took out my binoculars. I got a look inside at the courtyard. *That* was where the action was. I counted about twenty cars in front of the rooms facing the courtyard. There were all makes and models, sedans, pickups, and a minivan. The cars seemed to represent a true cross section of the economic spectrum. Lust was alive and well, if not thriving, in this pocket of Little Havana.

Foot traffic remained light, which was no surprise in a city where walking was practically a misdemeanor. I saw an old couple walking a dog who looked even older than they did. After I had waited the full thirty minutes, I got out of my car. I took in a few breaths of the hot, moist air, and had to fight off an impulse to return to the air-conditioned luxury that beckoned to me from inside the Mercedes.

I sprinted across the street during a break in traffic and paused in front of the stone pillars that marked the Ecstasy entrance. Then I walked into the office. It was impossible to see in from outside because the windows were opaque silver-colored glass. I suspected that it was really a two-way mirror, enabling the person behind the desk an extra moment or two to check out who was coming.

"Buenas noches," I said. Behind the desk was a middle-aged, paunchy, balding, and distinctly unclean-looking man. He was wearing a dingy *guayabera* and sipping a *colado*—a large *café* in a Styrofoam cup—smoking a cigar, and listening to Amor 107.5 while reading the *Diario las Americas*. I didn't need to use too many of my detecting skills to guess his ethnicity.

"Thirty dollars for a regular room for two hours," he said without looking up from his newspaper. "Fifty if you want the Jacuzzi. Cash up front, no plastic."

"I'm not here for a room," I explained. "I'd like to speak with you for a moment, señor, if I could."

He let out an enormous sigh, letting me know he was doing me a huge favor by taking time out from his busy schedule. He put down his paper and glowered at me. I opened up my purse, making sure he saw the Beretta inside, and pulled out my private investigator's license for his inspection. I also gave him one of my business cards.

"A private investigator?" the man asked, leaning over the desk to check me out head to toe. "A little beauty like you?"

"That's right," I replied sweetly. I put my purse on the desk so that the Beretta was within easy reach of my right hand. I could deal with being checked out. It was the "little beauty" part that made my hand itch to grab the gun.

"So what do you want?" he asked, leaning back again.

"Were you on duty here yesterday?" I asked. He grunted, which I took for an affirmative. The police report said the desk man's name was Pascual Menéndez, the same name I now saw on a little brass plate next to the wall clock. "I'd like to speak with you about what happened here late yesterday afternoon."

Menéndez puffed away on his cigar, blowing a big cloud of smoke right into my face.

"I've already talked to the police," he growled. "I have nothing more to say about it."

He lost interest in examining my chest and went back to his newspaper. I didn't know whether to feel relieved or insulted.

"I understand that," I said, summoning all my willpower not to wave the smoke away from my face. I don't mind good cigar smoke, it's the cheap stuff I can't deal with. "But sometimes people remember things after the fact. I only need a few minutes of your time."

With this, I smiled and leaned closer. I hated playing these games, but sometimes this was all that worked with morons.

Menéndez considered what I was saying and how I looked. "Well, just a minute or two won't hurt." He waved his hand to indicate the empty room. "But get on with it. I'm pretty busy."

I took out my notebook. I was pleased that the manager hadn't asked me for my specific role in the investigation, or who I worked for.

"Your name?"

"Pascual Menéndez," he replied, puffing out his chest a little.

"Señor Menéndez, can you tell me exactly what happened here yesterday?" I asked.

He shrugged. "It was a normal day until I heard Francia screaming."

"The maid?"

"*Sí,*" he said. "She was screaming like a crazy woman."

"Had you ever seen the man who was killed before?" I asked. I wanted to verify that it was Alexander who had come into the office to pay for his room.

"Not that I remember," Menéndez said. "But I don't look at faces much. We sell privacy here. You get it? I take the money, hand out keys, and ask them if they want anything to drink." He pointed to the racks of liquor and wine.

I thought for a moment, although it wasn't easy with a cloud of cigar smoke enveloping my entire head.

"So you don't know for sure if the man who was killed rented the room himself?" I said, my disappointment showing. "Do you know how long he was actually in the room?"

"No, I don't." He looked down and carefully refolded his newspaper. "I already told the police all this. Talk to them."

This interview was clearly over. I didn't want to antagonize him, and I knew I could ask him all I wanted during the discovery phase of the trial. I put the cap on my pen and closed my notebook.

As casually as I could, I asked, "What about the housekeeper, Francia? Is she around? I'd like to speak with her."

Menéndez snorted. "Yeah. Me, too. She didn't come in today. First time ever. She doesn't come in, she doesn't call."

He took a big gulp of his *colado,* then added, "That woman never misses work. She came in one time so sick she could barely stand up. The other maid wanted me to send her home. She told me, 'Don't you dare. I need the money.' "

Menéndez shrugged, as though he found such industriousness crazy.

"Maybe she's upset about everything that happened here yesterday," I offered, although my mind was racing.

"Her? That's funny!" He looked down at his paper. "She's a tough one. The only thing that surprises me is that she started screaming when she saw the guy with the knife."

Now I was beginning to worry. I was about to venture another question when a shady-looking guy came in dressed in black polyester from head to toe, giving off a strong smell of cheap whiskey. He passed a fifty-dollar bill across the counter.

"Jacuzzi?" Menéndez asked.

"Jacuzzi," said the man in a gravelly voice.

Menéndez tossed him a key. "Room 10," he said.

There were no concierge or bellhop services at the Ecstasy. Nor were any expected, to judge from the reaction of Mr. Polyester, who grabbed his key and shot out of the office. I figured that few patrons of the Ecstasy showed up with luggage.

"Thanks for your help," I told Menéndez, trying not to sound too sarcastic. He didn't bother to reply, instead immersing himself in the newspaper.

I came out of the office in time to see Mr. Polyester escorting his date toward Room 10. She was towering in high heels, poured into a two-sizes-too-tight silver pantsuit, her hair dyed a shade of red that would have made Lucille Ball blush. They moved fast, and were gone within a minute.

I stood outside the Ecstasy Hotel leaning against one of the stone pillars by the entrance, looking at the street where Tío Ramón had parked. Then I looked over at the used-car lot.

There were surveillance cameras there, placed high up.

Now I had an idea.

11

I CALLED MARISOL AT HOME EARLY THE NEXT morning. I usually didn't call her before noon, since I knew she had an active social life and it was likely she wouldn't be alone.

"Lupe, what's up?" Marisol had a distinctive raspy voice that always made me think she had just downed a glass of Jack Daniel's filled with cigarette butts.

Marisol Velez was a thirtysomething Venezuelan investigator unequaled in Dade County in the specialties of camera and video surveillance. She was tall with blond hair that never looked quite natural and recently had assumed a platinum sheen that resembled the silver icicles one might find on a Christmas tree. Marisol was so voluptuous that small boys and grown men alike were prone to bouts of confusion every time she walked past. And she dressed to elicit just that reaction.

Once one got over Marisol's physical appearance, then one could focus on her ability to film anything that moved from miles away. I always thought she was a well-kept secret, and that one day the covert branches of the United States government were going to snatch her away and keep her busy for the rest of her working life.

"How's your schedule?" I asked her. "I need your help on a case."

I heard rustling in the background—the sound of Marisol sitting up in bed and trying to sound businesslike. It wasn't an easy task, not with that Marilyn Monroe voice of hers, but she was a gifted investigator who always delivered outstanding work. Her personal affairs might have been a bit of a mess at times, but she was innovative, smart, and together in her professional life.

"Do you want me to come in today?" she asked. "I can be there if you need me in a hurry."

"That would be great," I replied. I was eager to tell her what I had in mind. If anyone could pull it off, it would be Marisol.

"Cool." And that was it; Marisol hung up. I wasn't offended at all by her abruptness. I figured she was entertaining a man when I called, and that she wanted to take full advantage of her time before heading to my office to begin the workday. She knew, as all investigators did, that her personal time would be severely limited once she took the case. In the meantime, she would finish up her personal investigation of the lucky man in her bed.

I had long ago figured out that Marisol was making up for the years she'd lost while married to her first husband, a low-level diplomat from Valencia, Venezuela. He had been posted to the Miami consulate as the third assistant consul in charge of issuing visas for students and au pairs. As soon as he completed his tour of duty in Miami he expected to return home to Valencia to raise a family with Marisol. Marisol had other ideas. As the saying goes, it's hard to keep them down on the farm after they've seen Paris. The charms of Valencia were no match for the Sodom and Gomorrah of South Florida.

Next I placed a call to the Suarez home. I wanted to go see Tío Ramón, but Tía Alina told me that he was still sleeping off his ordeal of the day before.

"Should I wake him?" she asked me.

"There's no need," I told her. "He needs his rest. Just have him call me when he feels well enough to meet."

After I hung up I heard the outer office door open; a moment later Leonardo poked his head in.

"*Buenos días*, Lupe," he said sleepily. "*¿Como estás? Café con leche?*"

What kind of question was that? Was the Pope Catholic?

"*Sí, gracias,*" I said.

Ordinarily I might have gotten up and kept Leo company in the kitchen while he was making the coffee, but that morning I was preoccupied and needed to gather my thoughts together. I took out the letter from the Spanish lawyer and thought about the offer made to the Suarez family for their properties in Cuba. I stared at it until something occurred to me. Alexander had died unmarried and without children. Tío Ramón was now the sole owner of the Cuban properties.

Well, in principle. Everything in Cuba still belonged to the government. But if and when property rights were reinstated on the island, they would become Tío Ramón's. The Helms-Burton Bill passed in 1996—after Castro's military shot down two civilian airplanes piloted by Cuban Americans over international waters—sought to regulate foreign companies that profited from doing business with the Castro government. It sought to penalize the accumulation of profit from enterprises that had once been in private hands but had been confiscated by the Communist government. As far as I could tell, the Spanish lawyer's proposal to the Suarez family wouldn't fall under the jurisdiction of the bill.

As Castro reached his final years—or days—people were anxiously waiting to see what sort of government was going to evolve after Fidel's passing. No one knew what the situation was going to be, but everyone seemed to agree that things would not continue as they had been. The old man's force of character and personality had kept his government alive, but that would end soon. Cuba wasn't a purely Communist state; it was a Fidel Castro state. And no man lives forever.

The effect of Alexander's death had been to place the Suarez family's Cuban properties in one man's hand: Tío Ramón's. Like it or not, it was a solid motive for murder.

Tío Ramón had assured me that he had told Alexander he wasn't interested in selling his half of the two mills in Camagüey. But Tío Ramón could have been lying about that. He could have lured his nephew to Miami under the pretense that he was ready to sell the mills, and that they should meet in an out-of-the-way place to discuss the sale. And then he could have killed him.

If there's one thing I've learned over and over during my years as a private eye, it's that nothing is as it appears to be. It was entirely possible that Tío Ramón had another motive for killing his nephew, something secret that I had yet to uncover.

Tío Ramón seemed to be doing very well financially, but appearances could be deceiving—especially in Miami, where so much of life was smoke and mirrors. Once Alexander was out of the picture, Tío Ramón would stand to gain three and a half million dollars from the sale— double what he'd have gotten after splitting the proceeds with Alexander.

But why bring me—a private investigator—into the situation? Perhaps to make himself look innocent by apparently inviting scrutiny just before the crime took place. I might be ready to believe whatever he told me, because of the close friendship between our families. Sometimes the

best defense was a good offense. It wouldn't be the first
case I'd worked in which the client was trying to use me.

I told myself to calm down, that this line of speculation would help no one. But I was paid to question what I
was told, even if those questions raised doubt about my
own client's credibility. I wrote down all my questions and
placed them in the Suarez file. Hopefully I wouldn't need
them later.

Just then Leonardo appeared with a big steaming mug
of *café con leche*. I had been so lost in thought that I hadn't
noticed his outfit until then. Not that there was much to
see—Leo was in danger of violating my eight-ounce rule
for office wear, which stipulated that any garment he wore
had to weigh more than a half pound.

This morning he was dressed head to toe in mesh. Not
just any mesh, mind you, but all in flesh tones. It was very
hard at first glance to see that he was wearing anything at
all. I stared at him, and my only reaction was deep gratitude that we weren't expecting any clients in the office that
morning. The fashion police would have called in a 911. I
really needed to speak with him at some point—some
offices had dress-down Fridays, but lately at Solano Investigations every day had been undress-down day.

I thanked him for the coffee and went back to work. I
read the letter from the Spanish lawyer again, and another
thought came to mind. If the Suarez family had received
such an offer, it was likely that the owners of other sugar
mills in Cuba had also been contacted. Tío Ramón had
told me that there were 156 mills in Cuba. That meant a
lot of owners who could be contacted. And then there
were other industries: tobacco, cattle, hotels. The same
sorts of offers might have been extended to dozens of exile
families.

I told myself to relax. I wasn't going to be able to

investigate a murder at the same time as exploring the state of all formerly privately held properties in Cuba. It was too much.

A moment later I heard the outer office door open and a woman's voice call out, "*Buenos días!* Anyone home?"

"Marisol!" Leonardo called out with genuine delight in his voice.

"Coffee smells great!" her voice rang out from the next room. "And what a great outfit! Can I borrow it sometime? We're about the same size."

I got up from my desk just as Marisol came into my office. She leaned over and kissed me hello. Then she whispered in my ear, "*Really*, Lupe. Shame on you. You obviously don't pay Leo like you should. He can't even afford enough clothes to cover himself!"

With this, she erupted in peals of laughter. I felt my ears turning red with irritation.

That did it. From now on the eight-ounce rule would be the law of the land. As soon as I felt like confronting my cousin about it, that is.

12

"SO WHAT DO YOU THINK?" I ASKED MARISOL AS we focused our binoculars on the video camera affixed atop a steel pole in the used-car lot next door to the Ecstasy. We were sitting in the Mercedes, street-parked alongside the wall bordering the hotel. I had backed the car as much as possible into a ficus bush, hoping to keep out of sight. But I knew that, if we could see the camera, then it could see us as well.

Marisol had yet to utter a single word. She was immobile save for her lips moving slightly; she seemed to be making some kind of calculation in her mind. I was getting antsy—no one ever listed patience among my many virtues.

Finally she spoke. "I think that camera has enough range to pick up what's going on on the street out here," she said. She nodded at the camera. "Watch the angle when it points left to pan the lot."

I pushed the binoculars so deep into my eye sockets that I feared leaving a permanent mark. It seemed to me that Marisol was right, that the camera might overshoot the perimeter of the parking lot. That meant there would be a video recording of street activity outside the Ecstasy at the time of Alexander's murder.

"I think you're right," I said, trying to keep the excitement out of my voice. I lowered the binoculars. "So you're familiar with that kind of video-surveillance equipment?"

"*Sí.*" Marisol stared out at the car lot. "Generally speaking, it works two ways. There's a video monitor on the premises, where a security guard watches what the camera captures. That is, if the business can afford a security guard. The other way is having the activity monitored from a central location, off the property itself."

"But in both cases there's a video recording of what the camera shoots?" I asked hopefully.

"Usually a seventy-two-hour recording, with the time and date stamped on every frame," Marisol explained. "The most common brand a business like this would use is Panasonic."

I thought for a minute. "And where would they keep the tapes?"

"If the surveillance equipment is kept on the premises, then that's where the tapes would be stored. If the monitoring is done at a central station, then that's where the tapes would be."

I looked up at the sign in front of the lot: AAA Best Preowned Cars. "What do you think about this place?" I asked.

Marisol thought for a moment. "I'd guess they use on-site monitoring," she said. "They're interested in capturing criminal activity on tape, so they want to make sure they have the visual records. They carry insurance to cover their losses, but this would be their fallback."

Marisol popped a stick of gum in her mouth; the smell of sweet artificial tropical fruit filled up the Mercedes' interior.

"There's a lot of activity here during business hours,"

she noted. "We've been here about an hour, and we haven't seen any security guards patrolling the place."

I thought for a moment. "This is my third time here. But I've always come during regular business hours, so I don't know what happens after hours. I haven't seen any security, but then I haven't really been looking."

Marisol nodded. "They probably have a security guard who stays in the office watching the monitor. He'd have orders to call the police if he saw anything suspicious going on after hours—and not to get involved or to interfere."

Marisol smacked her gum, a truly annoying sound. "You know the way things are today," she added. "If their security guard tried to stop a thief and someone got hurt, they'd end up with an expensive lawsuit."

If Marisol was correct, and AAA Best used on-site monitoring, then the record of what happened out there on the street on the day of Alexander's murder was somewhere in the car lot's office. I was gambling that this was the case, and that the camera might have recorded something useful. There were a lot of ifs, but at least it was something concrete to focus on.

Which left me with one question: How did I get that video?

Five o'clock that afternoon found me walking onto the lot of AAA Best Preowned Cars. I had the *Miami Herald* tucked under my arm and folded to the used-car section of the Classifieds. I walked around, looking at the cars, checking the prices, doing everything but kicking tires. No salespeople approached me for a while, which was fine. It gave me time to check out the place.

I had an idea how to get the video, but it was risky. I cruised the lot, thinking about what I had to do. I prayed it would work; otherwise I was going to become Tommy MacDonald's next client.

I was following a hunch, but nothing was going to be easy. I had called two video services in Miami and asked them about the turnaround time for duplicating a seventy-two-hour surveillance tape. Both gave me the same answer: seventy-two hours. It would cost me twenty-five dollars an hour. Which added up to $1,800. I decided that wasn't an option. I would have to think of something else.

I was going to have to steal the tape, I decided.

"May I help you?" a voice said from behind me.

"Oh, hi." I turned around. My luck was in. The salesman was a young Latino guy in his mid-twenties, his hair slicked back, gold chains around his neck, and a Rolex watch on his wrist. He was dressed for South Beach clubbing in body-hugging black polyester. His eyes were all over me, as though I were on sale like the cars in the lot. I knew how to play this one.

"Hi, yourself," the salesman said with a barely disguised leer. "Looking for something?"

"You bet," I said with a smile. "But let's start with a car."

"We have lots of them." He waved his arm. "Anything particular in mind?"

"Well, I used to drive a Jaguar, but I don't anymore," I said vaguely. I figured the salesman would assume I was talking about a boyfriend's car that was no longer accessible to me since we had broken up—leaving me single and available.

I had been in the area several times in the Mercedes over the past two days, so this time I had driven Leo's black Jeep and parked it a block away. I also wanted to make sure nothing happened to Leonardo's car in case something went wrong.

"I understand," the salesman said, feeling my pain. "So what can I do for you?"

"Maybe a used Lexus," I offered. "I've been reading that they're reliable, and they keep their value. They're also supposed to have a good maintenance plan."

"That's right," the salesman said eagerly, as though I had come up with the right answer to a trick question. "I can see you're a smart buyer."

He held out his hand and grabbed mine so quickly that I was almost frightened. "My name is Abel," he said. "And yours?"

"Margarita," I said. His eyes were burning into mine. "Margarita Ramírez."

He shook my hand with an intensity that reminded me of a blender making a milk shake. When he released me I suddenly felt the full force of the sun and the asphalt all around us. Abel was apparently used to these conditions—he looked cool and comfortable. I, on the other hand, was starting to feel like a limp dishrag.

"Would you like to look at what we have on the lot?" Abel said, seeming to notice my condition. "Or would you rather come into the office, out of this heat, and cool off while I tell you all about our inventory?"

"Going inside would be great," I said.

Abel opened up the glass door to the main office and escorted me inside. There was a big round open showroom featuring five cars in the center—each with a big colorful bow on its roof. A reception desk occupied one corner. I would have liked to check out the place more thoroughly, but Abel took hold of my elbow.

"My office is this way," he said, taking me to the second office on the right and opening the door with a flourish. "Please make yourself at home."

I sat down and thanked Abel, looking around the small room.

"Would you like something to drink? Coffee or a soda?" I could tell that Abel smelled a sale; I almost hated to toy with him like this.

"A glass of water would be great," I told him. I had seen a coffeepot by the reception desk and a soda machine in the showroom, but no water dispenser. I figured fetching water would send Abel on a longer mission.

"I'll be right back," Abel said with a little wink.

Now I had to think fast. I hadn't seen any room on my way in that obviously housed the video-surveillance equipment. There was no time to waste. I grabbed my purse and darted out of Abel's office. I heard his voice somewhere down the corridor, talking and laughing with another man. I hoped he would stay occupied for more than a few minutes, but it was a faint hope. Abel was hot on the trail of a sale—and maybe more.

There were six doors in the corridor, each identical to Abel's. They were probably all salesmen's offices, I figured.

There was another hallway branching off from the reception desk, more drab and utilitarian. There were no posters on the walls there, and it wasn't lit as brightly as the showroom or the sales section. This was my best bet.

Unfortunately there was someone at the reception desk—an overly made-up young woman stuffed into a granny dress. I immediately saw, however, that she was more interested in painting her acrylic nails a bloodthirsty red than she was in anything going on around her. I hoped she kept her attention focused on her beauty regime for a couple of minutes longer.

I brazened it out and marched right past her as though

I belonged there, and knew exactly where I was going. I had just turned the corner when I heard a nasal female voice call out, "Hey, you!"

My heart sank to my knees. I tried to decide whether to acknowledge that I had heard her. It would seem too suspicious to just keep going, so I turned around to face the receptionist.

Her freshly painted nails were so red she might have just finished slaughtering and deboning some small animal. She pointed to a horseshoe-shaped key ring hanging on the wall next to her desk.

"You forgot the key," she said in a bored voice.

Key? What key? And then I realized—she thought I was going to the ladies' room. Relief flooded over me.

"Oh, thanks," I said. "I didn't realize it was locked."

I took the key ring down from the wall and left the receptionist to the important task of blowing on her nails. I turned the corner, holding the key in front of me like a weapon. The hall was plain and deathly silent.

First I would try the rooms on the side of the hall that faced the car lot—I figured this side would be the best bet for the video equipment, because any security guard working there would have the added advantage of being able to look out the window. I opened the first door. It was a storage closet, filled with office supplies and paper towels. I quickly closed the door and opened the next one.

I gasped. There was no video setup in this room. Instead there was a balding old man sitting behind a desk munching a sandwich, a 7-Eleven Big Gulp at the ready.

"Oops!" I squealed. "Sorry, I thought this was the ladies' room." I dangled the key in front of me for evidence.

The man barely looked up from his meal. He pointed

down the hall and growled, "Two doors down. Across the hall. The one that says 'rest room' on the door."

When I closed the door my heart was beating so fast that I might have just finished a dozen *café con leches*. I'd only been in the man's office for thirty seconds at the most, but I hadn't seen anything in there that looked like video equipment. If I had to guess, I'd say that it was a billing office.

That left one more room on the parking lot side of the hallway. I prayed there would be no one in the room watching the screen during business hours, or else all of this would be for nothing. I held my breath and opened the door.

Bingo. A two-screen VCR machine with two recorders, small console, camera controls, and a lot of electronic cable. And against one wall, rows and rows of cardboard boxes; a quick look inside one revealed that they were full of videotapes. I read the labels on the stack of boxes. They were all from the year before, useless to me. I looked around, suddenly feeling desperate. Why the hell weren't all the tapes stored together? I knew I had, at most, another minute before Abel came looking for me.

There were two doors at the other end of the room, probably storage closets. I opened the first one and breathed a deep sigh of relief when I saw more boxes stacked up. But these were labeled with dates even older than the ones I had already looked at.

"Shit," I whispered. I was feeling the situation getting away from me.

Then I heard a voice in the hallway. "Margarita?"

I jerked my head up when I remembered that was the name I had given Abel. Oh, God. I couldn't think of what I would tell him if he caught me snooping around in the security room. I knew the receptionist had probably told him I was looking for the ladies' room, but that had been a few minutes ago.

I had no choice. I was in deep. Might as well find what I was looking for.

I opened up the other closet. More tapes and, finally, labels with dates from the current month. I heard Abel calling for me again. This time he sounded dangerously near.

The tapes nearest to me were recent, but still a month old. I looked around desperately, knowing I was down to my final seconds. I could easily be charged with breaking and entering if I was caught. I would certainly lose my PI license. I cursed my bad judgment and wondered what the hell I thought I was doing.

Then I found the most recent box. Trying hard not to hyperventilate, I found the latest tape. Its label listed dates ending three days before.

Three days. Each tape held seventy-two hours of footage. That meant only one thing—that the tape I was looking for was still in one of the two machines.

"Margarita?" Abel called out.

One VCR was labeled "SW camera," the other, "NE camera." I closed my eyes and tried to orient myself to the points of the compass. I pictured the ocean and the Everglades, my two usual reference points. Then I pictured the car lot and the street next to the Ecstasy Hotel.

I said a quick prayer to the Virgin for guidance, brushed my fingers over the medals pinned to my brassiere, and quickly pressed the eject button on the SW machine. I took the tape and replaced it with a blank one from my purse.

The instant I had the tape hidden away the door opened. Abel was standing there.

"What are you doing?" he asked. "I couldn't find you, and then I heard noises coming from in here."

"Oh, Abel. You must have thought I'd left," I said. I put my hand to my mouth as though mortally embarrassed. "I was looking for the ladies' room, and I must have opened every door in the place. You must think I'm a total idiot!"

"The ladies' room?" Abel asked, confused, looking around the office. "It's across the hall."

"You see, my doctor gave me these pills for female problems," I said. "They make me a little spacy."

I knew men—especially young, hip ones like Abel—hated to hear anything about female plumbing. My vague explanation worked; Abel looked away, as though he dreaded hearing anything more.

"So . . . you're not feeling well?" he asked.

"Oh, I'll be just fine," I babbled. "My doctor said I should be feeling better in a week or so."

I brushed past him and out into the hall. I didn't want to hang around the security room and have anyone discover there was a blank tape in one of the VCRs. I doubted that anyone ever looked at the tapes—unless there was a theft in the lot. Hopefully things would be quiet at AAA Best for the rest of the day.

"I got this prescription from the gynecologist," I said, uttering the dreaded word as Abel closed the security room door behind us. "He said they were strong, but I had no idea. I mean, they just make me into a real basket case!"

Abel looked worried. "Maybe you should go home and rest," he said. The situation was turning strange, and he seemed to be worried about getting in any deeper. "You can come back and look at the Lexus when you're feeling better."

"Oh, I'd like that," I said.

He took a business card from his shirt pocket and

handed it to me. "Make sure you ask for me," he said, recovering quickly. "And call me any time if you have questions."

We walked back to the reception desk, where I replaced the key on its hook. The receptionist was far too busy peering into a magnifying glass and plucking her eyebrows to pay any attention to me.

"I'll feel like talking business a little later," I said, giving Abel my best smile. "Thanks for being so understanding."

By now Abel was peering out at the parking lot, probably scoping the place for another customer.

"Feel better," he said as he opened the door for me.

Oh, I will, I thought as I patted my purse. Once I've had a look at this tape.

13

I SPED BACK TO THE OFFICE. DRIVING ABOUT
twenty miles over the limit. After what I had just done,
obeying traffic laws didn't seem quite so important. I knew
I was being paranoid, but I kept glancing in the mirror to
make sure I wasn't being pursued by the police. I even
drove with the radio off, so I could hear the sound of
approaching sirens.

I had bent a few rules in my time, but I had just taken
things to another level. I hoped it was going to be worth it.

When I was reasonably satisfied that my mug shot
wasn't going to grace any post office walls, I slowed down
and punched in Marisol's number on my cell phone. She
picked up right away.

"Can you come to the office?" I asked.

"Sure," she replied. "What's up?"

"I have something to show you," I said. "Get there as
soon as you can."

We hung up. I wasn't going to share any details with
Marisol about how I had come to be in possession of the
tape, because I didn't want to implicate her in a crime. I
was fully aware of the ramifications of what I had just
done. And anything on the tape that was relevant to
Alexander's murder would be considered evidence, which

meant that I would be obliged to turn it over to Detective Anderson. Even though Tío Ramón was my client, Alexander's death was an ongoing investigation.

And just because I had gotten away from AAA Best Preowned Cars didn't mean I was home free. I was counting on the likelihood that no one viewed the seventy-two-hour tapes on a regular basis. They were probably taken out, labeled, and stored. If anyone looked at my replacement tape, however, they would see something was seriously wrong. And Abel would surely remember the strange woman who mistook the security center for a ladies' room.

There was another problem. Detective Anderson might look up at the security cameras on the car lot and figure out what I had—that he had found a potential source of evidence. He might request the video, find it blank, and then the questions would start flying.

But Detective Anderson thought he had already found the guilty man. So how long would he keep his investigation open? The last thing most homicide detectives would want to do is muddy up a case by introducing doubt. But most detectives weren't Detective Anderson. He was honest and moral, and more interested in finding out the truth than inflating the number of cases he closed. So I would have to be very careful the next couple of days.

Marisol was waiting for me at the office when I arrived. I sat her down, told her what I wanted, and that I needed it fast.

"No problem," she said. "If there's anything there, I'll find it."

After Marisol left, I phoned Alvaro. I hadn't spoken to him since two nights ago, when I had to go meet Tío Ramón at the Dade County Jail. He was in his office, but in the middle of a meeting.

"I'm sorry," he said, "but I can't really talk."

"I understand. It's been crazy the last couple of days."

"Dinner?" he asked.

I agreed, noting that he sounded even more harassed than I did.

Next I called the Suarez home and asked for Tío Ramón. It was a while before he finally came on the line.

"Lupe," Tío Ramón greeted me. I was taken aback for a moment by how weak his voice sounded. "I haven't had the chance to properly thank you for your help."

"Oh, Tío Ramón, please," I demurred. It felt strange to have Papi's old friend in my debt. "I'm just glad I'm able to help you."

"I mean it. I don't know what would have happened to me if I hadn't been able to turn to you in my time of trouble," Tío Ramón said. He sounded more like his old self. I felt a little guilty for entertaining suspicions about him earlier.

"I need to ask you a few questions, Tío Ramón," I said delicately. "Please, if you could, answer them as thoroughly as possible."

I could have kicked myself. I sounded like I was reading from the Emily Post Book of Witness Interrogation. I had to get past the fact that I was dealing with a family friend. To any other client I would have said something along the lines of "Answer my questions and don't fuck with me."

"Of course, my dear," Tío Ramón said. "What would you like to know?"

I would have preferred this conversation take place face-to-face, so I could read Ramón's expressions and reactions. But I didn't have time to drive out to Key Biscayne, and I couldn't put off this conversation until later.

"When I came to your home two days ago, you retained me to investigate what was behind the offer the Spanish lawyer made to buy your family mills in Cuba," I said. "Are you in contact with any other Cuban mill owners in Miami? And if you are, have any of them received similar offers?"

"Actually, Lupe, I *am* in contact with other mill owners. We were friends in Cuba, and we continue our friendship in exile—the ones who are still alive, of course. It's been so long. More than forty years." A note of sadness entered Tío Ramón's voice. "There's an organization that most of us belong to, called the Cuban Sugar Mills Rightful Owners."

I was beginning to recognize the faraway tone that came into Tío Ramón's voice whenever he spoke about the sugar business in Cuba. As soon as the words were out of his mouth, I knew I was in for another stroll down memory lane.

"Our *ingenios*—sugar plantations—were located close together, and we socialized often," Tío Ramón said. "The *ingenios* were so far out in the country that there wasn't really much to do out there during the *zafra*. Of course we were there only during the sugar harvest; the other six months of the year we spent in Havana. After the *zafra*, it wasn't really necessary for the owners to be out at the *ingenios*. The administrators, managers, and other staff kept the mills running."

As I listened to Tío Ramón reminisce about the mills, I remembered something I had once heard Mami and Papi discussing at home years before. They were speaking about a woman who had arrived in Miami with her family a few days before. She had been the mistress of the owner of one of the larger *ingenios* in Oriente province. For years the mill owner had been trying to obtain an exit visa for her to join him in South Florida, and the Cuban government had finally granted permission for her and her children to emigrate to the United States. According to what my parents said, it was perfectly normal for a mill owner to have two families—his legally married wife and children in Havana, and his mistress and their children on the *ingenio* in the provinces. It was a practical arrangement, and Cubans are nothing if not practical. Each woman knew of the other and accepted the situation. The wife had no intention of rotting away on the *ingenio* half the year, and the mistress typically had no desire for city life. And eventually some of these men had brought both families into exile with them.

Tío Ramón continued speaking in idealized terms about life in Cuba as an *hacendado.* "Our parents and grandparents, even our great-grandparents, they were all friends and business associates. And we still keep in touch. One day, maybe, our children will be interested in the sugar business, and relationships between them will be as close as ours were."

As I listened, I wondered whether Tío Ramón had a second family, or if Tía Alina had been the only woman in his life.

"So there was a similar organization in Cuba?" I asked him.

"Yes, there was," replied Tío Ramón. "One for the sugar mill owners, the *hacendados,* and one for the *colonos,* the sugar farmers. We didn't always agree, because our interests weren't always the same, but generally we got along with each other. We were so powerful then in Cuba that we used to dictate sugar policy."

This probably wasn't the time to point out that if things had been so great in Cuba before the revolution, then

Fidel Castro might not have been able to take and hold on to power.

There was a long silence between us. Tío Ramón sighed and I could tell he was ready to step back into the present.

"To answer your earlier question, no. I haven't heard of anyone else receiving such an offer for a mill. That's why I was so surprised when Alexander called to tell me about the one he received."

"Is there anyone in the organization that I could speak with?" I asked. "Maybe one of the officers?"

"I don't see why not," Tío Ramón answered in a slightly puzzled tone. "Let me think of who you could call. I'll check to see who might be available."

"Thank you, that would be helpful." I took a deep breath. "Now I need to ask you about Alexander."

"I suppose we have to talk about him, don't we?" Tío Ramón said.

"Yes. We do." I decided just then to ask him only one or two questions. I would need to see him in person for more delicate matters.

"Before you went into the Ecstasy Hotel, as you parked and entered the courtyard," I began, "did you observe anyone at all around the premises?"

A moment's silence on the line. "No, I don't recall anyone. But keep in mind, Lupe, that I was thinking only about my meeting with Alexander. To tell you the truth, I didn't want to know much about anything that was going on around me in that place."

"I understand."

"Of course, if I'd known what I was going to find in that room," Ramón added, "then I'd have paid a lot more attention."

I thought I'd try a trick that had worked in the past.

"You might think this is silly, Tío Ramón, but bear with me. Close your eyes for a moment, relax, and picture the scene when you came into the courtyard."

"I'll do whatever you ask," Tío Ramón replied. "My eyes are now closed."

I could tell that Tío Ramón thought I was full of shit, but he had decided to humor me.

"Picture the street, the hotel, the courtyard, the hall-way, the doorway." I felt as though I might as well be dangling a pocket watch in front of Tío Ramón's eyes, but there was a chance I would get results.

I waited a full minute, then said, "What do you remember?"

Tío Ramón didn't respond. I hoped that was because he was concentrating so hard on what I was asking of him. But I was familiar with the mind-set of septuagenarian upper-class Cuban exile men. Doing a visualization exercise, for him, was probably on the same level as doing yoga and adopting a vegan diet.

"I'm sorry, Lupe." He sighed. "I don't think this is going to work."

"That's no problem," I said. "It doesn't work all the time. I was just hoping you might remember something new."

"Well, Lupe, what's next?" Tío Ramón said, in a tone that suggested he was reassuring me he didn't think I was completely nuts.

"I need to come see you—at your convenience, of course." I could have kicked myself again. I reminded myself that I was in control, not him. He was the client. I *had* to stop deferring to him. "We'll set up a time after I've spoken with one of your associates from the sugar-owners' organization."

"Of course," Tío Ramón said quickly. "I'll find an appropriate contact and get back to you right away."

The conversation seemed over when Tío Ramón added suddenly, "Just one thing, Lupe. It's a bit embarrassing." He paused. "I don't know if I should mention it at all, but I think you want me to be as thorough as possible."

My ears perked up. Here was a man facing a murder charge for a crime that took place in a love hotel. And he was embarrassed about telling his investigator something.

"You can tell me anything, Tío Ramón."

"Well, you see, you're a young lady from a nice Cuban family," Tío Ramón said haltingly. I could tell he had as hard a time dealing with me as I did with him.

"Please forget all that," I said. "I'm your investigator. You have to talk to me if I'm going to help you."

"Well, I did see someone at the hotel," Tío Ramón said. "She was coming out of a room, but she wasn't a . . . lady. Not a nice girl."

"What do you mean?"

Tío Ramón lowered his voice to a whisper. "I think she was a prostitute," he said.

I thought about what he had just said. I had planned to canvass the neighborhood and talk to prostitutes. But now I had a better idea.

14

"HOW'S THE CASE GOING?" ALVARO ASKED. THE
waiter had just finished taking our dinner orders at
Claudius, an Italian restaurant in Coral Gables. I hadn't
been able to give Alvaro my usual daily updates on cases I
was working. All he knew was that I had gone straight off to
the Dade County Jail from dinner at Smith & Wollensky's.

"It's early days," I said with a shrug. I didn't feel much
like talking about Tío Ramón, but I knew the situation
might change once the wine worked its magic. I had a lot
of unanswered questions, and I knew a conversation with
Alvaro would invariably raise a few more.

But I had another reason for not feeling like discussing the case right away. The last thing I wanted was for
Alvaro to know about the surveillance tape I'd stolen from
AAA Best Preowned Cars. Alvaro was a moralist and a
straight arrow, and I knew he would be angry with me.

The waiter returned with the wine, a perfectly chilled
Santa Margarita. We each took a few sips, and I started to
relax a little. I looked around the place. For some reason
the main dining room at Claudius always reminded me of
the Colosseum amphitheater in Rome, with its columns
and sandy-colored walls.

It had been only two days since Alvaro and I had been

together, but somehow it seemed like much longer. He looked good, and I was getting the familiar twinges that his presence typically caused in me. He looked great in his everyday work clothes—an open-necked work shirt and chinos. He could have been mistaken for a Gap or Banana Republic model, rather than what he was: a very successful immigration attorney with a thriving practice.

"Are you worried?" Alvaro asked, his brown eyes seeming to detect something in me. "I know this is no ordinary case, not with your papi and Ramón being such good friends."

"That's exactly right."

Alvaro took a sip of wine. "And because of that, you don't know whether you might be doing your client a disservice by staying on the case."

I squeezed Alvaro's hand, then leaned over and gave him a peck on the cheek. It was wonderful to have someone who could understand my predicament without judging me. My twinges were giving way to full-fledged longings. Two days was definitely too long, I thought, as I tried to concentrate on our conversation.

Alvaro dipped his bread into a plate of olive oil. "So where are you now?" he asked.

Over our first course of mussels marinara I brought Alvaro up to speed about Tío Ramón's version of what happened. I didn't tell him about my lingering doubts over Tío Ramón's innocence, feelings I couldn't completely erase. Maybe some part of me thought that doing so would have been disloyal to Papi's friend.

"I have to deal with two issues," I told Alvaro. "First I have to try to exonerate Tío Ramón from the murder charges and hopefully find the real killer." I drained the last of the Santa Margarita from my glass. "The second is to find out what's behind the offer to buy the mills in Cuba. That's what I was hired for in the first place, after all."

"That doesn't sound like it's going to be easy." Alvaro refilled my wineglass.

"But the two are related," I noted. "So maybe solving one situation will solve the other."

Just then my linguini in lobster sauce arrived. I dug in gleefully. There was no way to solve anything on an empty stomach.

THE SUN WAS STREAKING THE SKY RED WHEN I PULLED INTO THE driveway at home. I hoped no one would be awake at that early hour to see me just coming in. I was certain my family understood that I was no longer as pure as the girl in the silver frame on the altar table just inside our front door—in the photo I was wearing a white communion dress and a pearl-encrusted veil—but I didn't want to flaunt the fact in their faces.

Arriving home at 6 A.M., dressed in clothes from the night before, was not an image that I wanted to project to my family. And I didn't want to be a negative role model for my sister Fatima's twelve-year-old twin girls. Their son-of-a-bitch father, Julio Juarez, was bad enough. He had begun his married life by having sex with the maid of honor after the wedding ceremony in a ladies' room stall at the reception. Then he had pilfered money from Papi's construction business to pay for his mistress—which permanently took him out of the running for Husband of the Year.

Still, in spite of my complete contempt for my former brother-in-law, it was because of him that I became a private investigator in the first place. Had Julio not stolen money from Solano Construction to set up a little Cuban bonbon in an apartment off Eighth Street, then the family wouldn't have been forced to retain an attorney who in turn contracted a private investigator to track the missing money.

The investigator the lawyer hired was named Hadrian Wells, and he let me tag along while he went about his work. I was hooked from the beginning, absorbing Hadrian's every action as though I were a shrub in the Sahara during the year's only rainfall.

I was in my junior year at the University of Miami at the time, concentrating on a degree in advertising. But it didn't take me long to realize that I really wanted to get into investigations. Mami and Papi were predictably appalled. They ranted and raved that nice Cuban girls from good families didn't get into such a sleazy business.

Which was partly the point, of course.

We came to a compromise. I would graduate from the university as planned and, as soon I completed an internship at an established private investigator's office, I would hire my eighteen-year-old cousin Leonardo to work for me in my office. This would offer protection and company for me and would solve the problem of what to do with Leonardo—who was at loose ends. The family had been frantic with Leonardo at the time. He showed no interest in going into his father's profession: dentistry. And not only that, he didn't seem very interested in girls, which was a cause for much distress in a traditional Cuban family.

The hope was that Leonardo, by getting into what was typically a man's profession, would become interested in other manly pursuits. After eight years of working closely with Leonardo, I can say with certainty that the plan hadn't worked at all. If I had to categorize Leo's sexual preferences, I would use the word *confused*. I had never known him to have a relationship with anyone of either gender. Sometimes I wondered if Leo himself knew which sex he preferred.

It was rough going in the beginning; Leo resented going to work for a cousin who was just a few years older than he was. And I wasn't exactly ecstatic about having a family member around all day keeping an eye on me. But soon we realized that not only did we get along but we actually enjoyed each other's company. We became fast friends and confidants. I couldn't imagine running Solano Investigations without Leonardo, and I was sure he couldn't imagine working anyplace else. And by that time, frankly, I don't think anyone else would have wanted to work with either of us.

I was in a hurry to get upstairs and out of sight once I stepped inside the house, but I paused to look at the photographs in the foyer. The largest and most prominently displayed was that of Mami on her wedding day. She looked happy and shone with an inner radiance. It was one of the few photographs our family brought out of Cuba. There was another, of Fatima as a newborn, but all the other photos on the altar and spread throughout the house were taken after 1962—the year that my parents and my eldest sister left Cuba to go into exile. My middle sister, Lourdes, and I were born in the United States. There's so little photographic proof of my family's old life that sometimes it felt as though we didn't really exist until we went into exile. My sisters and I generally had to rely on oral accounts of what life used to be like in our homeland.

My grandparents, my parents, Fatima, Osvaldo, and Aida left Cuba together with little more than the clothes they were wearing. The Cuban government didn't allow departing citizens to take anything of substance off the island, and were known to strip people even of their shoes and false teeth at the airport as they boarded planes for other countries.

It's difficult to explain to someone who hasn't been forced out of his country. Exiles began life in a new country with different customs, a foreign language, and an absence of everything that was familiar to them. Adding to the struggle was a lack of favorite photos, books, and treasured family possessions that might have eased the transition. Cubans lost more than their family homes and businesses when they went into exile. They also lost the little things that, although they might have had little monetary value, reminded them of who they were and where they had come from.

It was a tragic situation that instilled the Cuban exiles with a deep and lingering sense of loss. One can always buy new things. But those things can never replace possessions that have been handed down from generation to generation within a family.

I considered all this, standing there in the entrance to my family home. I blinked back tears when I thought, as I had countless times, that Mami had died without ever seeing her beloved Cuba again. On her deathbed she had made Papi promise to bury her one day in our family's mausoleum at the Colon Cemetery in Havana. Papi decided that it wouldn't be right to bury her at Woodlawn Cemetery in Miami and then disinter her for a return to Havana. So he had her cremated and kept her ashes in a silver urn in his Hatteras, with the front of the boat facing south. Osvaldo polished the urn faithfully, and Papi waited for the time to come when he could take his wife home.

Papi didn't want to waste a single moment when this opportunity came, so it was Osvaldo's responsibility to keep the Hatteras stocked and ready to hit the sea at a moment's notice. My sisters and I knew that when Fidel died, we were supposed to congregate at the house and set off for the port of Havana. And we were all in agreement with the plan.

I was still standing there in the hallway, my fingers touching the photographs' silver frames, steeped in my family's history, when my cell phone went off. I was so startled I almost knocked over a picture of my sister Lourdes in her habit, photographed the day she took her religious vows.

I fumbled in my purse as it kept ringing. I found myself uttering curses in Spanish.

"Hello?" I finally said.

"Lupe," Marisol said in her raspy voice. "I hope I'm not calling you too early. But I'm finished with the video."

"Meet me at the office," I replied.

15

"YOU'RE SURE YOU GOT EVERYTHING. RIGHT?" I asked Marisol, quite unnecessarily, as I read through her report and looked at the photographs arranged on my desk. Marisol wasn't at all insulted; she knew my question reflected my own state of mind rather than any doubts about her abilities. I had gambled big-time to get that video, and I was acutely aware that it might turn into a mistake that could haunt me.

We met at my office less than an hour after Marisol called me on my cell phone, then started going over frames from the video surveillance taken in the hours before Alexander's murder. We watched the film on my office VCR, stopping and starting it to correlate with Marisol's written report. I had to keep rubbing my eyes as they smarted from staring so intently at my small TV screen.

I was instantly relieved to see that my initial hunch had been right—the camera at AAA Best captured an area outside the car lot's perimeter fence. The SW camera hadn't totally captured the street alongside the Ecstasy Hotel's outer wall, but it had filmed enough to give us something to work with.

Unfortunately, the camera angle was such that we didn't have footage of individual people arriving and departing as they parked on the street. All we could see of them was their shoes up to about their knees, but Marisol had been able to zero in on the car's license plates and extract still photos from the individual frames. She had blown them up into grainy black-and-whites—not much to look at, but the plate numbers became discernible under a magnifying glass.

As I watched the video and checked out the photographs, it seemed significant to me that Alexander had instructed Tío Ramón to park on the street rather than in the Ecstasy's courtyard. It would have been easier, and probably more discreet, to simply park in front of Room 7 and walk quickly inside. Alexander had said he would be looking for Tío Ramón, so he wouldn't have to wait outside the room any longer than necessary. Now the thought occurred to me that Alexander might have asked Tío Ramón to park on the street in order for the older man to be seen coming in.

But by whom? And why?

"I counted ten cars parked on the street during the five hours before your cousin was murdered," Marisol said. "Of course, after the body was discovered the place was overrun by official vehicles, and most of the cars already on the street left pretty quickly."

"No surprise there," I said.

Marisol laughed. "I guess none of the customers there wanted to be interviewed by the cops. Go figure."

I flipped through the photos showing the street several hours after the murder, after the police cars had left. There was one other car parked next to Tío Ramón's Jaguar. It was an American sedan that looked familiar, so I flipped back to a picture of the street four hours before the murder. I picked up my magnifying glass. I saw the same car in both pictures—it looked like a dark Ford Taurus.

I showed Marisol the two photos. "Do you remember seeing anyone arriving or leaving in this car?" I asked.

Marisol began looking through her report, seeking the precise frames that would show the vehicle arriving at the Ecstasy. "Give me a second," she said.

"Take your time," I told her. "It might be important."

I walked over to the windows and watched the parrots beginning their leisurely morning routine. I wished I was like them, sleeping until nine in the morning. Alvaro and I had slept only a couple hours the night before—we had a lot of catching up to do, after two days apart—and I was already starting to pay the price.

"I found it," Marisol said. She looked at her report, nodding. "The driver was a male. He arrived at 1:05:36 P.M. He parked and walked in the direction of the Ecstasy." She looked at another page of her report. "I have no record of the vehicle leaving. It was still there when the video ended."

"Can you pull up the frame of the man arriving?" I asked, motioning toward the VCR.

"Sure. Give me a minute." Marisol picked up the VCR remote control, then popped another stick of gum into her mouth to add to the considerable wad that had already taken up residence there. I think she must have had an entire rubber tree plant in there. I hated to see, smell, or hear anyone chewing gum—with such force that I almost wished Marisol would resume her two-pack-a-day cigarette habit.

I heard Leonardo come into the cottage, so I went out to greet him while I was waiting for Marisol. I had been sitting too long, and I was stiffening up.

"Buenos días," I said to Leo.

"Lupe!" My cousin seemed distressed to see me at the office before him for the second time that week. I could tell he didn't want this to become a trend. "Anything wrong?"

"Just following up on something Marisol found on a video surveillance," I said vaguely, hoping it was enough information to satisfy his curiosity.

"Lupe!" Marisol called out form my office. "Found it!"

"Back in a minute," I said to Leonardo, then sprinted back to my office.

Marisol was standing right in front of the TV screen, the remote control in her hand. She had frozen the tape to a moment where we could watch the actions of the Taurus' driver.

I nodded, and Marisol began running the tape, slowing it down so that it flickered frame-by-frame on the screen. She pointed at the car as it approached the front of the Ecstasy Hotel. The driver slowed down, then stopped just a few feet past the entrance. About a full minute later the door opened, and I saw a pair of trouser legs that obviously belonged to a man walk around the vehicle, toward the back. He stopped, paused in front of the trunk—presumably putting something inside or taking something out of it. It was frustrating to have such a chopped-off, truncated view of what was going on, but I reminded myself to be grateful for what I had.

Then the legs turned, walked toward the Ecstasy entrance, and went out of sight. As hard as I tried, I couldn't remember whether or not I'd seen that Taurus parked in front of the Ecstasy when I went there the morning after the murder. Tío Ramón's car had been impounded on the scene by the police, I knew—which was a service to my uncle, since such an expensive car never would have made it through the night unattended in that neighborhood.

I had Marisol advance the tape. Sometimes video was better than memory. Soon I saw that the Taurus *had* still been parked at the hotel the morning after the murder, while I was in the courtyard bantering with Detective Anderson.

My Mercedes would have been recorded for posterity as well, but I had parked far enough away from the surveillance camera's range to avoid being preserved on tape. It didn't really matter, anyway; running into Detective Anderson when I did ensured that my visit hadn't been a secret. In any case, my preference was always not to be caught on tape—anytime, anywhere.

"Leo!" I called out to my cousin. He came in and said good morning to Marisol. "I have a tag I need you to run for me. ASAP, please, *primo.*" I copied the Taurus's license-plate number from Marisol's report.

Marisol looked at me expectantly as Leo left the room. "So, Lupe, did you find what you were looking for?"

"I'm not sure. Maybe." I had a hunch about that car, but I wanted my suspicions confirmed before I voiced them. "You did a great job, Marisol. As usual."

She beamed, packing up her things. I was rarely effusive with praise, so I thought it meant a great deal when I offered it. And the fact that I overpaid my investigators— even more so on a rush job such as this one—never hurt, either.

"Do you need anything else?" Marisol asked, suppressing a yawn. "I'm beat. I worked through the night on that video."

"*Gracias, chica.* Go home," I told her. "I'll keep you posted if I need you again on this one. Right now I'm not sure which direction it's going to take."

I watched Marisol pick up her purse, exhaling deeply,

and wondered if I looked as exhausted as she did. I knew how I felt, which was worn out. I walked Marisol to the door and waved good-bye to her as she drove off.

I wondered if I had reached an age at which sleep deprivation was something I couldn't afford. Then I shrugged off that horrific thought. Give up sex for sleep? Never! I had my principles, after all.

16

ABOUT FIVE MINUTES AFTER MARISOL LEFT I GOT A
call from Tía Alina, telling me that Tío Ramón was feeling
much better after his jail stay and would be pleased to meet
with me "at my convenience." I would have preferred to
wait for the results of the tag search on the Taurus, but I
didn't want to delay meeting my client. My nap would have
to wait a little longer.

I drove to Key Biscayne with my mind focused on how
I wanted to pursue questioning Tío Ramón. I kept reminding myself not to defer to him because he was Papi's
friend, and to keep in mind that I wasn't sure he had been
forthcoming about Alexander. I kept reminding myself,
and I kept hoping it was working.

The same housekeeper opened the door for me as last
time, and she escorted me to Tío Ramón's study with such
haste that I knew she had been warned about my arrival.
This time, though, Tío Ramón was not waiting for me
alone. With him were three female family members: Tía
Alina, and his daughters, Teresa and Sofia. I greeted them
warmly, one by one, kissed them all, and declined an offer
of coffee.

"Please, Lupe, take a seat." Tía Alina indicated an
armchair by the window, where I had sat during my previous visit.

I made myself comfortable as Tío Ramón took a seat
directly opposite me. Tía Alina and her daughters pulled
three rattan chairs from a table in the corner of the room,
then joined us to form a circle.

Tío Ramón looked old, tired, and frail. But he looked
a hell of a lot better than he had at the Dade County Jail—
which was no great surprise. He was dressed in another
starched white *guayabera,* and equally starched dark brown
linen trousers. Tía Alina was showing the strain of the past
few days as well; her eyes were cloudy and ringed with a
tinge of purple. She was dressed casually in a royal blue
cotton pantsuit, with black low-heeled pumps.

In the moment before we began, I recalled what I knew
about Teresa and Sofia, the daughters. They were more
my older sisters' contemporaries than mine, but I had
spent some time with them in the past.

Both women lived in Miami, but their lives were very
different. Teresa, the older, had gone the traditional
Cuban housewife route—she was married with three young
children. Sofia was the career woman, and I remembered
that she was divorced with one son. And each woman's
clothes reflected the path she had chosen. Teresa wore a
flowery, mid-length, slightly faded skirt topped by a white
man's shirt, along with flat brown sandals, her hair pulled
back too tight, and no makeup. She seemed tired and har-
ried, probably as much from caring for her small children
as from her father's predicament.

Sofia was wearing an Armani teal-colored gabardine
suit—I instantly recognized it because I owned the same
one—and a pair of black Manolo Blahnik sling-back shoes
I would have cheerfully killed for. Her light brown chin-
length hair was professionally tousled and expertly streaked,
and her makeup glowed as if she had just applied it. Sofia
was the only person in the room who looked as though she

had actually slept at all the past few days. I recalled that she worked at a Spanish-language TV station as an anchor on a weekly news program. I was wearing jeans and a T-shirt, with pink plastic platform slides on my feet; next to Sofia, I felt like a reject from a local thrift shop.

"How can this be?" Tío Ramón broke the silence. "How can the police possibly say I would kill Alexander, Lupe?"

I took a deep breath. "You were seen covered in blood with a knife in your hand, coming out of the hotel room in which his dead body was found. You seemed to be running away," I said point-blank. "Your fingerprints are on the murder weapon. It's not a picture of an innocent man."

"I wasn't running away!" Tío Ramón protested, his eyes flashing with anger. "You know that I was going to my car to get my cell phone and call the police."

"That's not how the police see it," I said as gently as I could.

"Papa would never kill Alexander," Teresa interjected. "It's an insult that they could even think such a thing."

I noticed that she hadn't said her father would never kill *anyone,* only that he wouldn't kill her cousin. I wondered whether that meant anything, or if I was being hyper-sensitive.

I let the comment pass. "I need to ask some questions, please." I reached into my purse and took out a notebook and pen. "When was the last time you saw Alexander before the murder?"

I looked around the room. None of the four Suarezes seemed in a hurry to reply. I didn't get the impression that they were searching their memories; rather, it seemed they were all trying to figure out how to answer the question.

Tía Alina took the plunge. "It must have been three

or four months ago, when he came to the house to pay us a visit. Is that right, *querido*?" she asked, looking to Tío Ramón for confirmation.

Right away I smelled a rat. This wasn't working.

"Look, I know that sometimes it's hard to recall specific facts," I said slowly. "But right now I feel you're not being totally truthful with me. And if that's the case, I can't help you."

No one said anything, and all four family members avoided looking me in the eye. I knew I had hit the nail on the head. They were hiding something.

"Lupe is right." Sofia finally spoke up. "There's nothing to be gained in keeping this from her."

Tío Ramón nodded, stood up, reached into his pocket. He walked over to his desk and unlocked the bottom drawer. He produced a cigar, which he rolled around in his hand, pinched between his thumb and forefinger, and lit with the silver lighter on his desk.

"Ramón—" Tía Alina began.

"Papa—" Teresa said.

Tío Ramón silenced them both with a withering look. Things were apparently bad enough. The man wasn't going to deny himself a cigar.

He was still standing, enveloped in smoke, as he spoke. "Alexander did come to visit," he said. "But this was not a warm, family visit. He came to ask me for money. And he accused me of having cheated him out of his father's money."

Tío Ramón sighed sadly. "You see, I was the executor of my brother Julian's estate. That's why Alexander was unhappy with me."

"So you had a fight?" I asked. My heart was sinking inside. I suspected where all this was heading.

"Alexander threatened Ramón!" Tía Alina interrupted, almost shouting. "He said he would come back and get him. He actually threatened his uncle!"

"What did you do then?" I asked Ramón.

Tío Ramón sat down heavily. "I told him never to come back here again," he said sadly. "I . . . I told him that I would kill him if I ever saw him again."

Mierda.

I hated to ask my next question. "Did anybody witness you saying that?"

Tía Alina and Tío Ramón exchanged glances. "We let Alexander in the house when he came to see us, before we knew what he wanted," Tío Ramón said. "But as soon as he started claiming that I had stolen from him, I told him to leave. He wouldn't go, and we started to shout at each other. But when I threatened him, and he threatened me . . . well, I suppose that happened outside in the driveway. I think the maid and the chauffeur heard."

"And you never saw Alexander again after that?" I asked. "Alive, I mean." I made a mental note to speak with the maid and chauffeur, although I knew they probably wouldn't betray their employer by giving me any damaging information.

"No," Tío Ramón replied flatly. "I had no contact with him whatsoever, until he called to tell me about the letter from the Spanish lawyer." I noticed that he was clutching his cigar so tightly that he was in danger of crushing it.

Tía Alina nodded vigorously to indicate her agreement with what her husband was saying. Teresa and Sofía were staring hard at me.

"Okay," I said, knowing at that point I had no choice but to believe him. "Do you know anyone who might have wanted Alexander dead?"

All four Suarezes shook their heads. "We really didn't know much about his life," Sofia offered. "He moved to New York years ago. None of us kept in touch on a regular basis."

I thought about what Sofia had told me. "What about your brother Carlos?" I asked her. "He lives in New York, right? Maybe he had more contact with him."

"No, Carlos had nothing to do with him," Tía Alina said, perhaps a beat too quickly.

It seemed strange, considering that Carlos and Alexander were first cousins and almost the same age. And as far as I could tell, the rift between the families had occurred only after Julian's fairly recent death, which wouldn't account for such a lack of connection between what I had always thought were two reasonably close families.

"What exactly did Alexander do for a living?" I asked. Although I already knew what, I wanted specific details.

"He was an artist," Teresa spoke up.

"What kind of artist?" I asked, thinking maybe I should open up a sideline business pulling teeth—it would surely be easier than getting information out of the Suarez family.

Teresa glanced at her family, as though unsure whether she had permission to speak further.

"I'm not sure," she said. "I know that he went to NYU and that after he graduated he stayed in New York. He never came back home to live in Miami for any length of time."

I didn't buy this for a second. I knew well how close Cuban families were. I'd bet they even knew what kind of underwear Alexander preferred. What I couldn't figure out was why they were being so evasive. I was working *for* them, after all.

"His parents must have been upset. After all, he was an only child, and he was living so far away." I waited for comment, but no one picked up the bait. This session wasn't becoming much more productive, so I decided to zero in on what happened at the Ecstasy.

"Remember when you told me about walking toward Room 7," I asked Tío Ramón. "You said you saw a woman who looked like a prostitute coming out of one of the rooms."

Tío Ramón nodded slowly. "Can you tell me anything about her?" I asked. "Any details that you remember."

If it was possible for a man to blush while enveloped in a thick cloud of fine cigar smoke, Tío Ramón pulled it off. He was extremely old-school, and I knew it would be hard for him to speak of these things in front of his wife and daughters. Tough.

"Let me think, Lupe." More cigar smoke. I saw his wife and daughters glance up at the cigar, but no one was complaining. Obviously Ramón was taking advantage of his extraordinary circumstances. "The young lady was Oriental. Quite tall, but I'm sure she was Oriental. I was so far away from her that I can't tell you much else. I was very preoccupied at the time, thinking about what Alexander might want from me. Especially after the last time we had seen one another."

"Did you say anything to her, or did she seem to notice you?"

"It was strange," Ramón said. "I'm not sure, but I heard her say something—like she was talking to herself."

"What's so strange about that?" I asked.

"Well, I told you she was an Oriental," Tío Ramón explained. "But I could have sworn she said a couple of words to herself in Spanish. And without an accent."

I jotted this down. If Ramón was right, we were on to something. How many accentless Spanish-speaking Asian prostitutes were there in Miami?

"Tell me about the room, and what you saw when you got there," I said. "I know we've been through this before, and I apologize for dredging it up. But please, tell me everything."

The three Suarez woman cringed on cue, realizing they were about to hear in detail what had happened in Room 7 at the Ecstasy Hotel. I sympathized. It was never easy to contemplate violence and mayhem, and it was much harder when it involved someone a person knew.

"I . . . the truth is, I didn't really notice much in the room. I was looking for Alexander," Tío Ramón explained. "I admit it—I was a little frightened. I didn't know what to expect, especially since the last time I saw my nephew we were threatening each other. For all I knew, I might have been walking into some kind of a trap."

I nodded and pressed on. "Try to recall what was in the room," I said. "You stood there for a moment when you couldn't find Alexander. Was there anything on the bed or on the table? A suitcase, a briefcase, anything?"

Tío Ramón shifted so he could gaze out the picture window at the waters of Key Biscayne off in the distance.

"I'm sorry, Lupe," he said. "It's all a blur."

"Fine," I said. Tommy was going to have to deal with Tío Ramón's defense in court, and from what I had just heard it was going to take all of his skill. The evidence was damning—the estrangement, the fight, the threats, the blood, the knife. ¡Ay!

I stood up to leave; the Suarez family followed suit, getting up so quickly they might have been wearing springs on the bottom of their shoes.

"One last thing, Tío Ramón," I said. "Did you think of someone I could contact at the Cuban Sugar Mills Rightful Owners Organization?"

Tío Ramón hurried over to his desk, as though relieved to finally be of some help. He picked up a business card that had been placed under a glass paperweight depicting the Cuban flag.

"I gave a lot of thought to who you should speak with," he said. "I decided that, instead of putting you in touch with one of the old members, I would recommend you to Tomás Cardenas. He's the son of Miguel Cardenas, an old friend of your father's and mine."

Tío Ramón handed me the card. Tomás Cardenas was a name-partner attorney at Valdez, Johnson, and Cardenas, P.A.—a firm specializing in personal-injury litigation. I tried to remember where I had seen those names before. A few years ago I had done some work for them, I remembered, but not for Tomás Cardenas. I had worked for Sergio Valdez. This was no coincidence, since at one point or another I'd worked for most of the reputable law firms in Miami—plus, I'm not proud to say, a few of the less reputable ones.

"Thank you," I said, putting the card in my purse. "I'll give Tomás a call."

"I've already spoken with him, and told him that you will be contacting him," Tío Ramón said. "And I asked him to help you as much as possible."

"Please, Lupe," Tía Alina said suddenly, grabbing my hand and squeezing it tight. "Get your Tío Ramón out of this nightmare."

"I'll do my best," I said as she hugged me.

"If you need anything at all, just let us know," Sofia said; behind her cool, collected facade, I could clearly see that she was worried. She was right to be. I was willing to bet she was the only person in the room besides me who understood just how grave Ramón's situation was becoming.

Tommy had his work cut out for him. He had been a magician in court before. This time he was going to have to channel the spirit of Merlin himself.

17

LEONARDO HAD THE VEHICLE REGISTRATION CHECK
on the Taurus waiting for me when I got back to the office.
I was feeling so tired by then I feared I was going to drop,
so instead of sitting at my desk I took the report from my
cousin and reclined on the sofa in my office to read it. I
was tempted to close my eyes and rest them for a minute,
but I knew if I did, it might be a long time before I woke
up again.

The license-tag check came back with the results I suspected—the car was owned by a rental company. Sunshine
Rent-a-Car was a local company that advertised heavily,
catering mostly to South American tourists. It boasted in
airport ads that it had the best low-cost, no-frills trans-
portation rentals for visitors to South Florida.

The video surveillance showed that the Taurus had
been parked on the street hours before and after the murder. The tape ran out before I could see when the car was
finally moved, and who moved it. I hadn't seen it when I
went to the Ecstasy the next night, taking a better look
around and speaking with Pascual Menéndez, the Ecstasy's
manager. So I could conclude that it had been taken away
between my morning and evening visits to the hotel—some
time during the day after the murder, in other words.

I planned to operate under the assumption that Alexander was the driver of the Taurus. He was a visitor from out of town, he was trying to be low-key and nondescript for some reason, and in speaking with Tío Ramón he had emphasized parking on the street outside the Ecstasy. Obviously Alexander wouldn't have been able to drive the car away. So, unless the police had impounded it, someone else had taken it away. I only hoped it hadn't been stolen, in which case it would either have been cannibalized for parts or freighter-bound for another continent half the world away.

The list of possibilities also included tow-truck companies. They were notorious in Miami for towing cars at a moment's notice, and under the flimsiest of pretenses, and then demanding exorbitant sums for ransom. They were known to circle the streets, sometimes even towing cars that were legally parked. It was a scam and a hassle that most motorists had dealt with at one time or another.

In my current state of exhaustion, the thought of tracking the Taurus down seemed daunting. But it had to be done. I summoned all my energy to hoist myself off the couch, then went over to my desk to work the telephone.

I opened up the Yellow Pages to "Towing Companies." There were five pages of listings for Dade County alone. I flipped through and crossed out companies that were located too far away from Eighth Street. I narrowed down the possibilities to twenty-two companies that might have towed away the Taurus.

I called one. Then two. I had the make and model of the car, along with the license plate number. I called the third one. Nothing.

It was on the seventeenth call that I got results, to my surprise—I was beginning to think I must be completely on the wrong track. The youngish male voice on the phone told me that there was indeed a dark blue Taurus on the lot with plates that matched the number I gave him. Yes, he added, it had been towed from the address I gave him—the Ecstasy's. And yes, if I paid the towing and storage fees, I could pick up the car any time.

"We're open twenty-four hours a day," he added, "for your convenience."

I looked up at the clock on the wall. Five o'clock. I had been up for almost a day and a half, and I felt it all over. But I had just received too good a break to let pass for the ten hours it would take me to sleep and feel halfway human again. Leo had already left for the day, so I locked up the office and climbed into the Mercedes.

Ace International Towing was located as far west on Flagler Street as someone could drive without plunging into a swamp. Miami is the only city I can think of with city limits defined by the habitats of alligators, turtles, and egrets. I kept waiting for news that greedy developers had bribed Zoning and Planning into allocating the Everglades for commercial use; all the wildlife would be shipped off to an inhospitable preserve somewhere, and the developers would claim all the while that it was being done for the animals' benefit. God only knew what they would do then to the Miccosukee, the Native American tribe who lived there—maybe relocate them to Disney World.

The towing company's offices were in a shopping center, sandwiched between a bridal shop and a tanning salon at the very end of Flagler Street—right on the edge of the Everglades, which were as yet untouched, I saw. As soon as I looked at those three establishments in that location, two words came to mind: the first was "money," the second was "laundering."

I parked in a slot in front of the bridal salon, ignoring the hopeful reaction of the matron sitting in front fanning herself with a copy of *El Nuevo Herald*. I half waved to her as I walked toward the Ace International storefront. Signs in the window were posted in about twenty different languages, but they all told the same story: this esteemed establishment accepted only cash. That confirmed my suspicion about money-laundering behind the owners' primary source of income.

I pushed open the door and went in. The room was so small that I felt as if I could stretch out my arms and touch the walls on either side. Behind a minuscule desk was a pimply teenage boy. He looked to be about thirteen, with a buzz cut, dressed in an old bowling shirt with the name "Clyde" stitched over the breast pocket. His eyes were glued to a little six-inch black-and-white TV.

"Hello," I said. The room was so small it felt as if I were shouting even though I was using an everyday tone of voice.

There was no reaction from Clyde, or whatever his name was. He was totally engrossed in the TV. I peered over the desk to see what he was watching, and the second I learned what was captivating my young friend, I was sorry I had let my curiosity get the better of me.

Clyde was watching an explicit porno movie, where two naked women were having their way with each other. To one side of the screen I saw a man dressed all in leather, albeit with strategic patches cut away to reveal relevant body parts. I doubted that Clyde represented much danger to me, but I felt in my purse for my Beretta just in case.

"Hello," I repeated. "I called about an hour ago, about the blue Taurus your company towed off Eighth Street. Remember?"

Clyde was unable to tear his attention from the screen. I glanced over and saw that the man had joined the two women, and the three were performing an acrobatic maneuver that seemed intended as an insult to gravity and physics. I vaguely wondered where Clyde's parents were, and if they had any idea what their son was doing instead of his homework. I spotted a backpack on the floor in the corner, with some high school textbooks on top. Oh well, I thought, he was certainly getting his anatomy lesson.

"Lady, you owe four hundred and twenty-six dollars." Clyde spoke without taking his eyes from the screen. Without looking down at anything he itemized the charges from memory. "That's a hundred-dollar towing fee, three hundred for three days' storage, and twenty-six dollars in tax. We accept cash only."

"Look, I didn't really come here to get the car," I said quickly. I figured it didn't matter much what I was saying; by then a Doberman pinscher had appeared on Clyde's TV. It was getting extremely crowded in that bed. "My boyfriend rented that car. He's from New York, and he was here for a few days. We had a fight and I got out of the car, but I left a manila envelope in there. It isn't anything valuable to anyone but me, just some notes for an article I'm writing. But I really, really need it. Can I please just get that envelope out of the car?"

"No way," Clyde said without looking up. "Only authorized people are allowed to come into contact with the vehicles."

Great. Whoever spent twenty minutes training this kid should have been very proud of themselves.

"Please, I could get fired if I don't get those notes," I said. I knew time wasn't on my side. Even in a shoestring operation like this one there was bound to be some adult in charge. And whoever it was, he would probably be even tougher to deal with than my young friend Clyde.

"Sorry, lady," Clyde said. Now the dog was on the bed. I'm open-minded, but I had to look away.

"Look, kid," I said. "Do you know you're breaking the law?"

I reached over and flipped off the TV. Clyde looked up at me in complete shock, trying to focus his eyes back on reality.

"What the fuck?" he sputtered.

"You're under age." I pointed a finger at him, a no-no in my household that I hoped would get through to him. "Florida state law prohibits the viewing of pornography by minors who haven't been declared emancipated by their parents. Have your parents emancipated you to watch porn that, to top it all off, includes abuse of animals? They could be charged with negligence, kid. And you can go to Juvenile Hall!"

I had no idea if any of this was strictly true, but I knew that Clyde wouldn't, either.

"Hey, look, lady," Clyde said, appearing stricken. He paled, and for a second I almost took pity on him. "Please, my dad's out on parole. I don't want to get him sent back to jail."

Ay, mierda. Now I really felt bad—but not enough to keep me from what I had to do.

"Look, it's okay. It's just that I'm in trouble if I don't get that envelope." I sighed. "I don't want your dad to go back to jail. So let's make a deal. I take five minutes to get that envelope, and I don't report you to the police."

Clyde paused. "And you have to promise not to watch this garbage until you're old enough to know it's bad for you," I added.

"Okay, okay," Clyde said.

"One minute with the car, no more porno, and I'll be on my way," I told him. "I'll forget I ever saw a thing."

I could tell the last part was music to Clyde's ears. The hell with company policy—he reached around to the wall, where there was a corkboard filled with keys, and selected one. He tossed it to me.

"Hurry up. I could get fired for this," he said. Then he pointed to a steel door behind him. "The lot's in the back."

Clyde didn't have to say it twice. I went through the door, down a corridor, and out into the lot. There were only about fifteen cars out there, some of which looked as though they had been permanently abandoned by their owners.

After I had walked a few feet more it didn't take me long to find the Taurus. All I had to do was follow my nose. There was a sickly-sweet putrid odor coming from its trunk that was unfortunately familiar to me.

I popped open the trunk and was instantly relieved that I had skipped lunch that day.

I reached into my purse for the violet-scented linen handkerchief that Aida always pressed on me, insisting that ladies needed such accessories. She was right, it turned out, although I think she would have been surprised to find out why. I took another look inside the trunk, got out my cell phone, and dialed a number that had become all too familiar to me.

"Detective Anderson?" I said when he picked up. "This is Lupe Solano. I have some news for you."

18

"LUPE. LUPE." DETECTIVE ANDERSON MOANED IN AN exasperated tone of voice. "Please. You have to stop bringing me so many dead bodies."

"I'm sorry, Detective," I said with real contrition. "It's not like I'm doing it on purpose. I guess it's an occupational hazard."

Detective Anderson was making me feel like the Grim Reaper—and not for the first time. We were standing under an awning right outside Ace International Towing's back door. The crime techs were swarming all over the Taurus. Soon the car was going to be taken to the lab, so its contents could be analyzed in a controlled environment.

"So, Lupe, talk," Detective Anderson said in his laconic way. "You know the drill."

Both Detective Anderson and I knew that, as investigator of record on the Suarez case, I didn't really have to volunteer any information. As a private investigator in the state of Florida, my work was considered privileged under Florida Statute 493 and therefore came under the umbrella of attorney work product. But we both also understood that I had to give Detective Anderson some information, if we were going to continue to enjoy a good working relationship. That was just the way it worked; next time, the situation might work to my benefit.

I was reluctant to tie Tío Ramón's case directly to the Taurus, so I knew I was skating on thin ice. I felt a sharp pain in the pit of my stomach at the thought that Detective Anderson might follow up on how I found out about the Taurus—and that he would assemble all the pieces and deduce that I had stolen the surveillance tape from AAA Best Preowned Cars.

But stonewalling wasn't really a viable possibility. It might have worked in the short term, but not forever. Detective Anderson was too good at his job for that—not to mention the fact that we went too far back and respected each other far too much. I would have to walk a tightrope without a net to catch me in case I fell.

"Well, I had information that led me here to this car," I said carefully, nodding at the Taurus. "I had no idea what I was going to find. But I certainly didn't think it was going to be a dead body!"

Detective Anderson's eyes met mine for a moment; I could see that he certainly believed the veracity of my latter statement.

"You can't tell me what case it was that you were working that led you to the Taurus, can you?" Detective Anderson's intelligent blue eyes shone through his glasses and into mine. I was willing to bet my fees for the next six months that Detective Anderson was on the verge of connecting the body in the Taurus with Tío Ramón's case. It was too much of a coincidence for him to run into me twice in two days.

"I'm sorry," I said. "I can't."

"Well, at least you can tell me what's happened since you found the body," Detective Anderson said. He took out his notebook and looked at me with expectation.

Okay, I knew the drill.

"I didn't see anyone around the car at the time I found

the body," I told him. "The only person I've had contact with here at the towing company is that teenage boy inside."

"Lupe, come on. Help me out here." Detective Anderson pushed his glasses down his nose and rubbed his eyes. "Do you have any idea who this guy is? There's no ID on him."

I looked over at the crime scene, where the techs were zipping the body into a plastic bag to take to the medical examiner's office. I had my suspicions who the victim was. The question was whether I was going to share the information with Detective Anderson. I looked up at him, checking him out and trying to determine how far I could trust him. He looked back at me, knowing exactly what I was thinking.

"Lupe, this is me," Detective Anderson said. "We've worked together enough times for you to know that I'll do the right thing."

"I'm not sure who the victim is," I told Anderson. "But if I had to make a bet, I'd say he's a Spanish lawyer from Madrid. His name is Mauricio de Villegas."

The stench had been overpowering when I opened up the trunk, and he had been too decomposed for me to see his features—anyway, I had never met him in person. But I had recognized his suit as tailored in a European style, and his hand sticking up from the trunk bore a gold pinkie ring with de Villegas's initials.

"A lawyer from Spain. Shit." For the first time since I'd known him, Detective Anderson showed real dismay. "That changes the whole investigation. It's going to turn into an international situation, and the Spanish consulate is going to get involved."

"Sorry for all the problems it's going to cause you, but I'm almost certain," I told him.

"Well, if you're right about this guy's identity, then in reality I owe you a huge favor," Detective Anderson said, recovering his old stoicism. "And by now I know you well enough that I'm positive you wouldn't tell me his name unless you were a hundred percent convinced. You've saved me a lot of work—and with no guarantee that this guy wouldn't have ended up in the morgue as a John Doe when it was all finished because we couldn't ID him."

"No problem," I said, well aware that I might need to take him up on his offer of a favor.

"Is there anything else I should know about the victim?" Detective Anderson asked, knowing full well that it was very unlikely I was about to volunteer anything else.

"That's it, Detective," I replied. Now it was my turn to ask a question, although I suspected I already knew the answer. "What do you think the M.E.'s going to conclude on this guy, in terms of cause of death?"

I was interested in what Anderson thought, since it would be days before the medical examiner's official findings would be released. Detective Anderson had certainly seen enough dead bodies in his time to make a pretty accurate guess in advance. I knew, though, that he was likely to play it safe; there was no point saying anything at the scene that he might be held to later.

Detective Anderson shook his head slowly, meditatively. "Well, Lupe, you saw the condition of the body. Under normal circumstances—whatever *that* might be—a body isn't very pretty after even one day of being unattended." He glanced up toward the sun; although it was early evening, it was still blazing. "And out here, in a metal box, the process is a lot more brutal."

I still winced at the thought of the lawyer's body stuffed inside the trunk of the Taurus. The stench hadn't been the worst part about finding the dead man. It had been the results of two days' decomposition, aggravated by the extreme heat until the corpse barely looked human. I had barely been able to compose myself long enough to look around for clues in a panicked search for his identity.

"My guess—and it's only a guess—is that he was strangled," Anderson said, reflecting my own suspicion. "I mean, it's hard to tell with the body in such poor condition."

"I thought the same thing," I said. "The signs were there—the dark bruising on the face and neck."

Anderson gave me a thin-lipped smile. "You're tougher than you look, Lupe," he said. "You really did check out the victim, even in that condition. I know seasoned cops who would have thrown up on the asphalt after a sight like that."

I wasn't sure how to accept this particular brand of praise. I had been very shocked and upset by the body, and I had overcome my reactions in order to get my job done. It wasn't that I didn't feel for the victim; rather, I had trained myself to separate my visceral responses from my professional sensibilities. I had to, in order to do my job.

We both watched in silence as the body was loaded into the medical examiner's van. The van's double doors slammed shut with such a sharp, metallic sound that I jumped. Detective Anderson looked over at me with surprise.

"It's been a tough couple of days," I said.

"I know what you mean," Detective Anderson replied. "For me it's been a tough couple of years or so."

I was surprised by Anderson's statement, which verged perilously close to revealing something about his inner life. I almost asked him to expand further, but a uniformed cop ran over with a form to sign. By then, Anderson was back to his old self. We walked off the parking lot together, each lost in our thoughts.

Finally Anderson broke the silence. "There's something I forgot to ask you, Lupe."

"Yes?" I asked.

"You wouldn't happen to know who did this, would you?" Again the thin-lipped smile, with more of a sense of humor than I had thought the crusty detective possessed.

I shrugged and shook my head. We both knew it would be unlikely for me to tell him, even if I did.

"It was worth a try," Detective Anderson said. "One more thing, though, if you don't mind."

"Go ahead," I said with a yawn. My bed was calling out to me.

"I need to plan my week," Detective Anderson said. "Can you tell me if you're planning to call me up with any more bodies?"

I had to suppress my smile. "I sure hope not," I said.

19

AFTER I LEFT THE ACE INTERNATIONAL TOWING company I drove straight home. It wasn't an easy trip and, in retrospect, I was so tired that it might not have been a bad idea to pull over and sleep in a hotel instead.

I walked inside the house when I finally made it home, and poked my head in the kitchen to see if there was something to eat. I was starved, having not eaten a bite since breakfast hours before. I found Aida hard at work mopping the floor, a sure sign that dinner was over. Normally I would have been disappointed that I was too late to share a meal with my family—it had been too long, as usual, since we'd all eaten together—but in fact I was almost relieved. I wasn't sure I could have gotten through a sit-down dinner without taking a lie-down nap on the floor halfway through.

The whole way back from the towing company I had been buoyed by a single image: a steaming-hot bath filled with my favorite oil of gardenia, with a flute of perfectly chilled champagne sitting on the edge of the tub. After that, I wanted dinner on a tray while I watched mindless TV in my bed.

"Lupe," Aida said, spotting me standing in the doorway. "Lupe, you missed dinner!"

The word "again" was certainly implied.

"And we had *arroz con pollo,* your favorite," Aida said. "It came out perfectly. *Muy chorreado,* Lupe. Very moist. The twins had thirds!"

To Cubans, food means love. The amount of food consumed at the table is viewed as a direct correlative to the amount of love in the family. Going back for seconds or thirds was the equivalent of an extra hug or a kiss.

"*Ay,* Aida," I said, putting my arms around her and kissing her. "Is there anything left?"

We both knew this was an unnecessary question. Aida always cooked for an army. That was why we had two Sub-Zero refrigerators in the kitchen.

"You know there is." Aida looked me over critically. "You have circles under your eyes."

"I know," I said sheepishly.

Aida took my face in her hands and turned it first to the right, then to the left. "When was the last time you had a good night's sleep?" Without waiting for me to reply, she gave me an order: "You go upstairs and take a nice hot bath. I'll fix a tray and bring it up to you when you're done."

"Oh, *perfecto,* Aida. *Gracias.*" It was all I could do not to drop to my knees and weep with relief.

On the way to my bedroom I stopped off at the wet bar that Papi had installed on the second-floor landing and opened up the small refrigerator. I found a bottle of Veuve Cliquot, my favorite champagne for drinking in the bathtub. I filled a silver bucket with ice from the machine and put the bottle in it, along with one of the flute glasses from the cabinet. Thus properly prepared, I headed for my room.

While I was luxuriously lounging in the bathtub,

images of the Spanish lawyer stuffed into the Taurus trunk kept creeping into my mind. I was surrounded by the wonderful, overpowering smell of oil of gardenia, but the memory of the decomposing body permeated my senses. I kept sipping champagne, knowing it would be a little while before I could start to forget. Half a bottle of champagne and a long bath later, I still hadn't really succeeded.

I heard Aida's soft knock on the door announcing my dinner was ready. I got out of the bathtub and wrapped myself in a big fluffy terry cloth robe. Aida brought me copious amounts of steaming *arroz con pollo,* along with a healthy portion of *maduros,* the ripened sweet plantains that were a staple of any Cuban meal. I had a salad of avocados—the only vegetable that Cubans ever allowed to touch their lips—to finish off the main course. And as if that feast wasn't enough, Aida had given me a slice of her famous flan for dessert. On the corner of the tray was half a carafe of red wine—undoubtedly Sangre de Toro, the only proper accompaniment for such a meal. It was definitely comfort food, Cuban style.

I would sleep well that night. Finally.

THAT BIG MEAL AND GOOD NIGHT'S SLEEP WORKED THEIR magic. I woke up late the next morning refreshed and eager. I was still full from Aida's feast, so I just poured some *café con leche* into my favorite white ceramic mug—the oversized one depicting the Cuban flag fluttering in the breeze—before heading for the office.

As I drove north on Main Highway, I planned my day. It was going to be a busy one—if things went well.

Leonardo was already in the office when I arrived. I thought he was dressed rather sedately, in a dark blue unitard with just a slight hint of gold shimmer, and a pair of yellow Keds on his feet.

"*Buenos días!* You're late!" He scolded me playfully as I came into the office. I think he was relieved to see an end to the trend of my showing up earlier than he did. He got up from his desk with a stack of pink message slips in his hand. "Here, these are yours. You sure are popular these days."

"Anything urgent?" I asked, feeling the heft of the messages.

"All of them," Leo called out from behind me as I dropped my briefcase and purse on my desk. I was hoping my cousin was joking, but I couldn't be sure from the tone of his voice.

Before working my way through the messages, though, there was a call I needed to make first. I sat down at my desk and punched in a local number—I hadn't called it in a while, but I still knew it by heart.

"Hello?" Suzanne's breathy, girlish voice filled me with warm familiarity. Until that moment, I hadn't realized how much I missed her.

"*Hola, chica.*"

"Lupe! God, it's been a long time. How the hell are you?" Suzanne said, positively ebullient; I felt a twinge of guilt that I hadn't contacted her for something besides business.

"Great, great," I replied. "And you?"

"Staying out of trouble, *chica.* Thank God." In her high-risk line of work, this was the most that Suzanne could probably hope for. "So, Lupe, is this a social call? Or do you need something from me?"

Suzanne knew me too well—but then, knowing people was a big part of her profession. Suzanne was the most successful madam in Dade County, if not the entire southeastern United States. She was tall, blond, and impossibly beautiful, and she had slowly and methodically built up a stable of the most sought-after women and men in the business—all of whom were required to neither drink, take drugs, or even smoke cigarettes. Suzanne's clients came back to her time and again because of the quality of her staff and her rock-solid assurance of complete discretion.

Suzanne had, it turned out, started her career the same year that I did. And that wasn't the only similarity between us. We were born the same year, and within a month of each other. We were both successful in dangerous businesses, and we were ambitious risk takers. And we shared a wicked sense of humor. Last but not least, we both had a fondness for good food and drink. In a sense, we each thought of the other as a mirror image.

"This is a business call," I was forced to admit. "But let's combine it with pleasure. Are you free for lunch today?"

"Sure," Suzanne said, sounding delighted. "Let's go Cuban, okay? Haven't done that for a while."

We agreed to meet at Versailles restaurant—the Mecca for all things Cuban—at two.

I replaced the receiver and sat back in my chair. I glanced over at the picture window to see what the parrots were up to. Not much, it turned out, just a leisurely midmorning snack of avocados that had ripened on their branches.

Leonardo had organized my messages in the order in which he took them. It didn't sound like much, but it had taken me about five years to get him to do so. I made a mental note to buy him lunch as a reward when I was finished with the Suarez case.

Tomás Cardenas won the early-bird award for first call. The lawyer for the sugar-owners group had called promptly at nine, and asked me to call at my earliest convenience. The next call was from Tommy: he wanted to know "why the hell is your cell phone turned off." He demanded a call back ASAP. Next was Carlos Suarez—Tío Ramón's son—calling from New York to volunteer his help with the case. I thought that was interesting, and I wondered what sort of pressure his family was applying to make him get in touch with me. Marisol had also called, asking if I needed her for more work on the case.

I picked up the phone and decided to keep things simple. I'd reward the day's early bird with the day's first call-back.

"Mr. Tomás Cardenas, please," I asked the receptionist at Valdez, Johnson, and Cardenas. "Guadalupe Solano returning his call."

I had learned a long time ago that the best way to get past a receptionist was to say that I was returning rather than initiating a call—even when it wasn't true.

"Tomás Cardenas speaking." Well, well. The lawyer had a low, sexy voice that immediately sent chills up and down my spine. What can I say? I'm a sucker for telephone voices.

"Tomás, hi. This is Lupe Solano."

"*¡Lupe! ¿Hola, cómo estás?*" Tomás was successful in immediately making me feel as though I was the only person in the world with whom he wanted to speak at that moment.

"Fine, thanks," I said. I snapped back to business; the man's telephone voice was too good for me to let my guard down. "I assume you've already been in contact with Ramón Suarez about my need to speak with you."

"*Sí,* he did call," Tomás acknowledged. "What a shame,

this trouble Ramón is in. It's a tragedy. I'll be happy to offer my services, in any capacity you want or need."

"Thanks," I replied. "Would it be convenient for me to come to your office? I realize you're very busy, and I'll try not to take up too much of your time."

Silence on the other end of the line. "Listen, your office is in the Grove, right?" Tomás must have been sure of his information, because he didn't wait for me to reply. "I have a late-afternoon appointment on Mary Street. If you're available, we could meet for a drink then. We can discuss whatever you need to know."

"That would be fine." I found it a little surprising that Tomás would want to meet over cocktails, but it was fine with me. "I'll be in my office then."

"Great. I'm looking forward to meeting you," Tomás said. "I'll call you from my cell phone when the meeting is over. Should be no later than six. Is that a convenient time for you?"

I agreed to his proposal and hung up. For all his considerate manner, I had a feeling that Tomás Cardenas was no pushover, and no sufferer of fools. I would have to do some homework to prepare for our meeting.

Next I called Marisol and told her that, for now, I didn't need her services. I added that she should submit a bill for her fees and expenses.

"No problem there," Marisol said with a little laugh. "I'll fax it over in about fifteen minutes."

My hand was on the receiver to call Tommy when Leonardo came on the intercom to tell me that Detective Anderson was on the line.

"Lupe, I have something for you," Anderson said by way of greeting. I heard papers rustling. "Our victim in the Taurus was indeed Mauricio Mario de Villegas, a lawyer from Madrid. Forty-eight, father of three. Solo practitioner in international real estate law. Listen, Lupe, what do you know about that kind of law?"

"Not much. I guess it has to do with buying and selling properties between one country and another," I replied. Of course I knew what de Villegas had been up to recently, but I wasn't about to tell Detective Anderson. I had volunteered enough when I gave the detective the lawyer's identity.

"Well, that sounds about right," Detective Anderson agreed. "Listen, I don't want to press my luck with you, Lupe. But do you have any theories about why this guy got killed?"

It wasn't as though I hadn't devoted some time to trying to figure that one out. The body had been found in a car rented by Alexander Suarez. I wondered whether his urgent need to speak to Tío Ramón had anything to do with it—was he, for instance, going to confess to his closest relative that he had committed murder? I knew that the estrangement between the two families would vanish the second either side was in serious trouble. That was the way it was with Cuban families.

It was possible that Alexander had been unaware of the body in the trunk of the car he rented. I doubted it, given the footage of a man opening the trunk prior to going into the Ecstasy. But, of course, the footage hadn't been good enough to tell me *who* had opened up that trunk. The lawyer's body might have been placed in the trunk of the car sometime between the end of the video surveillance and the time it was towed to the Ace International back lot. This could have been done to implicate Alexander in the killing—he was dead, after all, and in no position to offer an alibi or an explanation. Whoever killed the lawyer must have known that the Taurus was rented to Alexander, and that therefore the car would be traced back to him. It would also be a matter of days at the most before Detective Anderson made the connection between Alexander and the Taurus, a short period of time in which I could work without his interference.

I had a lot of questions, and not many answers. And there was no way I could consult with Detective Anderson. He would pick up the trail soon enough, and I had to hope it wouldn't lead him to the surveillance tape that I had stolen.

"Sorry, Detective, I'm afraid I can't help you there," I replied. "I really have no idea who might have killed the lawyer."

"Well, Lupe, keep me posted if you get any ideas," Anderson said; his voice told me he was resigned to this game we had to play with each other. "And I'll do the same when I have some more details. Oh, by the way, your friend Charlie Miliken was assigned to be the prosecutor in the Alexander Suarez case. I don't know if that's good news or bad for you."

After dropping that little bombshell, Detective Anderson hung up. I knew what he meant, of course. Charlie Miliken was one of the smartest, toughest, and most thorough prosecutors in Miami. His conviction rate was somewhere in the stratosphere. That was the bad news. The good news, I supposed, was that he was one of my former lovers, and we still retained a spark of a friendship that we rekindled into a flame every now and then. He might cut me some slack or help me at some point. Very little was kept secret in the Dade County law-enforcement community, so I wasn't surprised to hear that Detective Anderson apparently knew about the history between Charlie and me.

I added the name of Charlie Miliken to my to-do list.

Next I placed a call to Tommy. Sonia, his secretary, told me he was in a conference and unavailable, but that he had asked her when I called to see if I was free for dinner. I agreed, but mentioned that I was having a late-afternoon meeting regarding a witness related to the case and that he should get in touch with me via cell phone.

I looked at the telephone slip on which Leonardo had written that Carlos Suarez had called. I would have to be careful dealing with this one. I was still unconvinced that all the information I had received from the Suarez family was correct and truthful—especially the part about Carlos and Alexander not having contact in New York. Cubans are very family-oriented, and these two men were first cousins, contemporaries, and single guys in the city. I didn't buy the idea that they hadn't kept in touch at all. Besides, what thirty-year-old man tells his family everything?

It was almost time to leave to meet with Suzanne, so I put off Carlos's call. I wanted to take my time when I spoke with him. I also figured that I could prepare for my meeting with Tomás Cardenas when I got back from lunch. I took a couple of minutes to add to my list. In addition to Charlie Miliken, I placed a star next to the name of Francia Alvarado, the housekeeper at the Ecstasy who had seen Tío Ramón coming out of Room 7 covered in blood.

I read over the list and groaned. A lot of ground to cover, with no sure direction. I touched the medals of the Virgen de la Caridad del Cobre, the Cuban Virgin, which my sister Lourdes insisted I wear for protection, pinned to the strap of my brassiere. I prayed, most of all, that I wasn't going to run across any more bodies. It would only increase my workload and, as Leonardo might have said, it was simply too much bad karma.

20

A QUICK LOOK AROUND THE CAVERNOUS RESTAU-
rant confirmed the fact that I had arrived at Versailles
before Suzanne—which was no surprise. Suzanne might
have been from Minneapolis, but I always suspected she
had some Cuban blood. She shared the characteristics of
my country's people, especially where punctuality was
concerned. Her streak of Cubanity was confirmed a few
years back, when in a rash moment she had a Cuban flag
tattooed on her ass—it waved proudly when she flexed her
muscles a certain way. I wondered how she felt about that
flag now that Cubans were personae non gratae in the
United States after the Elián González fiasco.

It was two, after the main lunch hour in most American restaurants, but in Versailles the place was crowded.
Nearly every table was occupied. I spotted a vacant one
toward the back and headed for it without waiting for the
assistance of the maître d'. In Versailles—the Cuban land-
mark in the heart of Little Havana—the law of the jungle
prevailed. It was first come, first served.

Versailles could exist only in Miami. It was open
almost twenty-four hours a day, shutting down only an
hour a night to allow for cleaning. And the food was
cheap, tasty, and very plentiful. Anyone who was anyone—

or who wanted to be someone—went to Versailles to see and be seen. It was considered the very nerve center of Miami's Cuban exile community. Whenever any news concerning Cuba occurred, the newscasters headed straight to Versailles to get the patrons' reaction. The place was a true and steady barometer of Cuban politics. It was rare for me to go there and not recognize at least a couple of the diners. Politicians—both Anglo and Latino—from Miami and from out of town were always dropping by campaigning, greeting their constituents, hoping to win support by stopping at each table and adding to the human gridlock. The waiters and waitresses would have to maneuver around them with heavily laden trays balanced perilously above their heads. It was the accepted state of things, like the cigar smoke that drifted everywhere in defiance of antismoking ordinances.

I sat down and made myself comfortable, then immediately ordered a pitcher of sangria and a platter of *mariquitas*—golden-fried plantains with garlic dip. Within seconds I was given a green plastic bucket filled with thin slices of Cuban bread dripping with butter mixed with garlic. My mouth watered like one of Pavlov's dogs.

Politeness decreed that I wait for my guest to arrive before beginning to eat or drink, but there were exceptions to every rule. I would defy Emily Post herself to adhere to every tenet of etiquette once inside the tantalizing confines of Versailles. So I was happily into my second glass of sangria, washing down mouthfuls of *mariquitas* glistening with oil and salt, when Suzanne came into the restaurant. I stood up and waved her over to our table.

"Lupe, *chica!*" Suzanne kissed me on both cheeks. She had to lean down to do so, because she was exactly one foot taller than I was. "It's great to see you."

"You, too," I said sincerely.

Suzanne grabbed a handful of *mariquitas* as soon as she sat down. "God, I love these things!" she enthused, dipping them in garlic sauce. She poured herself a glass of sangria and drained it in two swallows. "Oh, this is heaven," she said.

It was great to see someone unashamedly and unabashedly enjoying life like that—especially in the current climate of political correctness and low-fat health obsession. I was waiting for the life of excess to come back into fashion. I would continue to indulge until then, but I relished the thought of all the repressed people around me finally letting their hair down and enjoying life as it should be lived. It would certainly make things more interesting.

While Suzanne was enthusiastically digging into her food and drink, I had a chance to look her over. We never got to see each other as often as we would have wished, and the telephone was no substitute for regular in-person contact.

Suzanne turned heads everywhere she went and, at that moment, I caught nearly every man in the room swiveling his head to get a look at her. Versailles' clientele included many movers and shakers in Miami, men and women who had seen and heard it all. But nothing in their experience would have prepared them for this statuesque six-foot platinum-blond goddess who walked with the confidence of Moses parting the Red Sea. Her skin was milky white—a very unusual trait in tropical Miami, and one that she exploited to the fullest. She once boasted to me that she was the only woman in Miami without even the faintest trace of a tan line.

Today Suzanne was dressed rather conservatively in white Capri pants and a sky-blue T-shirt that perfectly matched the color of her eyes. Her long hair was tied back with a loose gingham blue-and-white-checked scarf. It didn't much matter—she could have worn a burlap bag and she would have looked incredible.

Since we were both regulars at Versailles, neither of us had to look at the menu. Suzanne ordered *camarónes enchilados*—shrimp cooked in tomato sauce. I chose *pollo Versailles*—grilled chicken cooked with onions, a specialty of the house. I had already worked through the first basket of Cuban bread, and another one was quickly brought to our table.

"So, Lupe," Suzanne said. "What do you want to know?"

I didn't feel awkward asking Suzanne for information, because we did favors for each other whenever we could. Years ago I had helped out Suzanne when she found out she had a stalker. And another time I had had Tommy help out one of Suzanne's girls who had gotten into trouble. Other times I had checked out clients for her to make sure they were legitimate. That was the nature of both our businesses. If it weren't for favors given and received, neither of us would have lasted long, to say nothing of being successful.

"I'm looking for a tall, Asian-looking working girl," I said. "Possibly a Latina. She was heard speaking Spanish without an accent."

"Tall, Asian, and Latina?" Suzanne said, frowning. "There aren't too many girls around who would fit that description."

"I guess not." Feeling a little dejected, I took a sip of sangria. Maybe Tío Ramón had imagined the part about hearing the hooker say something to herself in Spanish.

Suzanne suddenly snapped her fingers. "China Ramírez," she announced. "It might be China. But she's not one of mine anymore, she hasn't been in years. I didn't even know she was still in Miami. She's Asian, but one of her stepparents was Hispanic—I remember that. Why would you be interested in her?"

"I didn't really think she was one of yours," I told Suzanne. "She was spotted going into one of those love hotels over on Eighth Street. I know your girls don't work those kinds of places, but I thought at least you might know about her. She may be a witness to a crime—a murder, in fact, that one of my clients has been accused of committing."

"China was a nice girl," Suzanne said. "And popular. My clients liked her, and she had a lot of repeat business. She wanted to open up a hair salon, I think, after she got out of the life. She had her license and everything."

"What happened?" I asked.

Suzanne's blue eyes cast off a tint of sadness. "Same old story," she said. "A man. Drugs. Small-time rip-offs. You know my rules. I had to let her go."

Just then our food arrived. We watched as our waitress arranged the table, each plate somehow looking even more enticing than the last. We wished one another *buen provecho* and dug in.

Her fork held up in midair, Suzanne said, "I wonder how China is doing. It's been a long time since I heard anything about her."

"I'm not even sure it's China my client saw at the Ecstasy—"

"The Ecstasy Hotel?" Suzanne asked with distaste.

"That's the one."

"Unfortunately," Suzanne said, "that tells me all I need to know about how China's doing."

I wasn't positive it was China Ramírez who Tío Ramón spotted at the Ecstasy the night of Alexander's murder, but it was more than likely. Miami might have had a population of two million people, but in many ways it was really a small town.

Our conversation slipped away as we concentrated on our meal. In Versailles it was always impossible to eat everything put in front of you, and that day was no different. We were stuffed, although that wasn't going to prevent us from ordering dessert. There was always room for coconut flan, followed by two *cortaditos*. The coffee aroma emanating from the minuscule white ceramic cup placed before me was strong enough to give me heart palpitations, but I managed to persevere nonetheless.

I asked for the check. "So, do you know any way of contacting China?" I asked Suzanne.

Suzanne drained the last of her sangria. I started to pour some more for her, then realized that we had drained the pitcher. Actually, there wasn't much left on the table at all. It was a testament to two hearty appetites.

"Sorry, Lupe." Suzanne shook her head. "I haven't seen or heard a thing from her in at least two years. I haven't wanted to, either. I've learned to cut off people who get into hard drugs. It might seem cruel, but it's a matter of self-preservation for me."

I couldn't hide my disappointment. I felt that China might be important to building Tío Ramón's defense.

"Can you think of a way to find out where she might be living?" I asked.

"She was friendly with Marisa, one of the other girls. Marisa might have heard something more recent about China." Suzanne started to stand, folding her napkin and placing it on the table. "Be careful, though, Lupe. If China was working the Ecstasy, then she's not doing well. The Ecstasy is considered the lowest."

"I know," I said, standing. "And thanks for helping

me out. I wouldn't have bothered you with this if it wasn't important."

"I know that, *chica*." Suzanne bent over to kiss me good-bye. "Let me know if I can do anything else."

Suzanne and I walked out, single file. Suzanne went first, tall, blond, and regal. All heads turned as we progressed through the still-crowded dining room. Suzanne looked straight ahead, seeming oblivious to it all. But I knew she wasn't. She loved it.

I knew I couldn't compete with Suzanne for attention and looks. But I held in my stomach and forged on, making my best show of it.

21

BEFORE I BACKED OUT OF MY PARKING SPACE AT Versailles I glanced at the clock on the Mercedes's dashboard: three-thirty. I had planned to go straight back to the office after lunch with Suzanne, but since I was already on Eighth Street and just a few blocks from the Ecstasy, I figured I would swing by and see if Francia Alvarado—the maid who had stumbled onto Tío Ramón the night of the murder—had showed up for work.

I was extra mindful of the perimeter-post surveillance cameras at AAA Best Preowned Cars, so I parked well away from their range on the street. The ficus trees planted next to the wall surrounding the hotel didn't offer much concealment, but I stood next to the tree closest to the driveway leading into the courtyard. I hoped to have a look around without attracting notice.

I counted eight cars parked in the courtyard, two of which—a Honda and a Lexus—had backed into their spots. My private-eye instincts kicked into gear. I wondered if the drivers of those two cars might have parked this way so that their tag numbers wouldn't be visible from the street. It might also be possible that they were preparing for a quick getaway.

I told myself to stop speculating—after all, nearly every-

one at the Ecstasy had something to hide and would take
measures to hide it. I was there to find the maid, not to
uncover the secrets of other people's sex lives.

I knew the turnover rate at places like the Ecstasy would
be high, with most patrons renting rooms for between two
and four hours. The minute they left, the maids would
arrive to clean up for the next set of lovers. Time was
money in the love-hotel business, and the quicker the
rooms were cleaned, the quicker they could be rented out
again. Maids could be in any particular room at any given
time—unlike regular hotels, with regular cleaning schedules dictated by guests who actually spent the night.

I had been standing there for only a few minutes when
the door to Room 12 opened. A man and a woman paused
in the doorway. He was a tall Anglo man in an open-
necked shirt and jeans. The woman was almost as tall as he
was, dark-skinned, her black hair cut very short. She was
dressed in green surgical scrubs. They looked around to
see if the coast was clear before emerging. Apparently they
saw nothing that alarmed them because they quickly closed
the door behind them and walked to the silver Acura
parked in front of the room. The woman pointed her keys
at the car and unlocked it. She got in, then the man got in
on the passenger's side. They soon drove away.

A moment after the Acura's taillights disappeared
from view, a slim dark-haired woman dressed in shorts
and an El Salvador T-shirt began walking along the corridor toward the room. She was pushing a cart filled with
cleaning supplies. I wondered if it was Francia, and cursed
the fact that I had no photograph by which to identify her.

Standing there next to the ficus trees, getting bitten by
mosquitoes, wasn't getting me anywhere. So I decided to
approach the woman. Something told me she wasn't Fran-

cia—I thought that she had probably scrambled away as soon as the police got involved with the goings-on at the Ecstasy. I crossed the courtyard and knocked on the open door to Room 12. The maid inside was vacuuming, so she couldn't hear me above the noise of the motor.

I stood in the doorway looking around the room. I hadn't been able to see Room 7, where Alexander died, but I figured the rooms were all pretty much the same. This could have been any regular hotel room—well, except for the mirror on the ceiling, and the porno movie playing on the TV, depicting a man and woman giving each other sexual favors. The bedspread and curtains were made of matching chintz fabric, and there were pictures of hunting scenes on the walls. It was sort of Ralph Lauren meets Little Havana.

I walked in a few steps. After almost a full minute the maid noticed me. She looked up, uninterested.

"Francia?" I shouted over the moan of the vacuum cleaner.

The woman shook her head, her eyes widening as she checked me out. I recognized that look. It was the look of someone who lived in fear of authority—although, in my jeans and white cotton shirt, I didn't think I looked particularly menacing.

She flicked off the vacuum cleaner. "I'm Betty," she said. "Francia isn't working today."

"Do you know where I can find Francia?" I asked her.

"She's not working here anymore," Betty replied with annoyance. She leaned over, ready to turn on the vacuum.

I handed her one of my business cards. "Look, I'm not the law," I told her. "I'm a private investigator. I work for the attorney representing the man who was accused of the murder in Room 7."

"Yeah?" Betty asked, as though to say, *What's it to me?*

"My client is the older gentleman that Francia saw running out of the room," I added.

"What do you need Francia for?" Betty said with complete distrust. "She already talked to the police."

"I just want to hear the story from her," I replied. "That's all. Just a few questions."

Betty wasn't buying my explanation. I decided it was time to bear down a little.

"Francia is going to have to talk to me sooner or later," I told her. "That's the law, Betty."

I didn't want to go into the intricacies of the discovery period of a trial, but I would if I had to. I was convinced that Betty knew where Francia was, and that she didn't want to tell me. I didn't think it would be a good idea to read Betty the riot act—I didn't want to antagonize her or frighten her any more than I had—but I needed to get past the maid's defenses and her probable motivation of protecting a friend.

"I don't know where she is. I haven't seen or heard from her." Betty switched the vacuum cleaner back on.

Some people are such bad liars that they should never even attempt to utter an obfuscation. Betty was one of them. I handed her another of my business cards.

"Please give this to Francia," I said. "That is, if you happen to run into her."

Betty pocketed the second card without looking at it, then returned to her cleaning. If she pressed any harder on the carpeting, it was going to need replacement.

"*Gracias,*" I said, turning to leave.

When I got back to the Mercedes I took out my cell phone. Marisol answered on the first ring.

"Guess what?" I said. "I need you sooner than I thought I would."

I told Marisol what I needed her to do, and then I drove back to the office. There was a little time yet for me to prepare for my meeting with Tomás Cardenas.

IT WAS JUST AFTER SIX WHEN THE PHONE RANG AND I HEARD Tomás's low, sexy voice on the line.

"Lupe, sorry. I'm running a few minutes late. I hope I haven't inconvenienced you."

You'd almost think he knew I was a sucker for apologies. Especially when offered by someone with the sexiest phone voice I'd ever heard.

"No problem," I said. "I was still here working, writing up a few cases."

"So where is it convenient for us to meet?" Tomás asked. "I am completely at your disposal."

If only, I thought.

"You're in the Grove, right?" I asked, remembering what he'd told me earlier.

"Yes. But I can drive anywhere you want," Tomás replied.

I had never laid eyes on him, but I was already halfway in love with this guy. In Miami, people hate to drive. Taking to the road constitutes a real life-risking endeavor. I knew of couples who should have stayed together, but who had ended their relationship because they lived in different zip codes.

I thought about where we should meet, keeping in mind that I was having dinner with Tommy afterward.

"How about the bar at the Place St. Michel?" I suggested.

"Perfect," Tomás said. "See you there."

As I replaced the receiver, I realized that we hadn't told each other what we looked like so we could identify each other. I didn't think he was going to be carrying sacks of sugar around with him—nor did I think he expected me to be carrying a gun in a holster. Oh, well, I figured we'd work it out. The bar wasn't that big.

Plus, I could smell a lawyer anytime, anywhere. I had certainly known enough of them—and in a variety of ways.

22

I STOOD IN THE PLACE ST. MICHEL DOORWAY, checking out the crowd and looking for Tomás Cardenas. It took me only one pass to spot him leaning against the wall, a drink in his hand. He recognized me at the same time, and we walked toward each other.

Tomás's telephone voice had set up an expectation that, unlikely though it may seem, wasn't belied by his appearance in person. Never before had I seen a man who seemed more comfortable in his own skin. And what a skin it was. His big, luminous black eyes took me in with a glance, right down to my marrow. I hoped he didn't notice my slight shiver, since it would have been embarrassing and more than a little inappropriate. The bar's overhead lights shone down on his longish wavy black hair, making it gleam like polished marble.

The Place St. Michel bar was a place for the twenty-something crowd to meet after work for drinks, and there were perhaps a few dozen people already there. It took a while for Tomás to maneuver through them to get to me, so I was able to get a good look at him. He wasn't very tall, but he carried himself with clear authority—a man in control of himself and his surroundings. He was dressed in a khaki poplin suit with a blue-and-white-striped shirt and a wine-red tie. Formal, yet equally casual. The perfect Miami combination.

"Lupe?" he asked when he approached me. I nodded. "Would you like to sit down?" Without waiting for my response, he took me by the elbow and steered me toward an open table.

As soon as we were seated a waitress appeared, as if by magic. I suspected that Tomás was known at the Place St. Michel. We gave our order—Johnnie Walker Black for him, cabernet sauvignon for me—and looked one another over with undisguised curiosity.

"Ramón speaks very highly of you, Lupe," Tomás said. "He told me about all the trouble he's in and how much you've helped him."

"I've done what I can," I said. "He's in a very precarious situation."

Tomás nodded seriously. "We'll see what I can do to help."

Our drinks arrived. Both of us said, *"Salud,"* at precisely the same moment. The coincidence made us laugh.

Better focus on business. I reached into my bag and brought out a copy of the letter that Alexander had received from Mauricio de Villegas. I handed it over to Tomás and waited as he read it over.

"Were you aware of these offers being made to owners of mills and refineries?" I asked him.

"Yes. This is the third time I've heard about this happening." Tomás paused to think. "I'm trying to remember if this same lawyer made offers to the other owners, but I'm afraid my memory fails me on that point. I'd have to go back to my files and check the copies of the other two letters."

"Two others," I said, my mind racing. "Do you remember if the terms were the same? Ten cents on the dollar?"

"Yes, that much I remember. The other two offers were the same." Tomás shifted in his chair. "Look, Lupe, I'm sorry, but I can't divulge much more information than that. The individuals in question retained me as their attorney to represent them in any legal transaction that might transpire as a result."

I digested what Tomás had just said. "But you're a personal-injury attorney, not a real estate lawyer."

"You're right," Tomás admitted; he took a sip of his scotch. "I usually stick to my specialty, but this was a different situation. The individuals involved had met me through the sugar-owners meetings, and they got to know me through that organization. They're elderly, and by and large they haven't had too many dealings with attorneys. I happened to be the one they knew and trusted."

I could tell that Tomás was choosing his words carefully, acting more like a lawyer protecting his clients than a source willing to help me with mine. I sipped my wine and thought about what he was telling me. I wondered if the other two individuals he mentioned were thinking of selling off their properties, or if they had retained legal help to make sure they didn't somehow get cheated if they refused.

"Why do you think these offers are being made now?" I asked. "I mean, I've learned a few things—"

I flipped open my notebook to some jottings I'd made from an Internet search an hour before. "The mills certainly aren't productive," I said, and started to read from my notes. "Sugar harvests in Cuba have fluctuated in the past seven years, from 3 million tons to 4.3 metric tons, with all of it pledged as collateral for loans and sold in advance." I stopped to shake my head at the thought of an entire industry being ruined by greed, corruption, and neglect. "In comparison to the recent figures, the 1952 harvest yielded 7.5 metric tons of sugar. In 1999, the sugar harvest was forty-two percent less than in 1959—the year of the revolution."

Tomás smiled with admiration. "You've certainly done your homework," he said.

I acknowledged his compliment with a smile of my own. "So it's a given that there's really no money to be made from sugar. Tourism has replaced sugar as the main source of foreign exchange for the Castro government. So why would anyone be so eager to purchase sugar mills from Cubans who have been in exile for more than forty years?"

Tomás shrugged and gave me a boyish smile. "You would have to ask that question of your Señor de Villegas— and see what he says."

Tomás finished off his scotch and motioned toward my glass. "Would you care for another?" he asked.

I knew I would be leaving shortly for dinner with Tommy, which would entail a bottle of wine or two. I should be prudent and not accept Tomás's offer.

"Sure, why not?" I said. So prudence wasn't my strong suit.

Tomás signaled the waitress and, within seconds, we had new drinks and our old ones were cleared away. My guess was that Tomás was a big tipper.

I debated telling Tomás that I couldn't ask Señor de Villegas about his motives—because the Spanish lawyer was lying on a slab in the medical examiner's office suffering the indignities of an autopsy. But instinct told me not to volunteer the information. Tomás hadn't exactly been forthright with me, despite his stated wish to help Tío Ramón as much as he could.

We sat in silence for a moment. Then Tomás turned and flashed that devastating smile of his.

"Do you have any plans for dinner?" he asked in that sexy voice.

Why was I not surprised? I started to reply that I did have plans when my cell phone rang. I looked down and saw Tommy's number on the caller-ID screen.

"Excuse me," I said to Tomás as I picked up.

"How're we doing for time?" Tommy asked.

"Ready whenever you are," I said, although I was tempted to arrange another half hour to spend with Tomás.

"Good. Me, too," Tommy said. "And I'm starving. Do you want to go to the Beach for dinner, or would you rather stay in the Gables or the Grove? Whatever you want is fine with me."

It seemed the planets were aligned so that both Tomás and Tommy were extremely solicitous of my wishes. Whatever the reason, I was happy with both their attitudes.

"I don't really have a preference," I said quickly. I didn't want to stay on the cell phone too long; it felt rude, with Tomás sitting right next to me. And I didn't want Tomás to know too much about my personal life—specifically, that I was having dinner with Tío Ramón's defense attorney. And that sometimes Tommy and I had been known to discuss cases in bed.

Silence on the line while Tommy pondered. "Let's drive out to South Beach," he said. "How about Pacific Time? We haven't been there in a while."

"Perfect."

"Where are you now?" Tommy asked. "Do you want me to pick you up, or should we meet there?"

"Why don't we meet at my office?" I said, trying to sound as professional as possible. I could sense that Tomás was very interested in my conversation, and was probably trying to decode its content from my end.

Tommy agreed, and we hung up. The last thing I wanted was for Tommy to drive up to the Place St. Michel in his dark blue Rolls-Royce convertible to fetch me for dinner. That would have been a dead giveaway. What I couldn't figure out was why I cared what Tomás knew or didn't know.

"Well, have a nice evening," Tomás said sweetly, with a genuine smile. "Maybe another time."

"Maybe another time," I agreed.

TOMMY'S ROLLS WAS ALREADY IN THE DRIVEWAY WHEN I pulled into my regular spot outside the office. He waved to me as I got out of the Mercedes and activated the car alarm. I visually checked out the office from the outside, making sure everything was in order. Crime had been on the decrease lately in Dade County, but it never hurt to remember that anything could happen anywhere. Satisfied that the office seemed safe and secure, I walked toward Tommy.

"Hi, Lupe," Tommy said, stepping out of the Rolls to open the passenger door.

I kissed him lightly on the lips. He smelled as fresh and sweet as ever and looked especially good in his double-breasted gray pinstripe suit with a light pink shirt. I realized that my attraction to him hadn't diminished an iota from the moment I first laid eyes on him. I had unresolved issues regarding Tommy, as they would have said on a daytime talk show. Tomás, for all his charm, receded from my consciousness for the moment. And as for Alvaro, I had to guiltily admit that I hadn't really thought of him all day.

I wasn't going to worry about it. To paraphrase Scarlett O'Hara, I'll think about it tomorrow.

"Top up or down?" Tommy asked. It was the first time I could recall him asking my preference. I knew Tommy loved driving with the top down, especially on the causeway to Miami Beach, so I motioned for him to leave it down. My hair was pulled back into a braid, so it wasn't as though it was going to be irrevocably mussed up in the wind.

The Miami sky shone over us, lit by a quarter moon so bright I felt as though I could reach up and touch it. Tommy took a Montecristo Número Uno from his pocket, lit up, and took a deep drag. I smelled the rich odor of good tobacco mixed with the scent of the night.

23

"A BOTTLE OF ROMANÉE-CONTI, PLEASE." TOMMY said to the waiter at Pacific Time. "We'll settle on the rest of our order a bit later."

We were seated in the first banquette on the left side, a prime location for people-watching and also a place where we could have a private conversation without fear of being overheard. It was still early evening, and we were in no rush to deal with either dinner or business for the moment, so we relaxed and took in our surroundings while we waited for the waiter to return with our wine. I still couldn't get over how good Tommy looked and smelled.

The walls at Pacific Time were finished in a distressed cream color, with an enormous round wooden clock with a white face hung over the entrance—set, of course, to West Coast time. I noted with pleasure the cobalt-blue vases on each table filled with orchids and illuminated by votive candles, also in blue containers. The waiters and waitresses were dressed in spotless, perfectly ironed white steward's jackets and black pants; they floated about the large room, keeping a sharp eye on everything. Every table in the place was occupied, but the service was so seamless and attentive that each patron was taken care of beautifully.

We munched on garlic-flavored bread sticks while we waited. I had just started on my third one when the waiter appeared with two glasses in one hand and a bottle in the other. He put the glasses down on the table and, with great ceremony, opened the bottle and placed the cork in front of Tommy to examine. Tommy ignored the cork, and the waiter then poured an inch of red wine into his glass for approval. In all the time I had known Tommy he had never returned a bottle of wine in a restaurant, but he still went through the ritual of tasting it—mostly because it was a time-honored ritual, and also because Tommy didn't like to give servers a hard time. Tonight was no exception. Tommy took a tiny sip and then motioned for the waiter to fill both our glasses.

We tipped glasses in a silent toast and started to look over our menus. I hadn't realized how hungry I was until the smells from the kitchen reached our table. We decided to split the duck salad appetizer, then ordered lamb chops for Tommy and the Colorado beef for me. The desserts at Pacific Time were legendary, so I resisted digging deeper into the bread basket placed before us in order to save room for later.

Tommy sipped his wine, then cleared his throat and broke the ice. "So, Lupe, how's the case coming along?" he asked. "We really haven't been in contact much the last couple of days."

I thought back to the last time I'd updated Tommy; it had been upon discovering Señor de Villegas's body in the trunk of the rented Taurus.

"I'm waiting to hear back from a few people," I said. "Suzanne might be able to help me locate the prostitute, China Ramírez. I have Marisol on the trail of Betty, a maid at the Ecstasy, to see if she'll lead me to Francia—the witness on the scene. I'm contacting Carlos Suarez to see if he can shed any light on Alexander's life in New York. And Detective Anderson will get in touch with me once the M.E. draws a conclusion on de Villegas's cause of death."

"When do you think Anderson might call?" Tommy asked.

I shrugged. "I have no idea. The M.E.'s office is really overburdened." I couldn't resist the bread basket any longer; I cut a piece of pita in half, dipped it in olive oil, and popped it in my mouth. "I read that each M.E. in Dade County performs between two hundred and twenty-five and two hundred and fifty autopsies a year. All told, in Dade County alone there were more than thirty-five hundred autopsies performed last year."

Tommy looked at me with amazement. "Sounds right," he said. "But what I can't believe is how you remember things like that."

"It's a gift," I replied.

Just then the first course arrived. The duck salad was big enough to serve as a main course. Tommy and I dug in, and it was delicious. We polished it off in a couple of minutes.

"What else?" Tommy asked, dabbing his lips with his napkin. "Tell me about the witness you met this afternoon."

I told Tommy about how Tío Ramón had set up my meeting with Tomás Cardenas. I left out the parts about the phone voice and the black wavy hair.

"The main thing I learned," I said, "is that two other owners have received the same kind of offer that was sent to Tío Ramón."

"Do you think you could get this lawyer to tell you who

they were?" Tommy asked. "It seems to me that would be
relevant to Ramón Suarez's case. Can you work on him
some more?"

Tommy knew that I didn't give up easily. "I'll try," I
said. "But he was pretty adamant about it being privileged
client information."

The waiter returned to clear away our plates. Tommy
looked at how little wine we had left and ordered another
bottle.

"Right now I have to concentrate on who killed
Alexander," I said. "So I need to locate and talk to China
and Francia. Next I have to look into the lawyer's murder.
It's a matter of time before Detective Anderson links the
two—and then they might try to pin the second one on Tío
Ramón, as well. I mean, he was found in the trunk of
Alexander's rented Taurus."

"Alexander might have done it," Tommy mused.

"Or Tío Ramón, at least as far as Detective Anderson
is concerned," I emphasized.

"Well, what are we saying?" Tommy asked. "That your
Tío Ramón might not be as innocent as he claims?" An
amused twinkle infused Tommy's eyes. Tommy generally
assumed that his clients were guilty of something—if not
the crime they were accused of, then another crime that
they hadn't been charged with yet.

"I don't know," I admitted. "I'd like to think he didn't
kill anyone, but I guess I can't be sure. I mean, I've known
him all my life—he's one of Papi's closest friends in the
world. But no, I'm not sure."

The main courses arrived just as I was getting lost in
my uncertainty. I don't know which entree looked more
enticing—Tommy's lamb chops lying majestically on a
mound of mashed potatoes, or my filet served in a deli-

cious wine sauce. We postponed discussing the case any further while we devoured our food. We had our priorities in order.

"So, is it bothering you that your tío Ramón might be lying through his teeth?" Tommy asked when we had both finished. We had laid waste to our plates, and there was almost nothing left from either meal.

"Not so much that I can't work the case," I said. "I just need to get deeper into it, that's all. I'm frustrated that I have to wait to find the people who might help me determine one way or the other whether he's guilty."

The waiter cleared our plates and asked if we wanted dessert. He seemed to know the answer to his question before he even asked it.

We chose the chocolate bomb, the Key lime baked Alaska, and two double espressos. The perfect conclusion to a great meal.

No, I thought, there was an even better way to end the meal. I looked over at Tommy, who was watching me.

"Tonight?" he asked.

Somehow Alvaro seemed very far away from me, in both the emotional and physical sense. I knew what others might have thought about my going off with Tommy while I was in a relationship with another man, but I never played by others' rules and never would. I may have acted more like a man than a woman in my personal relationships, but I was operating in a man's world. Besides, I never cared what anyone thought about my personal life.

In my line of work and the life I'd chosen nothing was ever certain. I didn't really have the luxury of self-examination, and no use for recriminations over my behavior. I took full responsibility for my actions, and paid the price for my decisions. Besides, Alvaro knew my nature. That didn't justify what I was contemplating, but Alvaro had entered into our relationship with his eyes open.

Tommy was also an old friend. We liked and trusted each other, and that counted for a lot. We would be acting on old feelings and doing nothing we hadn't done before. We each knew the other would ask no questions later, and neither had any expectations.

It had been a long time for us, and I probably shouldn't have accepted his invitation. But I was always a sucker for a sweet-smelling man.

24

IT WAS SIX O'CLOCK IN THE MORNING AND I WAS standing naked in the middle of Tommy's palatial master bedroom. I turned my cell phone back on and checked for any messages that might have come in since I'd switched it off about eight hours before. Tommy was in bed sleeping soundly, so I left the lights off and was careful not to make any noise.

Marisol had called three times—the first two asking me to call her back on her cell phone ASAP, the last giving me an address in southwest Miami to which she had followed Betty, and where Betty had met with a woman who probably was Francia. The name on the apartment's mailbox had been F. Alvarado.

"I hope you're having a really good time," Marisol said sarcastically on the last message. "I'm out here following around maids while you're living it up."

I saved the message and moved on. The next one was from Suzanne, asking me to call her. Even though we were close friends and Suzanne kept some pretty irregular hours, I didn't think she would appreciate a predawn call from me.

Next was a message from Tomás Cardenas. He said to call him, that he had some information he thought I would be interested in hearing. Even though I was totally satiated from my night with Tommy, I still felt a flutter at the sound of Tomás's voice. Interesting.

The first order of the day was to get cleaned up, so I stepped into Tommy's shower and luxuriated in the sensation of steaming hot water coursing all over my body. I washed my hair with one of Tommy's coconut-scented shampoos, and finished off with a pineapple conditioner—I guess Tommy was an honorary native of the tropics. His soap was made with almond oil. When I was done, I thought all I needed was a little paper umbrella and I could have passed for a tropical cocktail.

After I toweled off I tiptoed through the bedroom and into the guest room, where I knew Tommy kept clothes left behind by various female house guests whom he'd entertained at one time or another. This wouldn't be the first time I helped myself to an outfit composed of other women's clothes—my sister Lourdes, the nun, called them "experienced" clothes. I knew they were all clean, because Tommy's maid was under orders to wash and hang anything left behind—and not to ask questions or offer comment.

From the closet I chose a pair of black Capri pants and a pink T-shirt, then underwear and a bra from a chest of drawers in the corner of the room. The only thing I was wearing that was originally mine was the pair of black suede slides I'd had on the night before.

I walked back into the bedroom and sat down on the corner of the bed. "Tommy, I'm leaving," I whispered in his ear. He reached out, his eyes still closed, and tried to pull me back into bed. "No, really. I have to get to work."

I had to admit that I was tempted, but I was clean and dressed. Tommy opened his eyes. "Well, I'll drive you back to your car," he said.

I pushed him back down. "I'll take a cab. You sleep.

I'll call you later." Tommy groaned, rolled over, and started snoring.

I located all my clothes from the far corners of the apartment, found my purse, and left. The concierge downstairs called me a taxi, which arrived within five minutes. In less than ten, I was at the office. The Mercedes, mercifully, was still where I had left it the night before, and in the same condition. I turned off the alarm and went inside the building.

My first stop was the kitchen to make some *café con leche*. I was going to be comatose without a morning jolt of caffeine. I prepared the pot and put the milk to boil, then went into my office.

There were several messages on the machine. I couldn't deal with them yet, so I opened up the window and looked out. Just as I expected, the parrots were nowhere to be seen. Seven in the morning was too early for them, sensible creatures that they were.

The smell of coffee was wafting through the office, and I went into the kitchen and poured a big healthy mug. I started to feel, after a couple of sips, that I was ready for whatever the day held in store.

The first message on the office machine was from Alvaro. He said he had been trying to reach me, that my cell phone must have been switched off, and could I call him ASAP. I heard more than a touch of annoyance in his voice. I couldn't deal with him yet, so I moved on. I had to straighten my head out first about what I had done, and what the consequences of my actions the night before were.

The other calls were duplicates of messages left on my cell phone—thankfully, there was nothing new that I had to consider. My only problem was deciding what to tackle first.

I had another long drink of coffee, and heard faint noises from outside the building. I got up to greet Leo, who I assumed was out there parking his Jeep. On my way through the reception area, I stopped off and poured him a fresh mug of *café con leche*. He was always bringing me coffee, and I thought it was time to return the kindness.

The steaming coffee in hand, I opened the office's outer door and called out for my cousin as I walked out onto the steps.

"Leo!" I said cheerfully.

And then the world turned all red. I felt my knees buckle, and my head exploding. Just before I blacked out, instinct compelled me to throw the mug of scorching coffee at whoever or whatever had just attacked me.

"Bitch!" I heard a man's voice cry out as the coffee hit its mark.

And then I felt the cold stairs against my cheek. There was a prayer on my lips as I faded away.

I AWOKE TO A SHRILL VOICE SHRIEKING MY NAME: AT FIRST I thought it might be an elderly woman, then I realized that it was Leonardo. I slowly opened my eyes—just in time to see two men in gray uniforms bending over me, placing a plastic mask over my nose and mouth.

"Lupe! Lupe!" Leo kept shouting over and over again. The sound of his voice was making my head hurt. *"¡Ay, dios mío!"*

I pulled the mask aside and sat up—much to the consternation of the two paramedics trying to tend to me. I soon discovered that sitting up wasn't a very good idea. The world started to spin uncontrollably, and I lay back down with a thud. My head was an entire universe of inflamed nerves and thunderstorms of pain. Leo's screams of concern, while well intended, were sending streaks of agony tearing through my skull.

"What happened?" I managed to ask one of the paramedics as he was attaching a black plastic monitor to my arm. I noticed, actually, that the guy was pretty cute, with black eyes and long curly lashes. I may have been knocked out, but I wasn't dead yet.

"Your cousin over here dialed 911." The paramedic motioned to Leonardo, who was leaning against the wall. My cousin had stopped screaming, but he looked hollow-eyed and traumatized, his thumb lodged in the corner of his mouth. "We got here immediately."

"I need to get up," I said.

The other paramedic stopped trying to replace the oxygen mask on my mouth and shook his head at me sternly.

"Look, miss," he said. "We think you need to be transported to a hospital for observation. You have a nasty bump and cut on your head, and you lost consciousness. You may have sustained a concussion."

I looked over at Leonardo. We both knew there was no way in hell that I was going to any hospital. Ever since Mami had died a long, painful death in one, I avoided them like the plague. I had spent too much time in hospitals and seen far too much.

I tried to sit up again, this time taking it much more slowly. The pain still throbbed in my head, but it was becoming almost manageable. I heard the whine of a police siren in the near distance and groaned. Of course, the police would have been called. It was standard procedure. And, of course, I still didn't know what had happened or how I had ended up on the ground.

While I was grateful for the paramedics' help, I wanted them to go and for the police to leave me alone. As soon as I saw the brown sedan roaring up my driveway and stopping a few yards from where I sat, though, I knew that my wish wasn't going to be granted.

Detective Anderson pushed open his door and jogged to me with an expression of genuine concern. "What happened?" he asked. "Are you all right?"

"I'm okay." I rubbed the side of my forehead, right at the hairline where the paramedics had placed a bandage. I summoned up all my strength, fought off a wave of nausea, and prepared to move. It wasn't easy, but I was heartened to see that I was still capable of standing up on my own—even if I was a little unsteady and had to put a hand on Detective Anderson's shoulder to keep my balance.

The paramedics finished writing up their report; there really wasn't much information for them to record, other than the fact that Leonardo had found me lying unconscious on the steps outside our office. I wasn't much help, because I had no idea who had hit me on the head. The cute paramedic cautioned me to take it easy as he packed up. His partner, the serious one, approached me one last time.

"You really need to go get checked out at a hospital," he said. "Come on. We're going that way. Let us give you a ride."

"Thanks for your help," I said. *"Gracias."*

The paramedic shook his head, got into the van with his partner, and drove off. Detective Anderson, Leonardo, and I watched them vanish into the distance.

"Did you see who attacked you?" Detective Anderson asked. He took my elbow to support me while I took a few wobbly steps up into the cottage.

"No, I have no idea," I said.

"I had the scanner on when I heard a woman had been attacked, and then your office address," Detective Anderson said. "I wasn't sure if it was you or someone else, so I wanted to come check things out in person."

I was surprised, and a little touched, that Detective Anderson had raced over to see what had happened to me. His tough-cop features were creased into an expression of genuine concern for me as I opened the front door and went inside. I knew I might not like what I saw, but I headed straight for the bathroom and the mirror there.

"Lupe, where are you going?" Leonardo called out from behind me. I heard him dogging my steps. "You need to lie down."

"Detective Anderson, have you met my cousin Leonardo?" I called out as I went into the bathroom. "I'm sure you've talked on the phone plenty of times."

You could never accuse Leo of having bad manners; he stopped his pursuit of me and extended his hand. While Detective Anderson and my cousin were getting acquainted, I closed the bathroom door, turned on the light, and faced the mirror.

Well, it wasn't as bad as I'd feared it might be. I looked pretty normal, in fact, save for a four-inch strip of tape holding a piece of gauze to the side of my head. I gingerly lifted one edge of the tape to see what was underneath the bandage.

I should have quit while I was ahead. The skin underneath the gauze was open, raw, and oozing blood. The gauze itself was already saturated, and I knew it would have to be changed soon. A bruise was starting to form around the wound, giving the side of my head at the hairline a blue-black tinge. I decided the bright lights of the bath-

room were painting too vivid a picture, so I switched them
off and stepped back out into the reception area.

Detective Anderson and Leonardo were waiting for
me. "Not too bad," I declared. They exchanged glances as
though to say they both knew that I was full of shit.

"So, Lupe," Detective Anderson said. He was leaning
over one of the chairs next to Leonardo's desk. "Feel like
talking about it?"

"Why not?" I replied. I was feeling a little queasy, so
I sat down on the sofa. "But there isn't really much to say.
I don't know what happened. I heard noises outside, I
thought it was Leo, so, coffee mug in hand, I went out the
door. And that was it. Someone got me before I had a
chance to see them."

"Did you get anything that might help us ID who did
this?" Detective Anderson asked hopefully.

I looked up at him. As usual, he was dressed in his
khaki suit and white shirt. The only difference this day was
his tie, which was a particularly bad number that could
have come right off the rack at Kmart. I wondered if he
owned one suit, or maybe six identical ones.

Leonardo, I noticed a moment later, looked like
Marie Antoinette in drag. He was in a unitard frou-frou
outfit of powder pink and sky blue, with ruffles at the
wrists and ankles. I stared at him for what was probably a
long time, wondering what it all meant. And I wondered
how long I would have to live before Leo showed up for
work in something like Detective Anderson's khaki suit
and white shirt with a tie.

"I wish I had seen something, but I didn't," I said,
shaking my head. The side-to-side motion of my head
sent pain shooting down to my toenails. "Not a damned
thing."

A frown creased Detective Anderson's forehead. "Look, Lupe, I know you're working under rules of confidentiality," he said. "But do you think this attack was somehow connected to a case you're working?"

Well, there it was, out in the open—the question that had been troubling me ever since I opened my eyes on the ground outside my office. Was my knock on the head connected to Tío Ramón's case? Had I almost joined Alexander and Señor de Villegas as victims?

On the other hand, Solano Investigations had worked out of the same cottage for eight years. We were public and visible. We'd never had a serious incident, but maybe time had simply run out for us.

"Okay, I know about the Ramón Suarez murder case," Detective Anderson pressed on. I pretended not to listen. "And I know about the Spanish lawyer found in the trunk of the Taurus. What I don't know is whether the two are connected."

"Lupe, that bruise is pretty ugly," Leonardo said.

"I know, I know," I replied.

"What I'd like to know is whether they're the same case," Detective Anderson said.

"Don't you think you should follow the paramedic's advice and get checked out at the hospital?" Leonardo asked like a mother hen.

"We'll see," I said to Leo, feeling ganged up on. I turned to Detective Anderson. "And you know I can't get into the details of my cases. Let's just say I'm treating the two incidents separately."

Detective Anderson examined me with his cool, dispassionate eyes. Well, I had done it. I had just very strongly suggested to him a piece of information that was patently false. Alexander's and de Villegas's murders were connected like links in a chain, as least as far as I was concerned. I wasn't sure why I'd said what I had, I just knew I needed some breathing space and some time.

"Well, anyway, you should listen to your cousin," Detective Anderson suggested. "If nothing else, you should get something for the pain. Because that's going to hurt like hell."

Suddenly I remembered something. I sat up, trying to ignore the drumbeat of pain in my head, and went to the office's outer door. I opened it up and started looking around the driveway.

"What are you doing?" Leo and Detective Anderson both asked, pretty much in unison, as they followed me out. I could tell they both feared I had totally taken leave of my senses.

"The mug of *café con leche* that I was going to give to Leo," I explained. "I threw it at the guy who hit me. It has to be around here someplace. That's why he left without finishing the job—because some of the coffee burned him. Maybe he grabbed it or picked it up—that would mean we have fingerprints on him."

"You didn't mention that you threw a mug of *café con leche* at the perp, Lupe." Detective Anderson came down the steps with a skeptical expression. "Are you sure it really happened?"

"What mug was it, Lupe?" Leonardo asked, looking around the grass and the plantings alongside the cottage.

"The big one with the moon on it—your favorite," I told him.

"Okay, Lupe, walk me through this," Detective Anderson asked me, finally getting with the program. "You were standing exactly where when the guy whacked you?"

I reenacted what happened as best as I could remember. It was almost more than I could stand, but I persisted, and I didn't allow myself to sit down on the stoop until I showed him where I had ended up, unconscious. Once I had gathered myself, I couldn't suppress a smile at the contrast between Detective Anderson's sober suit and my cousin's quasi-ballerina outfit.

"What are you smiling at?" Detective Anderson asked.

"Over here," Leonardo called out suddenly. "Found it!"

Detective Anderson strode over to where Leonardo was pointing, in the ficus bushes by the end of the driveway. "Don't touch it!" he said, making Leo back off. "I'll be right back."

Detective Anderson went over to his car and took a brown bag out of his glove compartment. He joined Leonardo, knelt down, slipped a pen through the coffee mug's handle, and gingerly dropped it in the bag.

"I'll have the crime techs take a look at this," Anderson told us. "Maybe they'll find something. We found the mug so far away from where the attack took place, it seems like the assailant had to have carried it there and dropped it. Maybe he thought about it and decided he didn't want to be carrying evidence in case he was stopped."

"Thanks," I said, getting up from the stoop. Detective Anderson met me halfway up the driveway. "And thanks for your concern. I really appreciate it."

Anderson waved off my thanks. "The good guys have to look out for each other, right?" he said with a wry grin.

As he got into his car, Leo and I waved good-bye. I was flattered that Detective Anderson considered me one of the good guys—almost enough to flag him down and tell him about the connection between Alexander and Señor de Villegas. But something stopped me. Anderson would find out soon enough, when he linked Alexander to the Taurus.

I was heartened to discover that, although I was still shaky, I was able to walk all the way into my office on my own. Once there, I lay down on the sofa and let out a huge sigh. I looked out the bay window and watched the parrots slowly moving in the branches of the avocado tree. I looked at my watch: nine o'clock. I guessed it served me right for being up and around so early in the morning.

I had just drifted off to sleep when I heard a soft knock at my door. Leonardo sat down on the edge of my couch, and I smelled a familiar sweet aroma.

"Here," he said, placing the joint at my lips.

"I don't—" I said.

"For medicinal purposes," Leo explained. "It'll make you feel better."

"What the hell," I said. "I'll make an exception."

25

BY THE TIME I WOKE UP IT WAS ALREADY NOON.
Leonardo had been right—his medicinal cure had made
me feel a lot better, although the bump on my head had
grown larger and more tender.

I sat up and walked over to my desk. The room was
staying on an even level, and I was able to focus my eyes on
the spot to which I was heading. So far so good. I needed
to go to the bathroom, but I was going to ignore the urge
as long as I could. I didn't want to confront the mirror
again and see how the damage on my head looked.

Given my state, I decided it would be best to spend the
next few hours as quietly as possible in my office, returning phone calls and writing up the case. I felt relatively
normal, but it wasn't time yet for tackling the outside
world. Besides, whoever attacked me was still out there in
Miami somewhere.

I didn't know for sure if it had been a random attack,
or if it had been related to the case. I would certainly have
preferred the former over the latter. But if it was connected to Alexander's murder, who would want me dead?
I couldn't imagine what I knew that would compel someone to kill me—or at least to put a big scare into me.

My head hurt worse the more I thought about it. In

fact, I got a wave of tingly nausea every time I pictured the last instant before I got hit. I decided to pick up the phone and make calls, at least to get my mind off the grisly recollection.

"Hey, Suzanne," I said when she picked up.

"Lupe, you don't sound so good."

"It's a long story," I said.

"Well, listen, I only have a second," she said. "But I haven't been able to find anyone who knows where China is. I'm really, really sorry. You know how much I want to help you."

"I know," I said. "It's all right."

"Lunch later in the month?" she asked.

"You got it."

We hung up. Not knowing China Ramírez's whereabouts was a blow, but not an unexpected one. And, all things being equal, it was a lot easier to take than the blow I'd received that morning on the front steps.

Next I called Tomás Cardenas back. I got past his secretary, and he picked up the phone within thirty seconds.

"Lupe." Tomás sounded delighted. "How are you?"

I didn't want to go into details, so I simply said, "Fine, thanks."

"I wanted you to know—I was contacted by another member of the sugar owners' group who received a letter similar to the one sent to Ramón Suarez," he said.

I thought for a moment. "And what is your client thinking of doing?"

"Now, Lupe," Tomás chided me. "You know I'm in no position to divulge that kind of information. I'm doing you a favor by calling you up and telling you this much."

"Sorry, Tomás," I said. The last thing I needed was for

the lawyer to get annoyed with me—and I knew how finicky attorneys could be about feeling pressed for information. "I hope you know how much I appreciate your help."

"Well, I don't think it's a breach of confidentiality to tell you that I have a new client who was approached in the same manner that we discussed last night, and by the same attorney in Spain," Tomás explained. "Although I did have to give the matter some thought before I called you."

"And I thank you for doing so," I said, reassuring him that he was doing the right thing. I decided now was not the time to bring up the untimely end of Señor de Villegas. Tomás would learn about that soon enough.

My head was starting to hurt again, and all of a sudden the room seemed stubbornly unwilling to stay put in one place. The combination of sitting up, thinking, and talking was apparently too much for me to sustain for very long. I realized I had to get off the phone before Tomás noticed that there was something wrong with me.

"Well, it's my pleasure," Tomás said, seemingly mollified by my expressions of gratitude. "So, Lupe. Are you available for dinner any time soon?"

Oh, God. I couldn't deal with this. Not while I was gripping onto the edge of my desk for dear life.

"Can we talk about it later, Tomás?" I asked. "Right now, all I can think about is this case."

"Sure, sure," he said, backing off. I guessed that, as an attorney, he knew well how quickly a date offer could be construed as sexual harassment. Although he might have also figured out that any female private investigator who became insulted over a proposition wouldn't last long in the business.

"Thanks again, Tomás," I said. Now the room was spinning; I couldn't even focus on the parrots. "I'll call you."

And, without even giving him a chance to reply, I hung up. I groped my way over to the sofa and collapsed. The room was pitching up in a counterclockwise motion and flickering like a frame of film caught in a projector. I hadn't felt this way even after splitting two bottles of Dom Pérignon one night with Tommy at the Forge.

My last thought before I blacked out was that the paramedic, Detective Anderson, and Leonardo might have all been right. I should have gone to the hospital and gotten checked out.

Not that I would have ever admitted it to any of them.

I WOKE UP AN HOUR LATER FEELING A LOT BETTER. OF COURSE I had felt pretty good the last time I'd awoken. Maybe that was the pattern: one hour up, one hour down. If that was the case, then I might as well put the time to good use.

I went to my desk and opened up the Suarez file. I flipped to the notes from my meeting with Suzanne at Versailles. Suzanne had mentioned that China's ambition in life had been to open up a hair salon. If it had been China hooking at the Ecstasy the night Alexander was murdered, she had apparently not reached her goal. Still, it gave me an idea about how to find her.

I picked up the phone. "Suzanne, hi. It's Lupe again."

"Hola, chica," Suzanne said. "You want to set up that lunch already? Maybe we shouldn't eat at Versailles again. I'm still trying to get my pants to zip up again."

"You name the place next time," I said, "but I'm actually calling about China."

"Sorry again about that one," Suzanne said. "Marisa lost track of her, and none of the other girls really ever knew her that well."

"Hey, no problem," I said. "But there's one thing I'd like to know. What is China's real name?"

Most of the women and men in *la vida* used street names. I assumed that China Ramírez's parents hadn't named her after the world's most populous country.

"China's real name," Suzanne repeated. "Hang on a second. I have it on file."

There was a click on the line. I knew it would be a little while before Suzanne returned because she kept her confidential business information in a safe sunk under the carpet into the floor of her apartment.

I had my head in my hands when the phone clicked back on. "You still there?" Suzanne asked.

"Pretty much," I said.

"China's real name is María Esperanza Ramírez," Suzanne said.

"*Gracias*, Suzanne," I replied. "I owe you one."

"You owe me more than one, *chica*," Suzanne said with a laugh.

After we hung up I looked at China's real name, which I had written down in front of me. María Esperanza: *Mary Hope*.

I dialed 411 and asked for China's listing. Nothing, of course. While I was still on the line I requested the phone number for the Department of Professional Regulation. After jotting it down, I actually accepted the phone company's offer to be connected directly for an additional thirty-five cents. I listened to the recording telling me there would be a delay while other customers were being helped, and realized that I was truly not feeling well at all. I always looked up numbers myself, and more than once I had declared that anyone who used 411 was morally corrupt. I decided that the mountain-sized bump in my head exempted me from such judgments.

"You want to verify that a beautician's license has been issued for a María Esperanza Ramírez?" asked the nasal-voiced clerk after I gave my request.

"Yes, please," I said. "I just want to verify that she's licensed."

I was put on hold, and I closed my eyes and thought of cool breezes and ocean water on my face.

"Ma'am?" asked the clerk when she got back on the line. "We have a license granted to a María Esperanza Ramírez, issued on December 12, 1998."

"Can you tell me the address on the license?" I asked. I didn't know whether this was confidential information, so I rustled some papers and tried to sound official. "It's a pretty common kind of name, and I want to make sure we're talking about the same person."

A moment of hesitant silence, then, "Well, the address I have here is on Northwest Fourth Avenue."

"Northwest Fourth?" I crinkled some more paper. "Are you sure? I have Southwest Fourth on the paperwork over here."

"Yes, here it is," the clerk said with confidence. "It's 301 Northwest Fourth Avenue. María Esperanza Ramírez."

"Well, I'm sure you're right," I said. "We must have made a mistake on this end."

"Anything else?" the clerk asked.

"No, thanks," I said. "We must have made a typo. I just wanted to verify the license. Thank you very much."

Well, at least China had followed up on the first part of her dream. You couldn't open up a beauty salon without getting a license first. But it was unlikely that she had opened up the salon, not if she was still hooking. The question was why, although I suspected I knew the answer.

I took a deep breath and stood up. The good news was that the room was staying in one place. The bad news was that I could no longer postpone my trip to the bathroom. I went inside and peed a river, which instantly made me feel much better. I left the light off so I didn't have to look in the mirror.

You see? I silently asked the empty room. *I'm feeling much better already.*

Then I realized that talking to myself wasn't a solid sign of a quick recovery. I went back to my office and gathered up my things.

I knew Leonardo would give me grief if he knew I was going out, so I waited about fifteen minutes until I heard him go into the office gym. A couple of minutes later it sounded like a wounded goat was giving birth in there—a sure sign that Leo was doing his upper-body workout and would be oblivious to everything for a while.

I felt steadier and stronger with every step I took. By the time I reached the Mercedes I had talked myself into believing that I was back to normal. If I could continue not to catch a glimpse of myself in the rearview mirror as I drove, then the illusion would be complete.

26

AS SOON AS I HEARD THE CLERK AT THE DEPART-
ment of Professional Regulation read off China Ramírez's
last known address, I knew that the would-be beautician
had fallen on hard times. That particular area of Miami
was known for its high crime rate, as well as its burned-out
and abandoned buildings, which served as crack houses.

I drove up Fourth Avenue, looking at the addresses,
and placed my Beretta in my lap so I could get to it in a
hurry. I drove past a group of young men, all generously
tattooed and dressed in oversized denim pants, designer
T-shirts, and unlaced high-top sneakers. They were
hanging around, smoking, fiddling with their jewelry, and
openly eyeing my Mercedes as I went by.

I hoped the bloody bandage on my head would make me
look like I lived and breathed trouble, and would keep any
ambitious muggers from getting too close to me. I hoped I
looked like a tough cookie, but I knew it was a long shot.

My attention was focused on looking out for smash-
and-grab artists—guys who threw rocks into the windows of
passing cars, so that they could reach in and take whatever
was available—and I almost drove right past China's building. When I saw it, I whistled to commemorate my good
fortune; in front was a tall chain-link fence topped with

concertina wire. Hopefully it would offer some protection from the social club of young men outside. I made a hard right turn and pulled into one of the open parking spaces in the circular driveway adjacent to the building.

China's apartment was in a three-story place that had seen better days—say, some time during the Carter administration. I took a quick look around, hopped out of the Mercedes, then locked it and set the alarm within about five seconds. I said a silent farewell to it, then jogged toward the building's entrance.

There was a list of residents posted on black felt posterboard by the front door. My luck continued to be good—M. E. Ramírez lived in Unit 5C. I pressed the buzzer next to that number and waited for a response. I hoped and prayed she would be home; otherwise I would have made the trip for nothing. I glanced at myself in the glass door, and saw that I didn't look like someone who had much excess energy to expend on empty errands.

I put my hand out and reached for the wall, feeling a little dizzy now that my adrenaline was starting to fade. But an instant later I heard the intercom crackle to life. A female voice called out in Spanish through considerable static.

"Who is it?" she asked.

"Lupe Solano," I replied, also in Spanish. "Sweet Suzanne sent me." I wanted to establish my credentials with China as quickly as possible, so I used Suzanne's nickname.

There was a little pause on China's end. "Suzanne?" she asked hopefully. "Suzanne sent you?"

As soon as I heard China's tone of voice, I knew that I had raised her hopes that Suzanne might ask her to come back and work for her again. I decided not to answer her directly, not until we were facing each other in person.

"Look, this isn't the best place to be standing around," I said. "Can I come up and see you for a few minutes?"

A couple of seconds later China buzzed me in. I walked through the graffiti-covered lobby and stopped in front of the elevator. After inspecting its apparent condition for a moment, I decided to take my chances on the stairs.

Climbing five flights of stairs in my condition took a lot of effort, but being trapped in that rickety elevator would have been a much worse fate. When I made it to the fifth-floor landing I stopped, leaned against the wall, and tried to catch my breath. I felt wetness on the side of my face and hoped it was sweat from the exertion of climbing—not blood trickling from my bandage.

China's apartment was at the end of the dimly lit corridor. As I walked down the hall my nostrils were met with a thick smell of spices and onions that made my eyes start to water. When I reached apartment 5C I tapped the door with the cheap metal knocker. A couple of seconds later I heard three sets of chains rattling, then a dead bolt being slid in its tracks. Finally the door opened.

Tío Ramón had said the hooker he saw at the Ecstasy was tall, and he wasn't exaggerating. The woman standing in front of me was easily more than a foot taller than I was. Reed-thin, with alabaster skin, almond-shaped eyes, and jet-black hair cut in a severe bob, she was wearing white short shorts and a blood-red tank top. She was a sight that would be hard to forget—it was no wonder she had impressed herself upon Tío Ramón's memory.

China stepped past me into the hallway, looking around with hunted eyes. I was glad that I'd slid my Beretta into my purse, where I could get to it quickly. It was obvious to me that China was living in fear, and of what I didn't really want to know.

"All right. Come in." China grabbed my arm and pulled me into the apartment. As soon as I was inside she started to replace the bolts and chains. This gave me time to get a good look at her arms. I stopped counting track marks at twenty. It wasn't a pretty sight.

Finally China turned around and leaned on the door. She looked at me and tried to smile.

"Suzanne sent you?" she asked.

"She told me about you," I said vaguely.

Still clinging to hope, China motioned to a ratty sofa by the window, indicating that I should sit there. China herself sat down in a leather armchair that looked as though it had been set upon by a carpet cutter.

China lived in a one-room studio. Apart from the sofa and the chair, there was an unmade twin mattress and box spring in the corner, and a Formica dinette set next to the little cooking area. The place smelled of dust and cigarette smoke. China's desperation clung to the place like an odor that had attached itself to the walls, the curtains, the carpet.

I decided that I should be as straight with her as possible. I took out a business card, leaned across, and handed it to her. China read it, then glanced at the bloody bandage on my head.

"I don't get it," China said.

I began by telling her that I was employed by the man who had been accused of the stabbing in Room 7 at the Ecstasy the night she had also been there. I described some of the facts of the case, and explained that I wanted to ask her some questions about what she may have seen or heard that night.

"What the fuck," China whispered.

The expression of utter disappointment on China's

face was heartbreaking. I knew the only reason she had let me come upstairs was a slim hope that Suzanne would take her back, restore her to some degree of respectability, maybe even fix her life. Now a cold, hard look came into her eyes as she got up to face me.

"How did you find me?" she asked in a voice tinged with a threat of aggression. "No one knows where I live."

I wasn't sure where this was going, so I spoke softly and gently. "I heard you wanted to open a beauty salon," I said. "I got your address through your business license. That's all."

China blinked, as though remembering a life never lived, and turned away from me. She took a cigarette from a pack on the stove top, lit it, and started pacing the room.

"Well, you wasted your time," she said, deliberately blowing smoke in my direction. Her movements were jerky and anxious, her eyes cold and wasted; otherwise, she might have been one of the most beautiful women I had ever seen.

"Are you sure about that?" I asked.

"I wasn't at the Ecstasy," she said. "I haven't been there in months."

She was too strung-out to hide the fact that she was lying.

"China, you won't get into any trouble with the law by talking to me," I told her. "Anything you tell me is private. I can't discuss it with the police—it's called privileged information."

"And I'm telling you that you wasted your time coming to the ghetto to see me." China ground out her cigarette in the kitchen sink, shaking her head with a mixture of sadness and anger.

"Look, if—"

"Leave. Now." China pointed at the door, not even looking at me. "And don't come back. I have nothing to say to you."

I gathered my purse and stood up. "You have my card, if you change your mind," I said.

China snorted, a pale attempt at laughter, then went to the door and angrily unlocked all her security measures. I stepped outside, and the door slammed behind me.

As I walked down the five flights of stairs, I tried not to dwell on China's total lack of cooperation. I had found her, that's what counted. Now I just needed a way to compel her to talk. By the time I reached the ground floor I had come up with a plan.

Miraculously, the Mercedes was where I had left it, and untouched. I got in and started it up. Before I put it in gear, though I checked out the street across from China's building, looking for the best place to set up a surveillance. There weren't too many choices. I backed out of my parking space and drove out of the lot. As much as I wanted to get off Fourth Avenue and back to my office, I couldn't leave. Not yet.

China was denying the fact that she had been at the Ecstasy the night Alexander was killed. So I had to find a way to place her at the scene, and then confront her with it. Just in case China was watching me leave, I drove away, heading west. Then at the corner I waited about a minute, pulled a sharp U-turn, and doubled back.

It wasn't easy to conduct a surveillance in a Mercedes in this neighborhood. For the moment the street looked quiet as I pulled under a banyan tree in the alley about a quarter-block from the entrance to China's building. I maneuvered the car so that I had good sight lines and maximum camouflage, then turned off the motor and

opened up the glove compartment. I took out my binoculars, as well as the Pentax camera with the zoom lens that I
kept for just such occasions. Then I settled back and took
a deep breath. So far, so good. I had a headache, but I was
still conscious.

It was about twenty minutes later that China came out
of the building and hurried down the street, heading east.
I adjusted the camera lens and saw that she had exchanged
her shorts and tank top for black jeans and a sweatshirt.
Wherever she was going, she was in a big hurry—and her
long legs carried her quickly. I managed to snap a dozen
photos of her in quick succession—getting a really good
one when she turned around to look both ways before
crossing the street. At least, I thought, she was still observing the rules of pedestrian safety.

I watched China until she was out of sight, then drove
away. Before I reached the office I stopped off and
dropped off the roll of film at a place that developed
professional-quality photos in a matter of a few hours.

When I went into the office, I was greeted by Leo all
worked up in a lather. He got up from his desk like a big
angry ballerina.

"How could you?" he fumed. "You sneaked out without telling me! You're in no condition to do anything!
Detective Anderson and I should have kidnapped you and
taken you to the emergency room! We're supposed to look
out for each other! How am I supposed to—"

I sat down and let him vent his frustrations. I knew it
would make him feel better. And I knew he was right. The
least I could do was let him enjoy his tirade.

27

AND LEONARDO WASN'T THE ONLY MAN IN MY LIFE who was completely pissed off with me. Detective Anderson telephoned a few minutes after Leo stopped yelling at me to catch his breath. I barely had had enough time to go to the bathroom to check out my cut—it didn't look good— before my cousin announced in an acid tone that the detective was waiting on the line for me.

"And I told him all about your little field trip," he added.

It was just as well that I didn't have much time to check out my cut. It didn't seem to be closing properly, and an ugly bruise was spreading across my forehead. I wasn't going to be entering any beauty contests soon. I looked as though I had gone into the ring with Evander Holyfield and taken a beating.

"Yes, Detective," I began. "Look, as far as Leo—"

"Forget that," Detective Anderson snapped. He sounded as though he was barely controlling his rage, which shocked me into paying close attention to what he was saying. "Look, Lupe. I just got the information back on the Taurus. Maybe we're backed up here, but I was going to get it sooner or later."

Okay. Now I understood why he was so angry with

me. "Oh. Really," I said, feeling like a schoolgirl caught cheating.

"And I'm sure you're aware—as I am now—that the man who rented the Taurus was Alexander Suarez." Detective Anderson breathed deeply, trying to calm himself.

"I can't discuss my cases," I said. It was a lame reply, but I didn't have much else available to me.

"You told me the two cases were separate," Detective Anderson barked. "You looked me right in the eye and told me a barefaced lie about a murder investigation."

I had to concede that he had a point. But the truth was, I was under no real obligation to help him out. I had been stalling for time, and now that time had run out.

No, that wasn't enough. And I knew it. Detective Anderson and I had a special relationship, one that some-times transcended the rules. And I also knew why he was so angry with me: his feelings were hurt. Well, how should I have known? He had never really showed any capacity for emotion in the past. I had started to take for granted that he was Teflon on the outside and all steel hardware on the inside.

"I'm sorry," I said. "But I didn't directly lead you to believe anything. You made an assumption based on what I told you. And didn't I help you out with the victim's identity in the first place?"

Okay, that wasn't a world-class apology. But he was still a homicide detective, and I was still a private investi-gator. I knew I was on dangerous ground, but I had to defend myself and get this conversation off any track that might lead him to accuse me of impeding his investiga-tion. It never hurt to remind him of the times I had actu-ally helped.

Detective Anderson was quiet.

"Okay, so that's the way it is," he said. "All right. Yes, you did save me time by giving me de Villegas's identity. Thanks again."

"I didn't mean to—"

"Enough about all that," Detective Anderson interrupted. He suddenly snapped back to his cold, dry self. "I didn't call you to unload. That happened unexpectedly."

"Well, what—"

"I ran the prints on the coffee mug from this morning," he said. "I came up with nothing. *Nada.*"

The attack this morning had seemed years past until Detective Anderson brought it up again. I had almost convinced myself that the wound on my head had been the result of some kind of accident. The last thing I wanted to think about was the fact that my assailant was still out there. And that he was likely to try again.

"Nothing," I repeated. *Damn it.* The quickest, easiest, and most reliable way to track the son of a bitch who'd hurt me that morning was through his fingerprints. Now I had no idea how to figure out who'd done it—and, maybe more important, why.

"Well, not exactly nothing," Detective Anderson clarified. "We found your prints. And another set, which was obviously the perp's. But we couldn't get a match with anyone on record. So we're stuck."

I knew my prints would have come up as a match on the police computer, because giving them was a requirement for getting a private investigator's license.

"Mierda." I didn't know how good Detective Anderson's Spanish was, but I figured I didn't need to translate that sentiment for him.

"I know." Detective Anderson's voice softened; obviously he understood my disappointment and uncertainty.

"We'll keep looking. I'll call you as soon as I find anything."

"I'll do the same," I replied.

"I hope so," Detective Anderson said. We hung up, and I made a promise to myself not to lie to him again. He was a good guy. We might have worked at cross-purposes sometimes, but he had never been anything less than stand-up.

I buzzed Leo and asked him to pick up the pictures I'd dropped off, which should have been about ready.

"That's more like it," he said. "Have me go. You stay here and rest. Maybe I've finally gotten through to you."

I paused. "Anything to make you happy," I said. "Now hurry up and bring those pictures back."

While I waited for my cousin to return, I opened up an envelope on my desk that had come while I was out tracking down China Ramírez. I hadn't had much luck yet with China, so now I needed to track down Francia Alvarado, the maid at the Ecstasy. I flipped through Marisol's report, hoping she had struck gold as usual.

She might have. Marisol's report indicated that she had done a surveillance on Betty, the other maid, and followed her from work to an address in southwest Miami just off Calle Ocho, not far from the Ecstasy. Marisol wrote that Betty had visited another woman there. Hopefully that had been Francia or another family member. I had reason to hope, since Francia was laying low and I had alerted Betty to the tightening investigation by showing up at the hotel.

I looked at my watch. It wasn't even five yet. This day seemed endless. Maybe I had a concussion, I thought, and had lost my ability to properly gauge time.

I was pondering this reassuring possibility when

Leonardo returned with the photographs. Per my instructions, the store had also enclosed a duplicate set.

Spreading out the pictures on my desk, I inspected them closely. I was by no means an accomplished photographer, but I thought I had done a passable job given the conditions under which I had been working. The pictures were taken at an odd angle, but in three of them China's face was clearly visible. Others showed her profile, which was striking and easily identifiable. All in all, anyone who had seen China would be able to identify her from these photos.

I wrote a quick cover letter explaining what I required, then called a messenger service to pick up a manila envelope and courier it out to Tío Ramón in Key Biscayne. That done, I slipped the extra set into the Suarez file.

I resisted an urge to check myself out in the mirror again as I prepared to leave for the day. I had one stop—to see Francia Alvarado—and then I was going home. I figured my skull would stay in one piece at least until then.

FRANCIA ALVARADO LIVED IN A THREE-STORY APARTMENT building that was kept in immaculate condition, from the perfectly tended front garden to the freshly painted white picket fence that encircled the property. Whoever owned the building took a lot of pride in it. I checked the place out, enjoying the light yellow paint that made the building glow in the late-afternoon light. I couldn't help but contrast it to China Ramírez's run-down building with its air of hopelessness and neglect.

There were a few other apartment buildings on the same block, each similar in size to Francia's, although none of them were as well maintained. Francia's building faced the street, with the ground-level apartments opening up to a publicly accessible corridor. Anyone could have gained access to the units; for all the attention the owner evidently placed on making his property attractive, he hadn't thought to devote as much energy into security concerns.

Unlike China's building, this one didn't have a driveway or parking lot in front. I was forced to street-park, which I didn't really mind. This was a modest neighborhood, but it seemed reasonably safe. The Mercedes and I stood a good chance of meeting up again, each in the same condition as we'd left.

I walked up and examined the highly polished brass mailboxes on the east wall of the building. The one corresponding to Apartment 8 listed the name F. Alvarado. I saw that Apartments 1 through 4 were on the ground level, so Francia's was probably on the second floor. I started climbing the stairs, which made my head throb again. I resolved to have someone who knew what they were doing look at my cut and bruise as soon as possible. And to start taking only cases that required no stair climbing.

Apartment 8 was at the end of the hallway on the second floor. I walked up to the door and pressed my ear lightly against it. Nothing from inside. I knocked, then knocked again a little louder when I heard noises on the other side.

"Who is it?" a woman asked in Spanish through the door. "What do you want?"

"Señora Alvarado, my name is Guadalupe Solano," I said in a clear voice. I half hoped that by evoking the name of one of the Virgin's apparitions I might lead Francia to believe that I was one of her emissaries. "Could I speak with you for a moment?"

Silence. "Really," I said. "I only want a few minutes. Please."

Just as with China, I heard a cacophony of chains and bolts before the door opened.

"Come in, come in," Francia scolded me as she stepped aside for me to enter. "Don't stand out there shouting at me for the entire world to hear."

She reached around me and closed the door so hard and so fast that it actually hit me on the ass before it slammed shut. We ended up standing inches away from each other, after Francia had finished locking up about half her collection of chains and bolts.

Francia Alvarado was almost exactly the same height as I was, so I was able to stare her straight in the eye—an unusual privilege for me, and one that I was taking full advantage of. Her black hair was cut short, and her face was youthful and wrinkle-free given her age—I'd say about forty. Her eyes lingered on my bandage and bruise, and she seemed about to say something but stopped herself.

The room I had just entered was clean, bright, and cheerful. It was furnished modestly, but it was apparent even from a quick once-over that everything inside had been color-coordinated and arranged with care and taste, from the framed prints on the walls to the sofas and chairs.

"Thank you for letting me in," I said. Francia was not only small of stature, she was small all over. Even her feet were tiny, smaller than mine. It was hard for me to imagine how she handled the physical workload of being a maid—especially at a love hotel, where each room had to be cleaned several times a day.

I reached into my purse, took out a business card, and handed it to her. Francia read it over slowly, then looked at me.

"Betty said you were asking about me at the hotel," she said.

I heard the unmistakable sound of a small child's whimpering from a room somewhere inside the apartment. A moment later I heard a soft woman's voice singing a lullaby that quieted the child.

"Sorry to bother you," I said.

"Then make it fast," Francia said, showing a flash of the tough side that the Ecstasy's manager had laughed about.

I began my explanation of how I was employed by the defense attorney retained to represent Ramón Suarez, the man accused of killing the occupant of Room 7 at the Ecstasy. I added that I only wanted to ask Francia a couple of confidential questions about what she might have seen that day.

When I stopped talking, I noticed that I was still standing only one step inside the closed front door. Francia showed no sign of inviting me in to sit down.

"I told the police everything," she said. She seemed more puzzled to see me than defensive or angry. "I don't understand why you have to come here to my home, asking me these questions. The police, they have all the information."

"I know. I have a copy of the police report," I told her. "But sometimes people remember details that didn't cross their mind the first time they were asked what happened."

I smiled at Francia and resisted the urge to sit down on the soft-looking sofa without being invited. My head was really starting to throb—in time with my pulse, and making me feel a little twinge of nausea with each drumbeat. At that moment I would have been willing to pay big money in cold cash for a glass of water.

"No, no." Francia shook her head, perhaps a little too vigorously. "I did not forget a thing."

Francia made a move as though to unlock the door. My window of opportunity was closing fast—along with the impending end of my ability to remain on my feet.

"The police report said you saw a man coming out of Room 7 holding a knife and covered in blood," I said quickly. "You started screaming. And I can understand why. It must have been very frightening."

Francia looked at me. "I don't scare easily," she said, then looked away. "But yes, it was a terrible thing."

"It would give me bad dreams," I said. "I mean, it sounds like something out of a nightmare."

"In Salvador, my country, I saw some very bad things," she said bluntly. "No one ever gets used to such sights, though. Or at least they shouldn't."

"Did you think the man was going to hurt you?" I asked.

"No, I never thought that," Francia answered. "I simply screamed because he startled me, and because I could tell what he had just done. But I didn't think he was going to hurt anyone else."

I reflected on this. Well, Tío Ramón had looked like a man who had just committed murder. At least he hadn't seemed to be in a rage, like a man who was going to continue killing anyone in his path.

We were still standing in front of the door, but I could tell that Francia was a little more interested in speaking with me. At least she had made no further move to evict me.

"How long have you worked at the Ecstasy?" I pressed on.

"Two years this month," Francia said without hesitating even a moment to stop and think. Nothing in her demeanor indicated whether she thought this fact was a good thing or a bad thing. "Betty started just before me. We've been working together all this time."

"You must have seen a lot, working there," I ventured with a smile. I started to reach for the wall to steady myself, but stopped. The wall was immaculate, and I didn't think Francia would appreciate fingerprints there.

"That's for sure," Francia said. She folded her arms and gave me just the barest hint of a smile. "But we're not supposed to notice what goes on. That's part of the job. Guests come there for privacy. Me and Betty, well, we hear nothing, we see nothing."

My heart beat a little faster. She hadn't mentioned "say nothing."

"But you notice things all the same, right?" I said. "I mean, I was thinking about it the other day, when I was talking to Betty. A hotel like that would be the perfect place to study human behavior."

"I mind my own business, just like I'm supposed to. And I don't stick my nose into other people's business." Francia's expression turned hard, as she suddenly stopped buying my sympathy act. "Look, I have nothing more to say to you. I want you to leave."

Francia moved toward the door, and the baby in the back room started to whimper again. Clearly this interview was coming to an end. I considered my rapidly dwindling roster of options and decided that I would simply have to level with Francia. I had a sense that, in spite of her reticence and suspicion, she was looking for someone who she could speak with. She had seen something jarring and awful, and she hadn't had a chance to unburden herself.

"Francia, look, I'm a private investigator working for Ramón Suarez's lawyer, just as I told you." I knew it would make my head hurt, but I took a deep breath before continuing. "But I haven't been completely honest, and I haven't told you everything."

Again I heard the baby's crying stopped by the soft

sound of a woman's voice. Francia glanced toward the back of the apartment, then back at me, as though to tell me to go on.

"I'm working so hard on this case because Ramón Suarez is my father's best friend." I knew it was a little dramatic, but I reached up and touched the bandage on my forehead. Francia watched me, becoming more and more interested. "They were best friends growing up in Cuba sixty years ago, and they're best friends now in Miami. I've known Tío Ramón all my life, and I know that he is not capable of killing a man. It's up to me to prove he's not the killer, and I need help from you in order to do that."

Like I said, it wasn't often that I looked into the eyes of someone exactly my own height. But in this case it worked for me; Francia gauged my sincerity and, apparently, I passed her test. She took me lightly by the hand and led me over to the sofa in the living room. I could have kissed her as I sat down with a sigh. I had never in my life been so grateful to get off my feet.

"Whatever I tell you—you will keep it confidential?"

"Yes," I said, my heart beating hard in my chest and, as far as I could tell, in the middle of my head.

"You're right. Betty and me, we notice what happens at the hotel." Francia sat down on the love seat across from me. "We talk about what goes on. It makes the time pass faster."

Francia, her hands in her lap, looked at me expectantly. "I know you saw Tío Ramón coming out of Room 7," I said. "Did you notice anyone going into that room or coming out before then?"

Francia thought for a moment. Then she gave a little shrug. "You mean, besides the dead man?"

"Yes," I said, clarifying my question. I would have liked to start taking notes, but it was a delicate moment and I didn't want to do anything that might make Francia stop talking.

"Well, I came to work at ten that morning, like I do every day. I work from ten until eight at night. It's the same with Betty," Francia explained.

"Did anything unusual happen earlier that day?" I prodded her.

"Well, you see, usually the rooms at the hotel are taken by couples," she said. "The man goes to the office to pay, and the woman stays in the car. Then he comes out of the office with the key to the room, the woman joins him, they go to the room. Sometimes they come in separate cars, but almost always the man goes and gets the key."

"I understand," I said. What I understood was that, like many witnesses finally unburdening themselves, Francia needed to tell her story in her own time, her own way. I hoped she told me something soon, though, because my neck hurt and I was starting to feel a strong urge to lie down and close my eyes.

"The man in Room 7, though, he arrived alone. He went to the office, he paid for the room, he went there." Francia shook her head, still puzzled. "I thought a woman would come meet him in a few minutes, you know. They pay for the rooms by the hour, so they don't like to waste time."

"And no woman joined this man?" I said. It was almost amusing. Alexander had claimed he wanted to avoid notice by checking into the Ecstasy, but by going there alone he had drawn a good deal of attention to himself.

"*Sí.* You know, I play a little game sometimes. When a man arrives alone, I try to guess what the woman is going

to look like. Then when she comes, I see if I was right."
Francia gave a little embarrassed shrug, as though to say
this was just a way of passing time. "This man in Room 7,
you know, he was very nice-looking. Very nice clothes. I
really wanted to see what the woman was going to look like
who was coming to meet him."

"And you saw no one," I offered.

"Well, he was alone for a few hours," Francia said. "I
went to work cleaning the other rooms, thinking that he
was going to be alone. I thought he'd been stood up. But
then something strange happened."

I held my breath, wondering what might be considered "strange" at a love hotel in Little Havana. "What do
you mean?"

Francia looked up from her clasped hands, her dark
eyes staring into mine. "It's funny, you know," she said.
"That was the first time I had ever seen a guest go from one
room into another."

I knew what I had just heard, but I was having a very
hard time figuring out what it meant.

"Let me see if I understand," I said shakily. "The guest
in Room 7, the murder victim Alexander Suarez, he left
his own room and went into another one?"

Francia shook her head. "No, no," she said. "I mean
that a guest in Room 6 went into his room—Room 7."

"You saw who it was, right?" I said.

"*Sí*. I thought I had been all wrong about that man,
you know, when I tried to guess what kind of woman would
be meeting him." Francia looked down at her hands
again. "He was so good-looking. I was sure he was meeting
a very attractive, very sophisticated type of woman."

I blinked, trying to clear the fog emanating from my
head wound. Something very important was happening,
and I was trying to see it from every angle.

"Who was it?" I asked. "Who came to see Alexander in Room 7?"

Francia sighed. "A whore," she said. She shook her head. "Like such a nice-looking young man needs to carry on with a Chinese whore. I mean, you'd think he could get a nice woman without paying. Wouldn't you?"

Oh, shit.

"Hey?" Francia asked. "Did you hear what I said?"

28

THE TWO TYLENOL P.M.s I'D TAKEN BEFORE GOING to bed had knocked me out so completely that I didn't at first recognize the ringing sound next to my ear as coming from my cell phone charging on the bedside table. I lay there, immobile and entombed in blankets, listening to the familiar ring, incapable of reaching out to answer.

I had planned to head straight home after leaving Francia's apartment—but one look in my rearview mirror at the bruise on the side of my forehead confirmed that there was no way I could arrive at the house in such a condition. So I stopped off at a walk-in clinic in the Grove, where the young doctor on duty cleaned and changed my dressing. I had no idea at all when I had gotten my last tetanus shot, so he also gave me an injection as a precaution against infection.

By then it was dark, and I knew I really shouldn't have been driving. But I was only ten minutes from home, so I gritted my teeth, concentrated, and got there in one piece. By the time I was home I felt like collapsing and falling asleep in one of Osvaldo's carefully tended flower beds.

As I got out of the Mercedes, I kept myself alert by replaying in my mind my interview with Francia. The hooker who had visited Alexander's room at the Ecstasy had obviously been China Ramírez. But now I had another question—who else had been in Room 6? I tried to think it all through, but I ended up holding on to the side of my head and walking up the driveway to my family's house.

I hadn't figured out yet what story to tell my family about my condition to keep them from being alarmed at the sight of me—there was no way I was going to tell them that someone had clubbed me in front of my office. It was one thing for them to know that I was a private investigator. It was another thing entirely for them to contemplate the notion that I might face physical danger from time to time.

As I tried and tried to think of a plausible explanation for the bruise and bandage on my head, I realized that my thoughts were spinning and getting nowhere. My brain had simply stopped functioning, from injury and fatigue, and I wasn't going to come up with a brilliant story. This wasn't like coming home at six in the morning on a Saturday night during my junior year of high school—as impaired as I might have been then, the teenage Lupe still had one over on my present self. I would simply have to wing it.

The Virgin must have been listening to my prayers. I was able to open the front door, walk inside, and make my way upstairs to my room without anyone noticing that I had arrived. I paused on the stairs and listened for a moment. My family was out on the terrace, having dinner together, laughing and telling stories. The reason they hadn't heard me come in was because they were having such a boisterous good time.

I took a couple of steps back down the stairs and peeked around the corner so I had a view of the terrace. I noticed

with a pang that my sister Lourdes was out there having
dinner with the rest of the family. She hadn't been home
in a couple of weeks, and I longed to go out there and join
them. But I simply couldn't. I would have ended up ruining the evening for everyone.

It had been too long since I had participated in my
family's everyday life, and I resolved that that would
change as soon as this case was over. I wanted and needed
it, and I missed them. I made my way slowly up the stairs to
my room, my footsteps heavy.

Once in my room I showered, put on a nightgown,
and dropped into bed. I was hungry, but I felt incapable of
the minimal effort it would take to procure some kind of
meal. It would be easier to skip eating and hold out until
morning. I was exhausted but wanted to make sure I slept
through the night, so I took those two Tylenol P.M.s,
which were guaranteed to help me avoid a middle-of-the-
night bout of insomnia.

And so it had gone—straight into oblivion—until the
phone started ringing. It stopped, then started ringing
again. Someone didn't want to leave a message on my voice
mail. I opened one eye and checked out the bedside clock.
I was surprised to see that it was a little after six in the
morning. It felt more like midnight.

Without turning on the light, I reached out and picked
up the phone. I made a sound that approximated "Hello."

"Lupe," Detective Anderson said, his voice loud in my
ear. He sounded out of breath. "Thank God you're all
right."

I shook my head, trying to wake up. What was he talking about? For a second I thought I was dreaming—until I
felt the throbbing in my head. No, this was real. I sat up in
bed and turned on the light.

"Of course I'm all right," I said to him. "Why wouldn't I be?"

"Do you know a woman named Maria Esperanza Ramírez?" Detective Anderson asked.

China? Now I was *really* awake. I knew that this could only be bad news. Detective Anderson might have thought I was a grim reaper, but he had his own intimate knowledge of nasty events.

"I know her," I said. "Why?"

"Her body was found a couple of hours ago in an alley in Little Havana," Detective Anderson said. "Off Calle Ocho. It looks like she's been strangled. I'm calling you from the crime scene."

"How did you connect me with her?" I asked.

"Because your business card was tucked under her dead body," Detective Anderson informed me.

"Exactly where are you?" I asked.

Detective Anderson gave me an address two blocks away from the Ecstasy. "Look, the crime techs got here an hour ago," Detective Anderson said. Now he sounded almost apologetic for having called me so early in the morning. "I've got maybe half an hour more here, and then I'm off. I just wanted to make sure you were all right. It was a weird thing, when we found your card."

"I'll be there in fifteen minutes," I said, and hung up before he had a chance to tell me not to come to the crime scene.

I had little time to waste, but I had to shake off the effects of a hard night's sleep. I jumped into the shower and soaped off furiously, cursing as the cold water hit my body. I brushed my teeth in the shower, then a minute later I was toweling off. I put on jeans and a T-shirt, sprayed some Chanel No. 5 all over, and was off.

IT WAS EASY FOR ME TO IDENTIFY IN WHICH ALLEY CHINA HAD been found. There were two squad cars with lights flashing blocking it off. The rear of the crime techs' van was visible between them. I couldn't see any news vans on the scene yet, but it was inevitable that they would get there soon enough—they would have heard the homicide call on their police scanners. I spotted Detective Anderson's plain brown car and parked right behind the crime tech van.

Detective Anderson, at the end of his shift, was dressed in his trademark khaki suit. He was speaking to another man as I approached the crime scene and, as I neared, I wondered for the thousandth time whether or not Detective Anderson was a real living and breathing human being. Didn't he feel the need to sleep, eat, or change his clothes? I'd never known him to do any of those things. I burned to know whether there was a Mrs. Anderson, or little Andersons running around in little khaki suits and sunglasses. In all the years I'd known him, he'd never made even a fleeting reference to having a personal life.

I didn't recognize the younger, casually dressed man Detective Anderson was talking to, and I nodded to him without saying anything. I saw his eyes focus on the bandage on my forehead, but he said nothing about it.

"Officer Morales, Vice," Detective Anderson said in a tired voice. "Lupe Solano."

We shook hands. The sun was just coming up, lighting up the horizon and promising another hot and humid day. There was no relief from the heat, not in Miami. The weather was hot, more hot, and even hotter, interspersed with hurricanes.

"Come over here." Detective Anderson guided me to the crime scene, leaving Officer Morales behind. He lifted the black-and-yellow plastic tape that cordoned off the area and held it up for me to pass underneath. We approached China's body slowly, careful not to step on any area marked off by the crime-scene techs.

"The M.E. hasn't arrived yet," Detective Anderson said. "It's been a busy night in Dade County."

We stopped. China was lying flat on her back on the ground, staring up at the sky. She was wearing the same black jeans and sweatshirt I'd seen her wearing earlier in the day when she was leaving her apartment.

Dawn had broken and the sky was brightening. Although the alley was in dark shadows from the buildings on either side, I was still able to see the ugly red marks across China's neck where she had been strangled. Her face and neck were dark red, and her eyes were bulging in their sockets. Her mouth was wide open as though she had been trying to scream.

I didn't feel very good. I felt like throwing up and, when I thought about China's beauty parlor, for a split second I felt like crying. I fought it all off by concentrating on the facts.

"How did you find her?" I asked. We were halfway up the alley, and China's body was partially obscured by a big green Dumpster.

"It was called in from the pay phone over there." Detective Anderson pointed across the street. "Anonymous. Of course. Female voice. Morales was working Vice a couple of blocks away, so he came right over. This is his turf, so he knows all the hookers who work around here. He ID'd her right away and saved us some time—she didn't have a purse or anything on her."

"Have you figured out how she was strangled?" I asked. I was flashing back to Señor de Villegas—it was the same

MO—and I knew Detective Anderson was thinking of him as well.

"No. We're still searching the area, but from looking at her throat I'd say it was a rope, and someone came at her from behind." Detective Anderson crouched down and, with a pen, pointed at the marks on China's neck. "Unofficially, of course. We'll see what the M.E. says."

I forced myself to look at where Detective Anderson was pointing. Maybe it was the early hour, maybe it was the bump on the head, maybe it was something else entirely. But I couldn't bring myself to look at China Ramírez's once-beautiful face.

"What about the time of death?" I asked. "Any estimate?"

"I'd say about midnight or thereabouts, from the condition of the body," Detective Anderson said. "But don't quote me."

I suddenly realized that Detective Anderson hadn't asked me why a hooker murdered in Little Havana would have my business card tucked under her dead body. His anger at me the day before was still fresh in my mind, and I wondered what was on his.

We took a couple of steps back when one of the crime-scene techs came over and asked Detective Anderson if he could speak with him. They walked off down the alley, leaving me alone. Suddenly I had no problem looking at China; in fact, I couldn't take my eyes off her. It was as if by staring at her I was going to find the answer to one of the countless questions that were popping into my mind.

Such as how China and Alexander had been connected. And why Alexander had been killed, and by whom. And who had killed the Spanish lawyer, and China.

And who had been in Room 6 at the Ecstasy Hotel the night this whole damned thing turned deadly.

By now traffic on the street was getting heavier. People were going to work or taking their children to school. Of course, everyone was slowing down to rubberneck at the police cars and trying to peek down the alley. One of the officers on the scene jogged down the alley toward the street, ready to tell everyone to move along. One would think we'd be inured to crime in Miami, but maybe we aren't. Maybe there's hope for us.

Detective Anderson came walking back toward me. "Well, Lupe, is there anything you're burning to tell me?" he asked. "Anything that I should know about this?"

Detective Anderson gestured at China, an impatient expression on his face. I waited a few seconds, then decided to keep it short and sweet. I'd give him minimal information while making it look as though I was fully cooperating. And I wouldn't lie. It was a tightrope act, but I thought I could pull it off.

At least I hoped I could.

"I interviewed her yesterday," I said, choosing my words. "I had been told she was a witness in a case I'm investigating. Ms. Ramírez denied being in a place where a witness had placed her, and then she asked me to leave her apartment."

"So she was lying." Detective Anderson didn't miss a thing. He glanced over at China again. "If she'd come clean with you, she might be alive right now. Is that what you've been thinking, Lupe?"

"Something like that," I said, wincing at the thought.

I knew I couldn't blame myself for China's murder, but it was too much of a coincidence that she'd been murdered just hours after I went to her place to talk to her.

And the business card placed under her body seemed to me like an obvious message. A strong possibility was that the killer was the same person who'd used my head for a snare drum the morning before.

Of course, China might simply have been holding the card when she was attacked. She might have changed her mind and been on her way to contact me. I didn't want to guess wrong, because the consequences might be deadly for me.

"I can't say for sure what happened, or what could have happened if she'd talked," I said to Detective Anderson. "But I would have helped her if I could have. I know that."

"I don't doubt it," Detective Anderson said softly.

At that moment the medical examiner's van pulled up to the scene. It was the same driver who'd come to the towing company lot to examine de Villegas's body in the trunk of the Taurus, and he nodded at me and Detective Anderson. The detective and I stood next to each other and watched China's body being prepared for transport to the morgue downtown. The whole procedure took only a few minutes—probably because the techs got so much practice working in Miami.

When the van was gone, Detective Anderson and I walked toward our cars. He escorted me to my Mercedes and waited until I had started the motor to head over to his own car.

Suddenly he turned and waved for me to lower my window. I did as he asked, and he leaned over my side of the car with a perplexed look on his face.

"The hooker and the lawyer were both strangled," Detective Anderson said to me. "And she was found two blocks from the hotel where Alexander Suarez was stabbed. You're working his case, and you talked to the hooker a few hours before she got herself killed."

I looked straight ahead and said nothing.

Detective Anderson, putting on his best Columbo act, scratched his head and chewed his lip.

"A lot of coincidences," he commented. "Don't you think so?"

I looked up at him and saw a flash of humor cross his features. If nothing else, he seemed to be getting an intellectual charge from all of this.

"I suppose," I offered.

"I thought so," he said. He stood up straight and thought for a second. "Watch yourself, Lupe. It's getting dangerous out there."

Detective Anderson patted the hood of my car and waved as I pulled out onto the street. I left him there staring into space, thinking of God knows what.

29

I WENT STRAIGHT TO THE OFFICE FROM CALLE Ocho. I hate to admit it, but after my experience of the morning before, I was a little skittish about being alone in the cottage. I circled the block twice, looking for an excuse to cop out, until I finally pulled into the driveway. Before I got out of the car I tucked my Beretta into the waistband of my jeans, then pulled down my T-shirt to disguise the tell-tale bulge. I felt a little silly, but the truth was that the gun gave me enough confidence to walk up to the building.

I walked up the path toward the entrance. I gave a little thought to the idea of going over to the Starbucks on the corner and hanging around until Leonardo arrived for the day, but then I told myself it was time to get over my fear. I had to be able to function in order to deal with this case—and, hopefully, find out who had attacked me.

It was too early for Leo to come to work, so I busied myself getting Solano Investigations up and running—I turned on the lights, checked the phone messages, and prepared an eight-cup pot of Cuban coffee, half of which I drank as soon as it was ready. Then I took down the painting of the Cuban royal palm that hung over the sofa in my office; it had been given to me in lieu of a cash pay-ment by a destitute artist a few years back, and was the per-fect size to hide my wall safe.

I whispered the safe's combination under my breath as I slowly twirled the knob to unlock it. It had been a while since I'd needed to open it up, but the combination leapt straight to the fore of my memory. The clicking sound of the lock opening was as sweet as ever.

I found what I was looking for right away—a shoe box, which I carried over to my desk. Inside it, wrapped in muslin cloth, was a second Beretta identical to the one I carried in my purse. I checked to make sure it was loaded, and that the boxes of magazines were full, before carefully placing it in the top drawer of my desk.

Only then did I take the Beretta out of the waistband of my jeans and return it to my bag. It wasn't just any black leather bag; in fact, I owed my life to it. When I first became a private investigator eight years before, I had searched all over Miami for a tasteful purse in which I could carry the Beretta without the gun's shape distorting the bag's. I finally found the perfect one at Chanel, and bought it at once. I have never for a moment regretted the king's ransom that it cost—I figured it had been a bargain, if I took into account how long I had carried it and what it had been through.

Several years ago I had, unfortunately, been forced to use the same Beretta to shoot an individual dead—and I fired the gun from inside my bag. The stitching that had been required to repair the bullet hole had eventually become almost invisible, but I knew exactly where it was. Sometimes I ran my finger over it, as a reminder that danger was everywhere. If I needed another reminder, there was always the bandage on my head.

I let my hand wander away from the old bullet hole, shaking my head at the memory. As a precaution, I put an extra magazine in the bag's zipper compartment before I closed it up. I was starting to feel like a walking NRA advertisement. Now that I was fully armed, I placed the empty shoe box back in the safe and replaced the painting on the wall.

By then it was almost nine. I wanted to speak to Tío Ramón, but Mami's voice was in my head telling me it was too early to call. Mami had taught me to abide always by the ten-to-ten rule: never call anyone at home before ten in the morning, or after ten at night. I knew it was old-fashioned, and that today few people adhere to any kind of social etiquette, but I always obeyed my mother.

Instead of calling Ramón, I took out his case file and looked through it. I reorganized everything based on the most current happenings. Then I read through the whole thing again. I had learned in the past that, as cases got complicated, it was easy to forget basic facts that were learned early in the investigation. I had since made a practice of reviewing my notes time and again and, if necessary, drawing up charts tying everything together. It was the only way to keep everything straight.

I heard Leonardo come in—this time, unlike the day before, I checked to make sure it was really him.

"How are you feeling?" he asked.

"Better than ever," I lied. "And busy."

"I can see that," Leo said, motioning toward all the papers on my desk. "Need help with anything?"

"No, no," I said cheerfully. "Thanks, though."

With that, Leo left me alone. He knew me pretty well, and he understood that the last thing I wanted to talk about was the attack of the morning before.

Soon the magic hour of ten o'clock arrived. I reached for the telephone and called Tío Ramón's house. I was surprised when a man picked up instead of the usual maid. I was disappointed as well, since I had wanted to speak to her about the episode between Tío Ramón and Alexander. I wanted to verify the version I heard from my client, although I didn't harbor much hope that she would contradict her employer.

"Señor Ramón, *por favor*," I requested.

"Who's calling, please?" the man asked politely, in English.

"Guadalupe Solano," I replied.

"Lupe? Hi, how are you?" he asked in a friendlier tone of voice. "This is Carlos speaking. Remember me?"

I remembered that I had neglected to return Carlos Suarez's call, which was more than a little embarrassing.

"When did you arrive in Miami?" I asked him. "I didn't realize that you were coming down."

"It was on the spur of the moment," Carlos said. "I wanted to be with the family during this difficult time. I wanted to say thanks to you for all your help. My parents have been bringing me up-to-date on everything that's happened."

I suddenly became aware that we had been speaking English this entire conversation, so I switched over to Spanish. Speaking in English with a fellow Cuban always gave me an awkward feeling.

"Well, it's very good you're here," I told Carlos. "I'm sure your family really appreciates it. I would like to speak with you at some point while you're here, if that's possible."

Carlos paused; then, when he spoke, his Spanish was stilted and hesitant. "Yes, sure," he said. "No problem. Whenever."

"I'll call again to set up a meeting, all right?" I asked. I was surprised that his Spanish was so rudimentary—most Cubans of my generation were fluent Spanish speakers. I figured that, living in New York, Carlos didn't have as much opportunity to stay in practice with the language as he would have in Miami. It was a pity.

"Yes, of course."

"For now, is your father available?" I asked him. "I'd like to speak with him for a few minutes."

"I'll go get him." Carlos dropped the phone as though it were a hot potato. He was really a lot nicer and more expressive in English.

A minute later Tío Ramón was on the line. "Lupe, how are you? I see you've learned that our Carlos has come down to be with us." The pride was palpable in Tío Ramón's voice. "What a nice surprise that's been."

"Yes, it's very nice," I agreed with the old man. "But, Tío Ramón, have you had a chance to look at the photographs I sent to you by courier yesterday afternoon?"

"Yes, I looked at them," Tío Ramón said, turning much more serious. "What do you want to know about them?"

I had included a note with the photographs. But Tío Ramón, being a Cuban man of his generation, did things his own way—which meant that he hadn't bothered to read the note.

"I need for you to look at the pictures carefully," I told him. "And tell me whether that was the young woman you saw at the Ecstasy Hotel the day Alexander was murdered."

"Lupe, you know I only saw her for a moment. But there's no need for me to look at the pictures again. Of course that's her, I'd know her anywhere." Tío Ramón paused, and I nodded to myself. I had found the right witness, only to lose her. "But how did you find her, Lupe? All I told you was that she was tall, an Oriental, and that I thought she said something in Spanish. That's not a very detailed description."

"I'm an investigator. Sometimes it's my job to find people," I told Tío Ramón. I decided this wasn't the time to inform him that China Ramírez was dead.

"Well, I certainly hope that she can help us somehow," Tío Ramón said hopefully. "Just think—she might have even seen the real killer before I arrived at that damned hotel."

I certainly wasn't going to burst his bubble—Tío Ramón hadn't had much to pin his hopes on lately.

"You told me you saw her coming out of one of the rooms," I said to him, changing the subject. "Can you remember which one?"

"Which one?" Tío Ramón repeated. "I don't . . . Wait, wait, let me think."

There was silence on the line. I heard Tío Ramón breathing. Maybe I was dreaming, but it was possible he was doing the visualization exercise I'd tried to teach him the week before.

"It was to the left of Alexander's room, to the left of Room 7, I think." Tío Ramón paused. "I don't know the number, but I'm sure it was the room to the left."

That would have been Room 6. Tío Ramón had just confirmed what Francia Alvarado told me the day before.

"Thank you, Tío Ramón," I said. "I'll be in touch."

"Lupe, everything is going to be all right, isn't it?" Tío Ramón suddenly blurted out. "I mean, you're going to prove that I didn't kill Alexander, aren't you?"

The happiness I had heard in his voice when talking about the arrival of Carlos was gone, replaced by raw fear. I cared about the old man too much to give him false hope.

"I am going to do everything I can, Tío Ramón."

And, with that, we said our good-byes and hung up.

I pulled out my address book and looked up a number in New York. It was for an investigative agency I'd worked with once or twice in the past. They cost a lot, but I knew they were discreet and careful.

I needed them to be, since I was going to ask them to dig up dirt on two cousins, one of whom was recently deceased.

After that, my next call was to Marisol. There was one more person I needed followed. Something wasn't adding up, and I wanted to know more.

30

AFTER I HUNG UP THE PHONE I PUT MY NOSE RIGHT back in my notes. There were about two dozen half-formed thoughts tugging at the coattails of my consciousness. First among them was that I was losing track of the initial focus of my investigation—the offer tendered to Tío Ramón to buy his family's two sugar mills in Cuba. I hadn't had a fraction of the time I needed to look into that aspect of the case, a facet of the situation that might prove to be the key to everything.

I picked up my notes from my conversation with Tomás Cardenas at the Place St. Michel. He had been contacted by two other members of the Cuban Sugar Mills Rightful Owners Organization who'd received the same offer as Tío Ramón—ten cents on the dollar for their family properties. That made four that I knew about. Probably other owners had received offers as well and were keeping the information to themselves—after all, these were big-money deals.

I sat back and thought about the consequences for the owners-in-exile of selling their sugar mills in Cuba. Why, to begin with, would someone accept such an offer? It was understandable if their motivations were purely economic—say, they were elderly and of limited resources, in which case the sale might finance a comfortable old age with a little cash left over as an inheritance for their children. If that was the case, then their actions couldn't be condemned. They had suffered enough because of the revolution and exile, and good for them if they found a way to cash in near the end of their lives.

Other owners in exile might feel that they were never going to get their property back in any case, and would figure that ten cents on the dollar was better than the nothing they would get by waiting to have their family properties returned to them at the end of the Castro regime. The mills had been confiscated by the Castro government in the name of "agrarian reform," which I supposed was a nicer term than stealing, and without any compensation whatsoever to the previous owners. If someone came forward decades later and offered the old owners money for property they might have considered long gone, then great.

Another group that might be receptive to selling the family mills would be the sons and daughters of owners who had died in exile. For them the mills had limited sentimental value, and they might welcome cash from the sale of properties they may have only heard about and never actually seen.

Finally there might be individuals who had become so disillusioned with their old homeland that they wanted nothing to do with the island's future. For them, selling the old mills might give them closure on a dead issue.

Any of these people might also feel that the sugar business had no profitable future, and that it was no use expecting to make money off the mills. The days of sugar-as-king were over for Cuba. Other sugar-producing nations had picked up the slack—and an offer of ten cents on the dollar might represent the last gasp of ever making money off the old family properties.

The more I thought about it, the more I realized that the offers to the old mill owners opened up the entire range of exile experiences. There were probably as many reasons to sell the mills as there were mills themselves. But still, I had to remember that there was such a thing as the Cuban Sugar Mills Rightful Owners Organization—which meant that there was still interest in what was going to happen to these properties. And there were men like Tío Ramón, who were well off and too proud to sell their family heritage.

The reasons for taking such a stand were also numerous, I realized. They might be sentimentally attached to their old land in Cuba, and they might feel there was a real possibility they could one day soon reclaim their property. Another reason for rejecting the offers was an unwillingness to sell off part of their homeland to foreigners—a sense of patriotism that would prevent them from giving up a property title to a non-Cuban. There were already plenty of foreign investors interested in Cuba, and perhaps some mill owners would balk at adding to their numbers.

Ramón's case was a little different, though, and less straightforward: he hadn't wanted to sell, but his nephew did. The problem was that they were legally co-owners. How to prevail in such a case—surely not by killing off relatives.

Then there was the matter of value and appraising the properties. Cuba was not a free-market economy. Everything was owned by the government, and even in joint ventures the government always retained majority ownership. Usually purchase prices were set at market value, but how would that be determined in this case? Obviously anyone accepting these offers for their family properties was also accepting the valuation of the buyers—and common sense dictated that these might be low-ball bids.

It was hard for me to see why anyone would want to buy property in Cuba at the moment, a country where a totalitarian government maintained control over every aspect of life, and where the rights of private property weren't respected. Investing in such a country was a big risk, with uncertain rewards at best in the future.

The Cuban government's control over foreign investment was so complete that foreign companies didn't even pay their Cuban employees directly; instead they paid the government a certain amount of money per employee. Then the Cuban government determined what wages it deemed the employees should receive. In one typical case, a foreign company paid the Cuban government one hundred dollars a month per employee; in turn, the government paid the employees five dollars and pocketed the difference. Another restriction was that the foreign company lacked the right to hire or fire its own employees— these rights were retained by the Cuban government. Given these kinds of constraints, it was hard to see why a company would want to invest a lot of money in Cuba.

Fidel Castro was seventy-five years old. Who knew what the future held for Cuba once he was gone. Anyone investing in Cuba knew that uncertainty was the rule for the immediate future.

Alexander Suarez had been killed, I was certain, because of the offer to purchase two sugar mills in Cuba from the Suarez family. Mauricio de Villegas had come to Miami and lost his life over the same transaction. The question was: Why?

The core of understanding what had happened, I knew, was finding out the identity of the individuals or group who wanted to buy the Cuban mills—and why they wanted them. One place to start would be by finding out the identities of the other three mill owners who had received the same offer as Tío Ramón.

Tomás Cardenas was representing members of the Sugar Mills Rightful Owners Organization—an organized group. I might be able to obtain the names of the group's membership, as well as the names of their mills and where they were located. But that wouldn't be easy—I had already seen how secretive both Tomás and Tío Ramón were about the organization.

Tío Ramón was my client, and I had known him all my life. Still, I didn't feel as though I could contact him and ask him to get that list for me. The truth was, I still wasn't certain about his role in the case. And it followed that I didn't necessarily want him to know in advance what trail I was following in my investigation.

And however much we enjoyed flirting with each other, Tomás Cardenas had made it clear that he wasn't going to divulge any confidential information to me. He had let out a few tantalizing tidbits to get me interested, then pulled back the instant I pressed him for details.

Tidbits weren't going to be good enough. Not if I was going to figure out what was going on with the remains of the Cuban sugar business. People were losing their lives over it, and I seemed to be the only person in a position to make the connection.

And I had better do it, I realized, before I became the next to go.

31

IT WAS ALMOST SIX IN THE AFTERNOON BEFORE I
returned to the office. I was hot, tired, dirty, and hungry.
I had a headache. I had been to two libraries and one
bookstore. My mind was bursting with all the information
I had just learned about the sugar business in Cuba. I felt
as though I could have written a master's thesis on the spot
on the subject if I'd been required to.

When I saw that Leonardo's Jeep was gone from the
parking lot, I circled the block twice to make sure I wasn't
being followed. It had been less than two days since I'd
been attacked, and less than twenty-four hours since
China was murdered. Whoever had done these things was
still out there—and might decide to come back and finish
his work on me.

Once I was inside, I locked the front door and turned
on the burglar alarm. I hadn't looked under the bandage
on my head lately, but I knew for sure that I didn't need
another knock on the head anytime soon.

I put all my books and papers on my desk, then made a
trip to the kitchen. The office was quiet and still, the
atmosphere almost eerie. I opened up the refrigerator and
checked out the wines inside. I remembered opening up
the Morgan a few days ago, so I poured myself a big glass.

Stopping at the window of my office before sitting down, I did a double take. I couldn't see a single one of my feathered friends—a first in the years since Solano Investigations first occupied the cottage. I was tempted to go outside and search for them, but I decided not to. The birds' absence was a little unsettling, and I felt better inside, behind a locked door, my Beretta within easy reach.

I made my way to my desk and switched on the lamp. It was going to be a long night. I still had plenty of information to digest.

First I reviewed what I'd learned about the current state of Cuba's sugar industry. The deeper I got into the facts, the more I felt that investing in sugar in Cuba was a totally foolhardy business decision.

First of all, no one could buy the properties outright. All business ventures had to be joint enterprises with the Cuban government—and with the foreigners as minority partners. Not only did an investor have to deal with the proven mismanagement of the government, but if a dispute arose it would be settled in arbitration by the Cuban Chamber of Commerce, an arm of the Cuban government itself. This ensured that things would go the government's way. And, to top it all off, investors would have to deal with a work force raised under communism with no concept of incentives for hard work and achievement.

The machinery that was being used in Cuba to grow, harvest, and process sugar was left over from prerevolutionary days. It hadn't been replaced or upgraded, and some mills had begun to cannibalize parts from other mills' machines in order to harvest and grind their sugar. One report I came across remarked how essentially none of the mills had a complete array of the necessary machinery in good working order.

And even the mills that were in relatively good shape were idle, because they lacked enough sugarcane to grind. The gist of several articles I collected indicated that this was because of bad management and incompetence, rather than natural disasters or crop failures. In order to speed up sugar production, the cane was harvested green by machines. The preferred technique was to harvest by hand, where the worker can cut each stalk in order to do the least damage to the plant and allow it to grow healthy again. Then there were the cattle, who were also allowed to freely roam over sugar fields, where they chewed the green sugarcane plants and damaged them.

Competition among sugar-producing countries was stiff. Times had changed since prerevolutionary days, when Cuba could claim a huge profit without having to match itself against lots of other countries. Quotas had changed, and there were new players in the business. It was becoming more difficult by the year to turn a profit in the sugar business.

So why on earth would anyone—especially a foreigner, with a world's worth of options—want to invest in Cuban sugar, given the present situation? And none of this even took into account the ramifications of the Helms-Burton Bill, which punished nations, banks, or companies that directed money to Cuba. The purpose of that American legislation was to strengthen international sanctions against the Cuban government and to tighten financial pressure against the Castro regime.

The bill went even further than the trade embargo already in place—it provided for legal action against investors who profited from American properties confis-

cated by the Castro government. That provision of the bill
stated that the rightful owners of these properties could
file lawsuits in American courts against foreign investors—
which brought me back to the Suarez case. Apparently
some hidden investors were hoping to buy title to the mills
to avoid the ramifications of the Helms-Burton Bill—and,
obviously, to avoid legal problems from the former owners after the fall of Castro's government.

I flipped through the pile of photocopied papers I'd
made earlier in the day, then came across a page describing the history of sugar in Cuba. I had to skim it to save
time, but I got the bare outline. It said that sugar was first
planted in Asia by Arabs, and brought to the New World—
specifically, the Dominican Republic—by Christopher
Columbus on his second trip across the Atlantic in 1493.
Sugarcane wasn't planted in Cuba itself until the early
1500s.

I had just started to become engrossed in the development of Cuba's sugar industry in the sixteenth century
when I heard a very loud sound that made me draw in my
breath quickly.

"What—" I began, then went quiet.

The noise had come from outside, I realized, a series
of crashes and thuds that I couldn't immediately identify,
all coming from the direction of the avocado tree. My
heart suddenly was beating so fast that I could see its
rhythm through my T-shirt.

In that split second I tried to convince myself that I
had imagined the whole thing. I had almost succeeded
when I heard more noises from outside my window—not
as loud this time, but impossible to explain away as the
product of fatigue and too much time spent poring over
old texts.

Someone was out there. Again. Just like yesterday morning.

I stayed at my desk and glanced out the window. It was nighttime, so I couldn't see very far outside. I knew that whoever was out there could see in, while I couldn't see out. I liked to have an unobstructed view of the garden outside my window, so I had never installed any shades or blinds. It had never seemed necessary, since the backyard was enclosed by a six-foot-high wooden fence that I had thought ensured my privacy as well as security.

All of a sudden I realized that I had been wrong.

The only other trespassers I had ever known to come into the yard were some of the cats that roamed at will all over Coconut Grove. Whenever the parrots decided their numbers had become too great, they would reestablish the balance of power by swooping down and pecking at the cats until they left for a while. These fights were noisy and not very pretty. But I was certain that the noises I had heard weren't the parrots. In fact, now I remembered that the parrots had been gone the last time I looked outside. I wondered if someone had scared them off.

Whoever was out there had a clear view of me, so I had to act as though I had heard nothing. I started rearranging my papers, trying to breathe deeply and calmly, when I accidentally knocked over a china mug filled with pens and pencils on the corner of my desk. It fell to the floor and shattered in a big noisy mess.

"Mierda!" I cursed at my own clumsiness.

I got out of my chair and went down on my hands and knees, as though to start picking up the pieces of the mug along with the pens and pencils scattered all over the carpet. My desk was wooden and old-fashioned, and it reached the floor on three sides. Whoever was outside my window wouldn't be able to see what I was doing.

When I was reasonably hopeful that I couldn't be seen from outside, I opened up my top desk drawer from a crouching position on the floor. I found the Beretta and placed it against my back, tucked into the waistband of my jeans. My heart was beating so hard, and I was breathing so fast, that I was almost worried that I was going to set off the gun.

I picked up pens and pencils from the floor along with pieces of the mug and deposited them on my desk, making a big show of shaking my head and staring regretfully at the pieces of broken china. Then I sat back down and pretended to gather up the papers I had been working on. My hands were so damp that when I picked up a pen, I had to grip it hard to keep it from sliding out onto the floor.

I didn't know what to do. I knew that raccoons were plentiful in the Grove, and that packs of them regularly terrorized the residential neighborhoods. The sounds I heard could have been a bunch of furry bandits looking for food. But there was no way I was going out the back door to see who or what was there.

Probably it was nothing. *Don't count on it,* a voice said inside my head. *Don't be foolish.*

Drops of sweat were falling off my forehead onto the papers that I was pretending to examine. Patience had never been my strong suit, and now it was almost unbearable for me to play this game with whoever might be out there. For all I knew, they had gone away as soon as they had fallen or bumped into the cottage.

I couldn't just sit there and wait for something to happen to me. I needed to get up without alerting the intruder that I knew he was out there. I stood up and yawned, as though bored and tired. In fact I felt so hot and panicked that I might have set off the smoke alarm. I stretched and picked up the empty glass of wine from the corner of my desk. Then I stretched a little more—this wasn't faking, I wanted my blood flowing for whatever was about to happen.

Each second felt as though it lasted ten. It took all my willpower not to look at the window, and not to drop to one knee and start shooting at my reflection in the glass.

I was halfway out my office door when I heard a blood-curdling screeching from the parrots outside. I almost dropped my glass. I knew what that sound meant—the big birds made it whenever they saw cats or raccoons or other intruders in the yard.

The parrots were warning me that there was danger outside.

I stopped where I was. I saw something out of the corner of my eye. I heard the sound of my own gasp break the silence in the room.

I instinctively dove for the floor as I saw the distinctive flash of a gun firing from the direction of the avocado tree. The window shattered, filling my office with noise and glass. I lay on the floor panting, praying, shaking, counting the two gunshots again and again that I had heard coming from outside. I lay there flat, knowing that whoever was out there couldn't see me unless he came right up to the open window. At least I had that in my favor.

I knew every inch of the backyard. I knew the spot from which the shooter had fired. And I knew it was only a matter of time before he came to finish the job.

Still on the floor, trying to catch my breath, I reached around my back and grabbed for the Beretta. I settled down flat on my back, the gun resting on my heaving stomach. I felt as though the rest of my life might be measured out in the next minute to come.

I closed my eyes and said a prayer to the Virgen de la Caridad del Cobre, the patron saint of Cuba, while touching the three medals pinned to my brassiere.

Now I was as ready as I ever would be. I groped for the wineglass lying on the floor about a foot away. Then I took a deep breath, jumped up, hurled it through the window in the direction of the avocado tree, and lay back down again as quickly as possible, but not before I saw the glass smash against the tree. Whoever was out there opened fire again—now I knew their exact position, right at the base of the tree.

In one motion I raised myself up on my elbows, pointed the Beretta right at the tree, squeezed off six shots, and hurled myself back down hard on the floor again. The noise made me feel as though my eardrums had shattered and, when it was over, I lay in a mist of fear, sweat, panic, and gun smoke.

I heard a moan outside, then the sound of someone falling to the ground. Then silence. One of the parrots squawked, then seemed to decide that it would be better to stay quiet and out of the way for the moment.

Still on my back, panting heavily, I looked around my office. There were two bullet holes that I could see in the wall above where I lay. Glass was everywhere.

I knew that I needed to call the police. It was very possible that I had just killed someone. And I didn't know if my attacker had come alone, or if there was someone else out there waiting for me.

I had to check it out.

There was a hole in the bay window big enough for me to step through, so there was no point walking around to the back door to gain entrance to the yard. Careful not to disturb the crime scene any more than I had to, I stepped through the window. I still held the gun tight in my right hand.

My attacker was lying facedown on the ground, his body contorted into a twisted fetal position. He wasn't breathing. I couldn't identify him without touching him, and there was very little light under the tree. The moon had gone behind clouds, and I couldn't see his face, I couldn't even see if he still held his gun or if it had fallen away somewhere. One thing I could tell was that there wasn't going to be a need for an ambulance.

Flipping over the body seemed like too much work, and I didn't want to disturb the scene. All of a sudden the weight of everything that had happened in the last ten minutes hit me, and I doubled over for a moment struggling to breathe. Underneath the bandage on my head, I felt a steady throb.

"Keep it together," I whispered to myself.

I retraced my steps back inside, returning through the shattered window. My movements were calm and deliberate, and I had to fight off the sensation that all of this was some kind of daydream.

When I got to my desk I picked up the phone and punched in a familiar number.

"Detective Anderson?" I said, and my voice broke. "It's Lupe. I regret to . . . I hate to say this, but there's another body."

Detective Anderson's first reaction was to unleash a series of expletives under his breath. But he composed himself quickly.

"What've we got, Lupe?" he asked wearily.

"You won't have to look for a shooter this time," I said.

"Why?" Detective Anderson asked. "Lupe, you sound strange."

"It was me," I said. "I'm the shooter this time."

"Where are you?" he said.

"At my office."

"I'll be right there."

Click.

It seemed like only a few seconds later that I heard the familiar wail of police sirens. They got louder and louder, filling the night. I laid the Beretta down on the corner of my desk and waited for the officers to arrive. I knew I wouldn't be needing the gun any more that night.

32

I UNLOCKED THE COTTAGE'S FRONT DOOR. TURNED on all the lights, and switched off the alarm in anticipation of the police's arrival. These small tasks seemed to drain what little energy I had remaining; slowly I walked back to my office, where I stood in the middle of the room and waited.

About a minute later I heard noises outside in the reception area, then a familiar voice calling my name. When Detective Anderson came into the room I moved toward him, then lost my footing on the broken glass everywhere underfoot. I fell hard against him, almost losing my balance.

The strain of the past two days caught up with me all at once, and I began sobbing and trying to explain to Detective Anderson what had happened. I shook my head hard, trying to keep control of my emotions. I know I must have looked terrible, soaked in sweat, an old bandage on my forehead, and bits of broken glass on my clothes and hair.

Throughout all this, Detective Anderson remained completely silent, holding me in a light hug and allowing me time to gather my strength. I saw him looking over the shattered window and the broken glass, then at the bullet holes in the wall. I tried to speak again, but once more my words dissolved into tears. Detective Anderson patted my back and told me to take it easy.

I could tell what he was thinking: that this was a side of me he hadn't guessed existed. I didn't like to show vulnerability, but at least I knew I could trust Detective Anderson. He led me by the hand over toward the sofa; then, when I had sat down, he went to the door.

"Give me five minutes alone with her," he said to the police officers in the next room. "Then we'll get started."

What Detective Anderson was doing was completely against police procedure, and I could have kissed him for it.

"I don't want to rush you, but I have to get started with the investigation." Detective Anderson gently sat down next to me and took a small notebook out of the jacket pocket of his khaki suit. "What happened here?"

"The body's in the backyard, outside the window," I said.

"I could have guessed that," Detective Anderson observed.

"I was sitting at my desk working on a report," I told him. "I heard a noise, and I got up. Someone started shooting at me—the first shot shattered the window, then there were a couple more. I fired back. And I got lucky. I hit him."

"Okay." Detective Anderson looked out; from where we were sitting, we couldn't see the body. "Who's out there, Lupe?"

I shrugged. "I'm not sure. It was too dark for me to see."

"You don't know," Detective Anderson said, a note of his dry skepticism entering his voice. "I guess we're going to find out together."

Detective Anderson then went through an abridged version of questioning me about where I was when I fired, how many shots I had fired, from where I had gotten the gun. He made a small diagram of the room in his notebook and put a small letter "L" where I had been. It was nice to know we were on a first-name basis.

Then he stood up and opened my office door. He went out to the reception area, and I could hear him instructing the crime-scene techs where they could find the body. He relayed the few facts that I had told him, then informed them they were free to begin their work.

"Can I go out there when they turn him over?" I asked Detective Anderson. "Maybe I can identify him."

"Wait here," he ordered me. "I'll be right back."

I sat on my desk and rubbed the side of my head. It was long past time to change my bandage. I could have used a general scrub, not to mention a good meal and about twelve hours of sleep. I squinted as the police suddenly flooded the cottage's backyard with light, making the place as bright as high noon. I saw about four men moving around slowly, collecting evidence, and every so often a flashbulb would go off. I watched all this activity in a daze, as though none of it pertained to me.

After about ten minutes, Detective Anderson came back to my office. I hadn't moved.

"The van from the M.E.'s office just got here," Detective Anderson said. "We ID'd him, but you can come out and take a look at the body before they transport it. If you still want to, that is. You look tired. You've already been through a lot."

"I need to see him," I told the detective, a little touched by his concern. I didn't give him a chance to tell me who my assailant was. I wanted to see for myself. I stood up and headed for the door—I didn't want to make a habit out of climbing in and out of my broken window.

I stood next to Detective Anderson as he spoke to the men from the medical examiner's office. The body was in a plastic bag on a stretcher, arranged so that I couldn't see his face.

"Come on," Detective Anderson said, leading me closer. "You still want a look?"

I nodded. Detective Anderson opened up the body bag. I found myself looking into the handsome face of Tomás Cardenas.

Dios mío. "I know him," I declared in as steady a voice as I could manage. "His name is Tomás Cardenas. He's an attorney. Personal injury."

I had shot and killed Tomás Cardenas, with his sexy phone voice and dark wavy hair. More shocking still, he had tried to kill me first.

"Yeah, we know who it is. He had his wallet in his pocket." Detective Anderson said. He turned to the medical examiner's staff. "Thanks, guys. It's okay to take him away now. I'll be in touch."

I watched Tomás being loaded up into the medical examiner's van. They slammed shut the back door and started the engine. Ingrained in my memory was the sight of Tomás's face on the stretcher—his features had been frozen in a painful wince, as though he had come across a piece of vexing information.

"Come on, Lupe. Let's go back inside." Detective Anderson took me by the arm and steered me back toward the cottage door. I felt cold, and wrapped my arms tight around myself as we walked inside.

The crime techs were packing up their equipment after going through my office and the yard. I knew that, pretty soon, it would be impossible to tell that they had ever been there.

Instead of walking me back to my office, Detective Anderson led me to the reception area, where he sat me down in one of the clients' chairs. I was glad to be given some kind of direction.

"Do you have anything to drink here?" he asked, motioning toward the kitchen.

"Of course." I paused, realizing he was on duty. "I can make coffee, if you like." Then I remembered who I was dealing with, and added, "I'm afraid we only have Cuban."

Detective Anderson had an amused look on his face. "Lupe, I mean something alcoholic." Then he actually smiled. "Look, I think we both could use it."

I couldn't hide my shock. I could never have conceived of Detective Anderson actually eating or drinking anything. Next he would be asking to use the bathroom, or loosening his tie.

"Great idea." Before he could change his order to water or motor oil, I got up and headed for the kitchen. "We have pretty much everything."

"A glass of wine would be terrific," Detective Anderson said. "If it's not too much trouble."

"Red or white?" This was a question I never thought I would be asking Detective Anderson. In spite of all the nastiness of the past two days, I had a sense of revelation.

"Red, if you don't mind." Ah, and the man had taste!

I went into the kitchen and opened up the pantry. I looked through several stacks of wooden boxes on the floor in which we stored our red wines, then chose a Châteauneuf-du-Pape that I thought was suitable for the occasion—whatever this occasion might be. That was one of the best wines Leo and I had at the moment. If I was going down in flames, I wanted to go in style.

I poured two glasses and gave one to Detective Anderson. "*Salud,*" I said, and we tipped our glasses at each other. We sat down in the reception area and sipped our wine in silence. The whole thing was completely surreal, but I felt strangely comfortable and at peace.

"Delicious. *Gracias.*" Detective Anderson lifted his glass to the light to admire the wine's color. After he took another sip, he sighed and his expression turned surprisingly grim. "I really need to talk seriously to you now, Lupe."

I thought all of a sudden that he was about to arrest me. But how, when he hadn't yet read me my Miranda rights? I told myself to calm down and stop being paranoid. Arresting officers didn't usually share a glass of great French wine with their perps. Still, Detective Anderson hadn't indicated whether he believed my version of events—and the thought of being charged with Tomás's murder after he tried to kill me was too horrible to contemplate.

"Of course," I said. I finished off my glass quickly, vaguely frightened that this might be the last wine I enjoyed for a while.

Detective Anderson saw that I was done with my wine; with a little shrug, he finished his off and poured us fresh glasses. He handed me mine, then sat back with a troubled look on his face.

"It's been quite a week, hasn't it?" he said. He cocked his head slightly and looked at me. "In the past seven days I've received notification of four separate murders in Miami that have all been somehow connected to you."

"Four. Really?" I said, acting as though I was somehow surprised by this information.

"Alexander Suarez. Mauricio de Villegas. María Esperanza Ramírez. And now Tomás Cardenas." Detective

Anderson's eyes widened a little, as though he was freshly impressed by this roll call of death. "So now we're going to talk. What's going on, Lupe?"

I considered my options. I could try to weasel out of giving him a truthful answer by claiming privilege. Or I could make him a proposal. I opted for the latter—but I would have to walk a fine line by explaining myself without betraying client confidentiality.

"You know that Ramón Suarez is my client in the case involving the stabbing of Alexander Suarez," I said, picking my words carefully. "Well, it didn't start that way. Tío Ramón hired me earlier to help him on a different matter. Later on it became apparent that this matter was intertwined with Alexander's murder."

"Ramón Suarez is your uncle?" Detective Anderson asked, seeming confused.

"No," I told him. "He's one of my father's oldest friends from Cuba. I call him Tío as a sign of affection and respect."

Detective Anderson leaned forward in his chair and sipped his wine. "And can you tell me about the matter your tío Ramón hired you for in the first place?"

"It had to do with the buying and selling of sugar mills in Cuba," I replied.

"What?" Detective Anderson asked. I could tell this wasn't the kind of answer he was looking for. "You're telling me all these people died because of some Cuban sugar mills?"

"I think so, Detective."

"I don't get it." Detective Anderson shook his head, staring into his glass of wine as though he might find the answers there.

All right, I had to tell him more. Especially if I expected him to go along with the plan I was about to propose.

"The Suarez family owned five sugar mills in pre-Castro Cuba—three in Oriente province, and two in Camagüey, and someone has made an offer to buy them," I explained. "The ones in Oriente are still in operation. They're not producing sugar at prerevolutionary levels, but they're still working. The two in Camagüey are idle—but those are the ones the Suarez family has received an offer on."

"But why—"

"I've wondered that myself," I said, anticipating his question. "And I don't know why someone would be interested in buying mills that aren't in operation."

Detective Anderson nodded, all his attention focused on me.

"Ramón and his late brother, Julian, were the heirs of the Suarez family, so they had a claim to ownership over the mills," I said. "Julian and his wife have both died, so his share of that ownership was passed on to their only child—Alexander."

"Go on," Detective Anderson said.

"A few weeks ago Alexander informed Tío Ramón that a Spanish lawyer named Mauricio de Villegas had contacted him about buying the two mills in Camagüey. He was prepared to offer ten cents on the dollar as purchase price in exchange for clear title over the properties."

"Ten cents . . . is this a common thing?" Detective Anderson asked me. "This is the first time I've heard of anyone offering to pay Miami exiles for their confiscated property in Cuba."

"It's very unusual," I said. "But then I figured—if the Suarez family had received such an offer, then maybe others had as well."

"Okay, that makes sense," Detective Anderson said. "So what did you do?"

"That's where Tomás Cardenas comes into the picture," I said. "He was the lawyer for several sugar-mill owners, and they retained him to deal with the offers. Several of them have been approached by Mauricio de Villegas's office as well."

Detective Anderson was frowning, his blue eyes narrowed. He was a very smart man, and I could see his mind racing.

"But that sounds like Tomás Cardenas was helping you out on your case," he said. "Why would he come after you and try to kill you?"

"There's only one reason. I must be close to finding out something that he didn't want me to know," I said.

"Do you think he was also the one who attacked you here yesterday?" Detective Anderson asked.

My hand went up involuntarily to the side of my head. "That I don't know."

Maybe I wasn't being entirely candid. I didn't really think that it had been Tomás who attacked me the day before because in my experience lawyers don't like to get their hands dirty. Shooting was the MO for a successful attorney. I hoped, though, that I was wrong. Because if I was right, there was someone else still out there who had it in for me.

Detective Anderson and I fell quiet for a moment. I kept thinking about the vibrant, sexy Tomás Cardenas that I had met for drinks at the Place St. Michel. It was almost impossible for me to imagine him out in the backyard, lying in wait, looking at me through the open window and waiting for his moment to attack.

Tomás was the second person I had shot and killed. I thought about the first time over and over after it happened, wondering and searching my memory to find out if it had been necessary for me to kill. I hadn't had a choice then, or with Tomás, but that didn't make it any easier. I would see Tomás Cardenas in my dreams for a long time, as I had seen Mariano Arango.

"That covers three of the dead," Detective Anderson said, finishing off his second glass of wine. "What about the hooker? How does she fit into your case?"

"Her street name was China," I said. "She was at the Ecstasy when Alexander Suarez was killed. I'm still trying to figure out if she had a role in all of this."

Detective Anderson nodded, then looked into his empty glass and chuckled softly.

"You know, Lupe, I have so many questions to ask you that I don't even know where to begin."

That was the opening I'd been looking for.

"I have a lot of questions, too," I said. "But I need to look into something before I can start to find answers."

I batted my eyelashes and smiled at Detective Anderson. A look of trepidation spread over his face.

"And I suppose that I can help you look into this 'something,' right?" he said. Without even waiting for a reply, he said, "What is it?"

And so I told him.

33

THE OFFICES OF VALDEZ. JOHNSON. AND CARDENAS
were in a two-story building just off Le Jeune Road in
Coral Gables. I hadn't been there since I worked a
personal-injury case for Sergio Valdez a few years back,
but I remembered that the firm owned the building.

It was after midnight by the time Detective Anderson
and I arrived there. The streets of Coral Gables were
deserted, so we had no problem finding a parking space
right in front of the building.

Detective Anderson and I had spent a lot of time that
night at Solano Investigations discussing the legalities of
entering the law firm's offices. Detective Anderson was
very much a by-the-book type of cop, and the only reason
he had agreed to my plan—reluctantly, and with plenty of
protest—was because I had convinced him that Tomás held
the answers to the other three murders. Detective Anderson had also agreed with me that Tomás probably hadn't
been acting alone.

"Lupe, look. The Fourth Amendment requires a jus-
tifiable reason to search the premises," Detective Anderson had said in my reception area. "Certain requirements
have to be satisfied, such as whether or not the individual
has a reasonable expectation of privacy, and whether the

police have a valid warrant. This situation doesn't satisfy either of those requirements."

"There's got to be a loophole," I said.

If there was one thing I had learned in eight years of being a private investigator, it was that there was always a loophole or an exception. Anyway, I wasn't going to give up that night because of legal technicalities. I'd been assaulted and shot at. I hadn't had any contact with my boyfriend in about a week—if Alvaro was even still calling himself my boyfriend after I had ignored him for so long. Probably he'd broken things off but hadn't been able to reach me to tell me it was over. And then there was the physical interlude with Tommy—I wasn't exactly overcome with guilt over that one, but I still had to deal with it on some level. I wanted this case over, I wanted people to stop hitting me and trying to shoot me. I wanted my life back.

As I watched Detective Anderson wrestling with the Fourth Amendment, I couldn't help but shudder at what he would think of my stealing the surveillance tape from AAA Best Preowned Cars. I had done more than violate the Constitution—I had violated a commandment, the one about not stealing.

"Maybe we can do this," Detective Anderson finally said, speaking slowly. "What you said about a loophole got me thinking. There are certain exceptions to not being able to enter premises without satisfying the general requirement that a warrant be obtained prior to the search."

I smiled at him, starting to feel a little rush. I knew that if anyone could find a way to do this, it was Detective Anderson.

"What is it?" I asked. I had to fight off the impulse to grab him and shake the information out of him. He was so slow, methodical, and straitlaced that I felt like screaming.

"Well, the exception is if someone's life is in danger, or if evidence might be destroyed or made to disappear before a warrant can be obtained," Detective Anderson said. "We can argue that both of these conditions apply in this case, right?"

I couldn't agree quickly enough. "Yes, my life could be in danger," I said. "Tomás tried to kill me tonight, but he might very well be involved with other people who want to see the job finished."

"That might be enough," Detective Anderson mused.

"It's not like you can appear before a magistrate at midnight," I added. "You want to, but it's not possible. Besides, if you wait, evidence could be destroyed or disappear. Tomás's accomplices are going to find out that he got killed tonight. They might go to the office to get rid of any evidence that links them to the crimes"

"That's it," Detective Anderson said. He stood up and straightened his tie. "We're going."

"I'm ready," I said. I would deal with my appearance later. For now, I could almost reach out and touch the answers I knew lay in the files at Tomás Cardenas's office.

"What about that bay window?" Detective Anderson asked, motioning toward my office door. "It's completely open. Anyone could get in."

"I'll deal with it in the morning," I replied. "This is more important."

I grabbed a piece of paper from Leonardo's desk and wrote him a note explaining that the glass in my office had been broken and asking him to call someone in to fix it. I would tell him the rest of the story in the morning.

We left the office in Detective Anderson's plain brown

official car. As I sat on the hard, no-frills seat, I realized
that this was the first time I'd ridden in a car with him. I
couldn't resist a look around as Detective Anderson drove
the short distance to the law offices. In Miami, most people spend such a great percentage of their lives in their
cars that they personalize them in some way—whether it be
with baby booties, photos, CDs, or assorted junk. Detective Anderson had done nothing to personalize his car. It
was like a rental—completely clean and impersonal, ready
for the next customer.

When we reached the building we got out and walked
together past a streetlight. We spotted a security guard who
looked as though he was still in his teens, dressed in a
dark green uniform several sizes too big and sleeping in
an uncomfortable-looking chair in the lobby. Detective
Anderson rapped hard on one of the double-glass front
doors, trying to rouse him. It was only on the fourth try
that the kid woke up, looking around with an annoyed
look on his face.

Detective Anderson flashed his badge, which instantly
turned the kid's expression of irritation to one of fear—
more, I thought, than the situation warranted. From his
reaction I figured that he wasn't the regular guard on
duty, that he was pinch-hitting for someone. Either that
or he was an undocumented alien in terror of being
arrested and deported. It was common knowledge in
Miami that the INS had been on the prowl that month
looking for illegals.

His hands were shaking so hard that he had a hard
time unlocking the front door. As he let us into the lobby,
I saw that up close he looked even younger than I'd
thought. I almost felt sorry for him.

Detective Anderson told him that we had business in

Tomás Cardenas's office and that we were going to be there for a while.

"Okay, okay," the kid said. "Whatever you say."

I don't know what the kid was up to, but he was far too shaken up to question this strange visit from a policeman and an unidentified woman. I sensed that we could do pretty much anything we wanted as long as it didn't involve him. I glanced at the name of the security company on the kid's shoulder patch, and made a mental note to myself never to use it for any reason whatsoever.

Tomás's office was on the second floor, facing west—that was a break for us, because that meant turning on his lights wouldn't make us visible from the street. Given his profession, it was also likely that Tomás worked late hours, and that no one who knew him would think twice about seeing his office lights on.

Detective Anderson flicked the switch in the small, sparsely furnished reception room. A quick look around yielded nothing of interest—just a couple of chairs next to a coffee table, and a secretary's desk. We moved on to a door behind the desk, where Tomás's name was engraved on a brass panel and recessed into the wall.

When we went in, my first thought was that Tomás had saved a lot of money by keeping the reception area spartan, then spent it all on his own office. It was practically a showpiece. I looked over at Detective Anderson and saw that his jaw had dropped open a couple of inches. No one worked out of rooms like this on a cop's salary.

Tomás had re-created the interior of a sailing ship as the theme for his office. It could have passed for the captain's quarters of one of the ships that Columbus sailed to the New World. The desk was made of such thick mahogany that a forest in Honduras must have been cut

down to make it, along with the oversized credenza under
the window. There were paintings of clipper ships everywhere—originals, not prints—and the windows themselves
were round and framed in wood to resemble portholes. A
big wooden bookshelf was filled with navigation charts and
antique sailing paraphernalia. Cubans were island people
who revere the water, but this was ridiculous.

"Come on, let's get to work," Detective Anderson
said, shaking us both from our reverie. "We shouldn't stay
here a minute longer than we have to."

In less than half an hour we had found what we came
for, neatly stacked among the dozen or so folders on the
credenza. I held up the file for Detective Anderson to see.

" 'Cuba: sugar mills/purchase offers,' " he read aloud.
"Looks like what we're after."

I opened it up and started reading. And smiling. It was
always gratifying to know that one of my hunches had been
correct.

34

I WAS BACK IN THE OFFICE FIRST THING THE NEXT morning, after a couple of hours' sleep. I felt awake and alert, maybe because the Suarez case was coming together in my mind, or perhaps because I was relieved to have survived the events of the night before.

Leonardo usually showed up at around nine—if the planets were aligned correctly—which gave me about an hour to clean up the place as well as I could. I went into my office to survey the wreckage, braced for the worst.

Well, it actually wasn't that bad. No one had broken into the cottage through the open bay window. Sipping my first *café con leche* of the day, I opened up the Yellow Pages and called a twenty-four-hour emergency glass repair service. I told them I was willing to pay their usual fee for replacing a window on one hour's notice.

I must have been speaking their language—the front doorbell rang about ten minutes after I put down the phone. Two guys in jeans and uniform shirts came in, measured the window frame, then went out to their truck. They returned with a piece of glass that fit perfectly; they slid it into place, puttied it, and cleaned up their mess within ten minutes. Then they handed me the bill, and my jaw dropped. I was in the wrong business. Glass replacement was definitely where the smart people were working.

"Lady, you want some help cleaning this up?" one of the guys asked me, motioning toward all the broken glass on the floor. "No extra charge."

"Sure, thanks," I said.

They brought out a huge contraption from their truck that vacuumed up all the glass shards in a flash. Suddenly all physical evidence of what had happened the night before had vanished—save for the bullet marks on the wall. I knew there was a jar of spackle someplace in our storage area, but for the time being I hung up a framed photo of central Havana over the worst of the holes.

I took out my Chanel bag to get my checkbook. As I wrote the check I glanced at the patched-up hole in the bag's fine leather. It made me think of the time I fired the Beretta through the bag, shooting a man. I wondered how often I would think of shooting Tomás Cardenas, and how long it would haunt me.

I handed over the check and the guys left. I lingered in my office, looking at the open Suarez case file on my desk. Just twelve hours before I had been sitting there, sipping a glass of wine, with no idea that someone was outside watching me, a loaded gun in his hand.

Leonardo was due to arrive in a few more minutes, and I wasn't sure what spin I could put on last night's events. He would freak out if I told him the story straight out, and I didn't want that to happen. Leo was fragile, and he was also protective of me. It wasn't always the best combination when things went wrong.

I took a couple of sips from my rapidly cooling *café con leche* and sat down at my desk. I read and reread the Suarez file, waiting for answers to spring out at me. I must have been sending out strong signals because a moment later there was a knock at the front door. I glanced outside and saw a FedEx truck.

"Lupe Solano?" asked a young woman in uniform and hat, clipboard in her hand.

"That's me," I said, signing for an overnight envelope. I looked at the address of the sender and saw it was from New York. Suddenly I realized that I was in luck. "Aha!"

"Looks like good news," said the woman.

"The best," I replied. "Thanks."

I had almost forgotten about the background checks I'd ordered from the investigative firm in New York—first on Alexander Suarez, then on Carlos Suarez. They had taken longer getting back to me than I'd expected, and part of me had almost taken for granted that they weren't going to arrive in time to be of use to me. And now they had arrived just when I needed a break. I whispered a prayer to the Virgin. Surely this wasn't just a coincidence.

I took the envelope to my desk and ripped it open. Inside were two smaller manila envelopes. I opened the first one, marked with Alexander's name. It contained four typed pages.

Alexander Suarez had indeed been an artist, that much was true, and his address and vital stats were the same as Tía Alina had given me. As I paged through the file, a very interesting piece of information seemed to leap out.

The property search revealed that Alexander Suarez owned a house on Fire Island, which he had bought in 1995 when he was twenty-five.

That gave me pause. Fire Island was located just south of Long Island. It was known primarily as an upscale vacation spot that catered primarily to a gay clientele. Alexander was thirty when he died and was unmarried. I didn't want to jump to conclusions, but this was staring me in the face.

I knew the macho male Cuban mentality. It seemed

likely to me that Alexander had stayed away from Miami and his family because he was gay. His parents might have effectively paid him off to stay away—they might have thought it was a disgrace to have a gay son. They were old-fashioned and conservative, and they wouldn't have understood—much less approved of—their son's way of living.

Another possibility was that Alexander's parents were oblivious to their son's sexual orientation. Every time he came to Miami they might have pressured him to marry a "nice Cuban girl." He was an only child, after all, and if he didn't marry and have children their branch of the family tree would end with him. There might have been many layers of denial, deception, and pretense.

I didn't want to fall into stereotypical thinking, but I had to be realistic about the facts as they were presented to me. I knew what conservative upper-class Cuban exiles thought about alternative lifestyles—in short, they were about as open-minded and progressive as the Spanish Inquisition. I figured I had just nailed down the heart of Alexander's alienation from the rest of the Suarez family. And I wasn't surprised that Tío Ramón and his family had said nothing to me.

There was a second envelope on my desk, this one pertaining to another male in the Suarez family. It was marked "Carlos Suarez," and I opened it up even more eagerly than I had the first one.

I tried to search my memory for recollections and impressions about Carlos. My sisters and I used to play with him when we were children. But as time passed, we all developed divergent personalities and interests, so our contact had dwindled to sporadic family get-togethers. Even though I had spoken to him on the telephone, it had been years since I had seen Carlos—now that I thought about it, I hadn't seen him since he moved to New York after graduating from the University of Miami.

He was the youngest of the three Suarez children, and the only boy. I knew he had grown up spoiled and pampered, the little prince of his traditional Cuban household. I took out a couple of sheets from the envelope—because I had ordered the check on Carlos as an afterthought, his report wasn't as detailed as Alexander's.

I was looking for anything that might have linked Alexander to Carlos. I still found it hard to believe the family's contention that the two cousins had little to do with each other. They had both been living in New York for about eight years, and until the uproar after Julian's death the two families had seemed harmonious. If Alexander was gay, that might have accounted for an estrangement between the two cousins—their lives might have been very different. But blood held Cuban families together. They might not have approved of Alexander's life, or they might have not wanted to know about it, but there would still have been a bond.

As I glanced through the report, I made a note to myself to remember not to bill Tío Ramón for the background check on his son. This one was definitely coming out of my own pocket.

Carlos Ramón Suarez lived in downtown Manhattan, on Bleeker Street, in an apartment he had been renting for the last five years. He worked in the private-finance division of a major bank—First Intercontinental—in a position he'd held for the last three years. Prior to that he had been employed by a smaller bank, as an officer in their commercial lending department. There wasn't much here for me to work with.

I was just beginning to turn the page when I heard the outer office door open.

"Lupe!" Leonardo called out, sounding chipper. "*¡Buenos días!*"

A couple of seconds later Leo appeared in my office doorway. That morning he had opted for a cowboy look, with brown suede pants and a body-fitting black cotton shirt with fringed sleeves. His accessories included a black leather belt with silver studs and a big buckle, and a brown leather band around his neck that looked tight enough to choke him. I bit my tongue and gave him a smile.

"*Buenos días* to you, too," I said to him. "There's something I have to talk to you about. It's a serious matter."

Something in my tone frightened my cousin; he perched himself delicately on the corner of my sofa, his hands pressed together.

"What is it?" he asked in a high voice, the band around his neck pulsing. "Is something wrong?"

"I was here alone last night working," I began. "And . . . well, there was someone outside under the avocado tree. He started firing shots at me."

I told Leo what had happened, sparing him the more graphic details. Leo went pale and covered his face with his hands.

"Oh, my God!" he said. "This is horrible. Why are you here? You need to be at home—"

"I need to work the case," I interrupted. "Look, it wasn't much fun. But it's over now. I'm sorry to worry you, but I wanted you to know."

"Oh, but you need to—"

"I need to wrap up the case, Leo," I insisted. I was touched by his concern, but this was no time to let the events of the past week get to me. The wound on my head had healed to an acceptable level, and I felt I had just enough in me to finish the job Tío Ramón had hired me for.

"Okay, there's no point talking to you when you're like this." Leo sighed and got up from the couch. "Just let me know if there's anything I can do. And when this case is over, I'm going to check you into a day spa for some serious relaxation."

"We'll do that, I promise," I said. "You can come with me."

This seemed to please Leo; he left the room with a renewed spring in his step, no doubt fantasizing about some exotic mud wrap or colonic irrigation.

I picked up the phone and punched a button on the speed dial the moment I was alone again. Tommy's secretary answered and she put me through right away.

"Lupe," Tommy purred, sounding happy. I knew his good feeling wasn't going to last, not after he heard what I had to tell him.

"I need to speak with you as soon as possible," I said. I felt like a real bearer of gloom and doom, but there wasn't any way around it. "In person."

Tommy paused. "All right," he said, sounding wary. "I have a meeting in Coconut Grove in about a half hour. I can stop by your office right after that."

"That would be fine," I said.

About ten seconds after I hung up the phone rang again. It was Detective Anderson.

"I don't have anything new for you," he said. "I was just calling to see if you're all right."

"I'm doing fine," I said. "Well, in fact."

I hoped I was right.

35

"SO. LUPE. WHAT'S SO IMPORTANT THAT YOU HAD to see me in person?" Tommy asked as he entered my office, his expression a mix of both amusement and trepidation. "Not that I object, of course. I haven't been to Solano Investigations in a while."

Tommy was impeccably dressed as usual, this morning sporting a three-piece charcoal-gray suit with a light pink shirt. He looked every bit the English gentleman, rather than the bane of Dade County's prosecutorial community. I dreaded ruining his day, but it was time to bring him up to date on what had happened. He knew already how the Suarez case was progressing, but the events of last night were a different matter entirely.

"Good morning. Now sit." I greeted Tommy with a kiss on the cheek and led him over to the sofa.

I had a strong sense of déjà vu as I gave Tommy an account of the night before. Unlike my description to Leonardo, this telling omitted no details. I also told Tommy about going to Tomás Cardenas's office afterward with Detective Anderson.

"All right. I can see why you wanted to speak in person. This is serious business." Tommy said. He paused and looked into my eyes. I could never hide a thing from him. In that moment I could see that he knew how much the events of the past days had affected me. His expression softened, and he said, "What now, Lupe?"

It was sometimes hard for us to balance our professional and personal relationships. We both wanted to reach out and embrace each other; he wanted to comfort me and I needed the comfort. But the reality was that I was the private investigator on the case, and he was the criminal defense attorney. We would be derelict in our duties to our client if we allowed ourselves to lose sight of that.

"It's down to loose ends, at least in my mind," I told him. I had always kept my theories to myself on cases, and I would continue to do so until I had hard facts to back them up. Tommy wasn't at all interested in speculation, only in reality. So I never consulted with him on what may or may not have happened. Our arrangement had always been a success in the past, and we saw no reason to change it.

"That's great," Tommy said with a slightly wry expression. "There's not much more I can do on the legal end, not until you've completed your investigation and submitted your findings to me."

"It hasn't been that long," I said, feeling a bit defensive. "It's been just a week since this whole thing started."

"I just think it's more complicated than you're letting on," Tommy commented. "Cardenas wanted you dead. That means—"

The buzzing intercom interrupted Tommy mid-thought. Leonardo's voice announced that Detective Anderson was on the line and wanted to speak with me.

"Tell him I'm in a meeting," I said.

"I already did, Lupe," Leo explained. "He says it's important and that he has to talk to you right away."

I had a very strong feeling that this was not good news. I frowned at Tommy as I walked over to the desk to pick up the receiver.

"Hello, Detective, how are you?" I said by way of greeting.

"I'm afraid I don't have good news." Detective Anderson never had great phone manners, and this morning he dispensed with even the barest of formalities. I wasn't about to complain. The last man I met with great phone manners and a sexy phone voice ended up trying to kill me.

"What's up?" I asked. His tone of voice offered no comfort.

"Aurora Santangelo is after your ass big-time," Detective Anderson said. "Seriously."

"So what else is new?" I attempted bravado, but in reality my heart was sinking. Detective Anderson wouldn't be calling me with this unless it was truly serious.

Aurora Santangelo was my nemesis at the State Attorney's Office. She had been a universally disliked, moderately successful Dade County prosecutor for about the last ten years. She was probably on her way to becoming a chief assistant in her office unless she screwed up somehow. To me, she was like a nasty recurring rash that cropped up again just when I had forgotten about it.

The woman hated me with every bone in her body, ever since I had showed her up in a case about five years ago. She had been overconfident that she would have a slam-dunk and had arrived in court essentially unprepared. As a result, she had lost the case and had been publicly embarrassed.

Instead of accepting her defeat gracefully and moving on, Aurora had tried to exact vengeance on me. She had accused me of witness tampering and forced me to defend myself—successfully, I might add. Her nasty scheme had backfired big-time, and she had been sent in disgrace to the traffic division in Hialeah to atone for her actions. Since then Aurora had blamed me for just about everything that went wrong in her life—a considerable number of things, from what I had heard—and used every opportunity to trash me both in public and in private.

In the years since, she'd accused me of breaking the law in just about every conceivable way. I had heard that she even once considered accusing me of arranging the killing of a baby albino alligator, after she saw a matching purse and pair of shoes that I was wearing. The albino part was a real joke—anyone who knows me knows that I never wear white. I could have also sued her for defamation of character and slander for stories she spread about my sexual practices and proclivities, but in a sense I always enjoyed the tales when they made their way back to me. At least the woman had imagination.

I didn't really consider her a worthy opponent, to be truthful, but she was scheming and slimy enough to be dangerous. Aurora was like a mosquito always buzzing around—annoying, but capable of drawing some blood. Because she wasn't very talented at her job, she didn't get a heavy caseload and had a lot of time on her hands to plot against me. And it looked like she was back in my life.

"Aurora wants charges pressed against you for killing Tomás Cardenas last night," Detective Anderson informed me. "As soon as word got out that you were involved in a shooting, she started nosing around and trying to figure out what had gone down."

"You know I shot that man in self-defense," I said, my voice rising. "He was trying to kill me. Come on, you were the investigating officer. I don't have to explain myself to you."

"No, you don't," Anderson agreed. "But Aurora is talking about convening a grand jury."

"Oh, God." I was breathing hard as I sat down behind my desk. "Listen, hold on for a second."

I put Detective Anderson on hold and told Tommy what I had just learned. Tommy made a face that looked as though he had just bit down hard on a lemon peel.

"Don't worry, Lupe, she's just trying to frighten you," he said. "She hates you, you know that. She's just being a conniving bitch, trying to pile on in a moment of weakness."

I pressed the button to bring Detective Anderson back on the line, but this time I put him on the speaker.

"I'm back," I said. "Now what exactly is she doing?"

"She's going around the State Attorney's Office claiming she heard you and the victim had something romantic going on, that you had some kind of lovers' quarrel," Detective Anderson said. "She's trying to persuade the chief not to quickly accept your explanation of self-defense. She says a more thorough investigation is needed. I can go to bat for you, Lupe, but I don't know how much good it's going to do."

I thought about this. "Why?" I asked. "Is anyone going to believe her, knowing about all the bad blood between us?"

"She says you were seen having a drink with the victim," Detective Anderson said, sounding almost apologetic. "This was supposed to have happened in a bar in Coral Gables a few days ago."

Tommy raised one eyebrow and looked at me. I knew what this meant: the situation wasn't going to just go away.

"And how does Aurora claim to know this?" I asked,

careful not to deny or confirm my meeting with Cardenas. I wondered if the woman was having me followed. That would have been extreme, even for her.

Detective Anderson was quiet for a moment. "Listen, Lupe, I'm going out on a limb just telling you about this," he said. "But we have a good relationship. I don't want you to be blindsided by some trumped-up bullshit."

"I appreciate it," I said sincerely.

"I may be out of line here," Detective Anderson added. "But you might not have as many friends as you think at the SAO. Watch your back. And take care of yourself."

With this, he hung up. I pressed the button to disconnect the phone, shaking my head. I knew I would never win a popularity contest among Miami law-enforcement officials, but I didn't think that anyone at the State Attorney's Office—except for Aurora—had anything against me.

I looked up at Tommy. His hands were folded, his expression neutral.

"I guess working on the criminal defense end of so many cases isn't going to endear me to too many prosecutors," I said.

"Welcome to my world," Tommy replied.

"But I've always been fair and professional," I said.

"Look, Lupe, this can't come as a complete surprise." Tommy sighed. "Your job has been to tear apart prosecutor's cases. They don't like that. They tend to forget that part of the Constitution about being innocent until proven guilty. Prosecutors assume suspects' guilt before going to trial, and sometimes you help shoot them out of the sky and make them look bad. I might add that you do it awfully well. And you get better at it the more you do it."

"Thanks," I said. I accepted the compliment because Tommy rarely doled them out. "And now what do I do about Aurora?"

Tommy didn't skip a beat. "You know what to do."

And so I did.

I MADE A CALL THE MINUTE TOMMY LEFT MY office. As usual, the phone rang about a dozen times before Charlie Miliken finally picked it up.

"Lupe, hello." Charlie's distinctive voice came through the wire, sounding as always as if his vocal cords had been immersed in cigarette smoke and bourbon. "I thought I might be hearing from you soon."

Well, word sure got around fast.

"Can we meet?" I asked him.

"Sure," Charlie replied. "Do you want to come here into the nest of vipers or should we meet someplace else?"

Much as I dreaded going to the Justice Building, I wasn't about to be frightened away by Aurora.

"Your office will be fine, Charlie."

"Okay," Charlie said, and that was it. He hung up.

Charlie Miliken was brave, no doubt about it, and he never believed in playing—or even acknowledging—office politics. That might have explained why he was never made division chief at the State Attorney's Office. Charlie was the best prosecutor at the SAO, with a conviction rate unequaled by anyone else there, but that fact wouldn't be readily apparent to anyone who just took a look at him. He was perpetually disheveled, his suits all out of style and ill-fitting on his tall, gangly frame. He walked around the Justice Building with two-foot-thick burgeoning files, papers falling out and leaving a trail behind him. But his appearance belied the fact that he had a genius intellect and a photographic memory. Criminal defense attorneys cringed when they saw Charlie's name as the prosecutor on a case, and more often than not changed their strategy and started talking to their clients about accepting a plea bargain.

Years ago Charlie and I had enjoyed a pretty torrid relationship—the kind that ended either in marriage or a breakup. We chose the latter, but had remained in close contact ever since. Every so often we slid back into a brief fling, sometimes even fantasizing that things might work out between us, but then we would experience a mutual reality check and part ways before too much damage was done. It had actually been about six months since I had last seen him.

I set off right away for the Justice Building in northwest Miami. As I drove there, I realized that it had been only a week ago that Tommy and I had been to visit Tío Ramón at the county jail across the street. It seemed like years had passed.

Traffic was fairly light, and I got there in about twenty minutes. I parked in the lot in front of the building and crossed the street—all the while looking around to make sure Aurora Santangelo wasn't lurking somewhere. I wasn't frightened of her, but I was in no mood for a public confrontation.

I had left the Beretta in the Mercedes's glove compartment, so there was no trouble for me at the security-check metal detector. I rode the elevator upstairs, not seeing anyone I knew. Charlie's office was at the end of a long corridor. His corner office didn't reflect power or status; rather, his chain-smoking habits had led to exile at a point as far as possible from his colleagues. I knew that strict regulations, public scorn, and smoke detectors could do nothing to make Charlie cut down on his habit.

I smelled the sharp odor of Camels as I approached Charlie's door. He opened his window to smoke, thinking that cut the nicotine fog somewhat. It didn't work.

I knocked and waited for a response from inside. Nothing. I knocked again with the same result.

"Mierda," I cursed under my breath. I should have set up a specific time to meet rather than just stopping by.

I was about to turn away when I heard a voice from inside the door. "Come in, Lupe!"

I opened the door. "I almost left, you know," I said as I stepped inside.

Charlie was sprawled on a wooden chair, tipped back as far as he could go without falling over backward. He was reading a five-inch-thick case file resting on his lap, with his feet propped on a disorganized stack of files on his desk. He had a cigarette in one hand, a diet Coke in the other. He looked up, his blue eyes twinkling behind the glasses perched on the end of his nose.

"I knew it was you, I recognized the sound of your walk," he said with a grin. "I just wanted to see if you were going to give up. As usual, you don't disappoint me."

Charlie's personality hadn't changed one bit. He was still testing me, seeing how I would respond. And his appearance was the same as the last time I'd seen him. His wavy, sandy-colored hair still begged for a trip to the barber. He was tall, about six-five, and was all arms and legs like a gangly teenager. He wore the same type of outfit as

he always had—a blue work shirt, brown rope belt, and
wrinkled khakis. I knew that if I opened the closet door
behind him, I would find the old navy-blue jacket and tie
he wore for court appearances.

There were monumental, teetering stacks of files every
place: on the floor, the desk and credenza, on every available surface. It was a good thing earthquakes didn't hit
Miami. Charlie would have been crushed beneath his own
files.

Charlie got up and cleared a chair for me to sit down.
I said thanks as I maneuvered my way over, feeling grateful
for the tetanus shot I'd been given two days ago as I worked
through the clutter.

Just as I walked past him, Charlie reached out and
pulled me tight in a big hug. The differences in our
heights had always presented a challenge, and now my face
was pressed against three pens he had in his shirt pocket.

"I've really missed you, Lupe," Charlie said in a quiet
voice.

My knees almost gave out when I smelled his familiar
scent—cigarettes, Jack Daniel's, and Canoe aftershave.

"Me, too," I replied, surprising myself a little. We
stood there for a moment, awkwardly prolonging our hug,
but then I miraculously regained my sanity and reminded
myself that this wasn't a social visit.

"Charlie," I said, pulling away from him. "I know
you're the prosecutor on the Ramón Suarez case."

"Ah, Lupe," Charlie said ruefully. "I guess it's business first."

Charlie walked around his desk and took his old place,
dropping the file on his desk and sending a pile of pencils
to the floor.

"Yes, I've been assigned the case," he told me, then he

laughed. "And I know you're working it with your old flame Tommy. Your client is in good hands."

"I didn't come here to discuss the Suarez case specifically." Well, that wasn't completely true. I did intend to discuss the Suarez case, but I wanted to talk about my personal situation first.

"Aurora?" Charlie asked.

"I hear she's coming after me in a serious way."

Charlie made a gesture as if he was swatting a fly. It echoed my own sentiments.

"She needs to get a life," Charlie commented. "Look, Lupe. I don't know much about it. People here aren't exactly dying to keep me up-to-date on the latest, if you know what I mean. At least not the incompetents like Aurora."

Charlie had heard nothing more than vague whispers, so I went into the details—all the while omitting Detective Anderson's name. I left out nothing—it would have been counterproductive, like holding out on a doctor or lawyer. He listened intently. We might have been on different sides of the law—he on the prosecution, me on the defense—but we trusted each other completely. It was the basis of our relationship, whatever that relationship might have been.

When I was finished, Charlie just shook his head.

"Christ, Lupe," he said. "I heard Aurora thought she had something on you, but I didn't know anything about a shooting. Are you all right?"

"As right as I can be."

"And your source for this is pretty good?" Charlie asked.

"Very reliable," I replied.

Charlie reached for the phone and punched in a few

numbers. He swiveled in his chair so his back was turned, my cue not to listen in. I heard only a couple snippets of his whispered conversation, knowing that Charlie wasn't trying to be rude or evasive. He was trying to protect both of us in case some problem came up in the future.

Charlie hung up the phone and turned back to me. "Yup," he said. "Your source was solid. Aurora's working hard to get you indicted for the murder of Tomás Cardenas."

"You know I would never kill someone, Charlie, not unless it was in self-defense."

"Sorry," Charlie said.

I got up and tried to pace the room—no easy task, with all the files and papers stacked every place.

"What can be done to stop her?" I asked.

"Let me think," Charlie said. "Give me a minute."

His last cigarette gone, Charlie lit up another one. We both knew that there was probably little Charlie could do for me. It was well known that he and I had been involved romantically in the past, and he wouldn't be considered a disinterested party. But he was senior enough in the office that there might be some hope.

"Charlie, I could lose my private investigator's license." I instinctively looked at my purse, where I had my blue *Private Investigator's Handbook*. The booklet detailed all the professional standards and ethics that investigators are held to under Florida Statute 493. I had read and reread it so many times that it was falling apart.

"What's the procedure for that?" Charlie asked.

I didn't have to refer to the book to answer the question.

"If a private investigator is charged with the use of deadly force while working a case, the Florida Department of State, Division of Licensing, launches its own independent investigation into the charges. They'd read the police report, talk to witnesses. There's no hard and fast role on revoking a license, but it's a real threat to me."

Charlie got to the point right away. "So if you're charged, you not only have to undergo a police investigation but the Department of State's investigation as well."

"That's right," I said. "And my license could be suspended pending the investigation. That would mean I couldn't work the Suarez case—or any other, for that matter—for whatever period of time it would take to clear up the whole mess."

"Not good," Charlie said quietly.

I felt my eyes watering, and I blinked rapidly. "And I would also have to defend myself against the criminal charges. This whole thing could take over my life."

"So you're fucked if Aurora succeeds in getting you indicted." Charlie, having successfully stated the obvious, opened the bottom drawer of his desk. For the first time in a while, I saw that he looked gravely concerned. "Not just a little fucked. Really fucked."

Charlie pulled out a bottle of Jack Daniel's from his desk, then two plastic cups from a bag. He poured healthy amounts into each, then handed one to me.

"*Gracias,*" I said. It was early in the day, but desperate times called for desperate measures.

I stared at the amber-colored drink, contemplating the dimensions of my predicament. My most immediate and pressing concern was that there still might be someone out there who was ready to kill me. Then came Aurora, who might sandbag my entire life with murder charges that would get my license revoked, if only temporarily. What would happen to Tío Ramón then? Whatever happened, I felt a strong sense that time was working against me.

I took a sip of the bourbon. I would have preferred a *mojito*—a double.

"To the confusion of our enemies," Charlie said with a wincing grin as he raised his glass.

I could certainly drink to that.

37

THE JACK DANIEL'S FROM CHARLIE'S OFFICE WAS still warming a nice place beneath my sternum as I drove back to the Grove. The return drive wasn't as smooth as the trip over, unfortunately, so I had plenty of time to think as traffic inched along. I knew the only way to spare myself the mess of a grand jury indictment—and to keep my license—was to figure out who was behind the crimes associated with Tío Ramón's case. I had a suspect, but a real bankable motive was just beyond my grasp. Hunches were fine, but only cold hard evidence was going to produce results.

When I got back to the cottage I went straight to my desk, where I took out the pages I had copied from the file in Tomás Cardenas's office. I was specifically interested in the letters that several sugar-mill owners-in-exile had received from Mauricio de Villegas. Each letter, like the one that Tío Ramón had received, constituted a written offer to buy their properties at ten cents on the dollar.

I laid the letters out side by side on my desk. Next I took out the pages I'd copied from the library, which listed the owners of the one hundred sixty-one Cuban sugar mills in 1958.

Looking up the name of one sugar mill de Villegas claimed his clients were interested in buying, I cross-checked it against the 1958 list. Then I did the same for each mill for which an owner had received a purchase offer. I took out the chart that indicated the current status of each of these mills, to see if they were operating or were idle. It turned out that half were currently in working order, albeit not operating at prerevolutionary capacity; the other half were idle or had been dismantled, with their machinery cannibalized for other mills.

I had not been a business major in college. But, looking at the facts before me, I could see that de Villegas—on the surface—was representing clients who were making a pretty bad investment.

According to the dates on top of the lawyer's stationery, the six letters to mill owners had all been sent out within a thirty-day period. I reminded myself that the letters in front of me might not have constituted all the offers made to exiled mill owners. Other individuals might have received letters and gone to other attorneys, or could have decided that they would handle the situation on their own.

One thing was for sure: this situation didn't make sense on the surface, so there had to be something more to it. There had to be a common thread that I was missing. I read the letters over and over, positive that they contained a clue that I had yet to discover.

About an hour had passed since I first sat down. I moved the letters to the side of my desk and decided it might be enlightening to return to the background checks on the Suarez cousins.

Carlos's background check was much less extensive than Alexander's. I knew that I could have him fill in the blanks in person—a luxury I no longer had with Alexander—but I was reluctant to do so until I had filled in as many blanks as I could ahead of time.

Carlos worked in the private-banking division of First Intercontinental Bank, a multinational corporation. That gave me an idea. I picked up the telephone directory and paged through it until I found the listing for First Intercontinental's Miami branch. I recognized the address—in one of the smaller but prestigious office buildings on Brickell Avenue.

Before I placed the call I jotted down a few questions I wanted to ask. As soon as I felt I'd prepared a sufficient script, I picked up the phone and punched in the number from the listing. I called from my office's private line, the one that didn't give out information to recipients using a caller-ID box.

A female operator with a strong Spanish accent answered the line in English. "Good afternoon, Intercontinental Bank. May I help you?"

"Yes, thank you," I replied in Spanish, having shuddered hearing her struggle to pronounce the bank's name in English. "I am interested in opening an international account."

I hoped that, by making my request in such a vague manner, I might be connected directly to a bank officer.

"An international account?" the operator asked. Her accent was so thick that she reminded me of Charo on methamphetamines.

"Yes, an account for everywhere in the world," I said, purposefully becoming even more confusing. "A world account. For every place."

That last comment must have been more than she could take. She said, "One moment, please. I will connect you to an officer." And she promptly clicked the line over to Muzak purgatory.

I had listened to that Celine Dion song about the sinking *Titanic* three times back to back—and in three different languages—when I finally got a human to pick up the line.

"This is Manuel O'Flannigan," the man said. "May I help you?"

"I hope so, Mr. O'Flannigan," I replied. "You see, I expect to be doing business all over the world. I want to have an account in a bank that also does business all over the world."

"We are an international bank," O'Flannigan said, sounding a little perplexed. Who could blame him?

"Where are your international branches?" I asked. "Could you please name them?"

Manuel O'Flannigan took a deep breath. It might have been because there were simply too many branches for him to list off the top of his head. And it might also have been because he was trying to be civil to a woman who was wasting his time and would almost certainly turn out to be a complete nutcase. He sounded patient, though; I figured that with a name like Manuel O'Flannigan, he'd had all sorts of life experiences.

He then named six cities in South America, four in Central America, and eight European capitals. Madrid was among them. I spared him from moving on to Asia and Africa; I interjected, "Very good, thank you."

"Is there anything else you would like to know?" he asked. "Ms.?"

"Ms. Enriqueta González," I said. "Thank you for your help. Actually, I do have another question."

"Ms. González, perhaps you would like to make an

appointment and come into our office," O'Flannigan asked, his impatience coming to the surface. "Then I could answer all your questions in a prompt and thorough manner."

"Does your bank subscribe to the KYC theory?" I asked, breaking through his attempt to get rid of me.

Suddenly I sensed a shift in O'Flannigan's attitude. "The KYC?" he asked. I could tell he knew what those initials stood for.

"That's right. Know Your Customer," I replied. "I've been told that a bank such as yours doesn't delve as deeply into a customer's background—provided that customer is referred by someone the bank knows is reputable."

I had heard about banks' screening procedures; none of them wanted to end up inadvertently laundering drug money, whether it be from South American or Asian cartels, or the new players on the scene that had sprung up from the former Soviet Union. But I also knew that a good referral went a long way toward circumventing these screening measures.

"That's what the term refers to," O'Flannigan agreed. "Ms. González, I strongly advise you to come to our bank for a meeting with one of our officers. We can provide you with all the information and assurances you might require to feel your account is in safe hands."

"I will," I said. "I'll call back. And I'll ask for you, Mr. O'Flannigan. You've been very helpful to me."

And he certainly had.

ABOUT TEN SECONDS AFTER I HUNG UP THE PHONE. LEONARDO buzzed on the intercom to tell me that Charlie Miliken was on the line.

"Aurora's going to the grand jury on Thursday," Charlie announced in a somber tone. "You've got three days."

"*Mierda,*" I spat out.

"Thought you might like to know."

"Thanks," I said. "I owe you for this one."

In the past, whenever I heard people talk about their blood running cold, I thought they were full of shit. Well, I owed them all an apology. It was indeed possible to feel one's blood freezing in one's veins—and it was happening to me that very moment.

"I'll keep my eyes and ears open and let you know what else I hear," Charlie said, trying his best to sound reassuring. "I'll snoop around and see if I can get some idea what kind of case she's putting together against you."

"*Gracias.* I really appreciate anything you can do, Charlie."

I hung up, got out of my chair, and walked over to the bay window. The parrots had come back in force after the craziness the night before. They had, in fact, alerted me to the danger in the backyard and in effect saved my life. I didn't know how to show my gratitude—I couldn't exactly open a bottle of champagne to share with them—so I stood watching them, letting them know I was still there. I hoped I gave them some small measure of the comfort they gave me. And I needed all the comfort I could get, what with Aurora about to drag me into court and totally disrupt my life and livelihood.

Feeling the need for some fresh air, I opened the door leading out to the backyard. I seldom went out there—I was more an indoor person, content to interact with nature from behind glass in an air-conditioned room.

The crime techs had been pretty careful going about their business so, thankfully, the yard wasn't too torn up.

The sun was starting to go down, and the yard was cast in a golden glow. It seemed a shame that Leo and I didn't really use this garden space. We might have put up a table and chairs out there under the avocado tree, cleared out a patio for dining al fresco. In time I might even be able to forget the image of Tomás Cardenas out there, watching me, waiting.

I was visualizing a positively bucolic scene when my eye caught on something shiny amid a clump of parrot excrement and leaves scattered ten or so feet from the base of the avocado tree. I quickly knelt down, picked up one of the large avocado leaves, and started scattering the small pile of poop with it. At first I thought I had found a bullet, which was strange. I thought the crime-scene techs located all the bullets I had fired.

"Hello there," I whispered when I had cleared away most of the bird doo.

It wasn't a bullet. It was a small gold key attached to a tiny silver key ring. My heart began to beat faster as I stood up, turning the key over and over in the dwindling daylight.

The key was clean, with no rust or dirt, just some dried bird shit. That meant it hadn't been on the ground for very long. It was only the long low-angle sun of twilight that had afforded me the chance to spot it.

I looked down again at the now-bare spot where I had retrieved the key. It was about ten feet from the place where Tomás Cardenas had fallen after I shot him, and directly below one of the largest tree branches.

It *had* to be his. There were only three people who went into the backyard at all: me, Leonardo, and Osvaldo, who came there once every couple of weeks to cut the grass and take care of landscaping.

It was possible that the key belonged to one of the crime-scene techs who had arrived after the shooting, but they surely would have phoned or returned to locate their lost property. No one had called or showed up. And that was because dead men didn't come back for their keys.

I got down on the ground again and started searching the area under the avocado tree. There were a lot of leaves, and they broke in my hands. Buried as it was in the bird poop, it was no surprise that the techs had passed over the little golden key. Finally, finding nothing more, I stood up and brushed off my jeans.

I went into the office and caught Leo, who was getting ready to leave for the day.

"Look familiar?" I asked him, tossing the key on his desk. I hoped he wouldn't be able to identify the flakes of bird shit still encrusted on the metal.

"No," he said. "Should it?"

I picked up the key. "Not really," I said. "Just checking."

"What are you up to now?" Leo asked, frowning. "You need to go home and get some rest. I don't think I really need to remind you what's happened to you in the last few days."

"I'll rest soon," I told him. "And that's a promise."

"You're still taking me along to the spa?" Leo asked, folding his arms.

"That's another promise," I said.

I went into my office and dumped out a ceramic mug full of pens and pencils. Among them was a small magnifying glass. I put the key down on my computer's mouse pad, turned on the desk lamp, and inspected the key under bright light. Carefully, I brushed off the last of the bird poop with a tissue. I started to make out some letters, so I adjusted the lens for a better look.

I had thought I was looking at letters, but there were numbers as well. I read the name of the Canton Key Company, which had presumably manufactured the key. Below this was the number 135, which looked as though it had been etched on by hand.

I put down the glass and looked at the key sitting there under the light. It was small and narrow, not like an ordinary car or house key. It looked to me as though it would open either a mailbox or a safety deposit box.

I had to make an assumption. And that assumption was the following: the key belonged to Tomás Cardenas, and it opened a safety deposit box. It was after banking hours, so I picked up the phone and asked the 1-800 directory assistance operator for an after-hours extension at the First Intercontinental Bank in Miami. It was a big company, and I assumed they would have round-the-clock customer service. I was correct.

A minute later I was on the phone with the bank. I told the service representative who answered that I was interested in opening an account at the bank's Miami branch—but that, before proceeding any further, I wanted to know whether First Intercontinental offered a couple of specific services.

The rep on the phone must have been either bored or chatty. Because we soon launched into quite a detailed conversation about the bank's services and operations. When he stopped to take a breath, I asked about the availability of safety deposit boxes.

"We have some available locally," my new friend said. "And we guarantee total safety and security."

"Are you sure?" I asked. "I know about all the crime in Miami. I want to be entirely certain that no one can break into the bank and empty out the contents of the boxes."

"Oh no. Not in this bank," the rep insisted, sounding affronted by the very idea. "Anything you put in one of our boxes will be there when you come back for it."

"I don't know," I said. "I want to put away some family jewelry for safekeeping. These are irreplaceable items."

"They won't be stolen," he insisted. "We can promise you that."

I pretended to ponder for a moment. "What kind of boxes do you use, anyway?" I asked. "And what kind of key would I be issued if I rented one? Can you give me brand names?"

"Box and keys?" He paused for a moment, and I held my breath. But then he said, "Hold on a second. I can get that information for you."

I listened to a light jazz Muzak rendition of "Feelings"—someone hadn't changed his phone tapes in a *long* time—until the bank representative came back on the line.

"The boxes are made by Wellington and Company, and the Canton Key Company makes the keys. These are two of the oldest and most respected names in the banking business," the rep said with pride. "So, you see, we guarantee security and the highest level of service."

I had to hand it to him, he was right. And he had also told me a lot about that key sitting there on my mouse pad.

"Well, I'm convinced," I said. "I'll definitely come in to open up an account."

"That's what I was hoping," he gushed.

And I *would,* if I ever needed another safety deposit box. For the moment, though, I had other, more pressing concerns.

And not much time in which to resolve them, if Aurora Santangelo had anything to do with it.

38

I LEFT THE OFFICE EARLY THAT AFTERNOON. TRY-
ing to ignore the feelings of guilt that washed over me as I
drove home. I was feeling much as I had in college, when I
had crammed as much as I could for an exam and any
more effort would be tantamount to overstudying. I was
living and breathing the case, and I was in danger of losing
the perspective I needed to see how all the pieces fit
together. I needed to get away from it, if only for one
night.

Happy to have the whole family home for dinner, Aida
outdid herself. She made a particularly delicious dinner
of *arroz con pollo*—chicken and yellow rice, the unofficial
Cuban national dish—and *tostones*, green plantains. There
were two kinds of flan for dessert, mango and coconut,
and lots of Cuban coffee. Dinner was accompanied by several bottles of Marques de Riscal, a hearty Spanish wine
that was the perfect complement to such a meal.

We laughed and joked throughout the hour, as always a
loving family that enjoyed each other's company. Looking
at Papi, my sisters, and the twins seated around me at the
dining room table, I realized how fortunate I was to have
such a family. And I couldn't help but think of how happy
Mami would have been, seated at the far end of the table

across from Papi. Even though it had been nearly ten years since she'd passed away, her place was empty and no one could replace her.

Papi was across from me at the dinner table; though I could see the curiosity in his eyes, he refrained from asking me anything about Tío Ramón's case. I knew he wouldn't want to bring up such a sensitive and private matter in front of my sisters and, in particular, my young nieces. Once, while Aida was clearing away the plates, I met Papi's eyes and gave him a little nod of confidence. Now all I had to do was live up to the gesture.

After dinner I decided that a steaming hot bath would be the perfect ending to the day, so I kissed each member of the family good night and headed upstairs to my bedroom. I found myself so tired that I yawned uncontrollably as I took off my clothes and ran the bath, filling it with scented oil.

I had just decided it was time to get out of the tub when something came to me: why the old Cuban sugar mills might have been attractive to a foreign investor.

With a huge splash of water I got out of the tub and put on my terry cloth bathrobe. Not even bothering to get properly dressed, I jogged downstairs to the library.

One huge bookcase there was devoted to a single theme: Cuba. On each spacious shelf, books were crammed into every available space and even stacked one atop the other. I looked them over until I found just the one I wanted—a detailed illustrated survey of the island's geography.

I curled up in the red leather club chair that Papi normally occupied. I shifted this way and that, trying to make myself comfortable, but it was a hopeless effort. Papi had spent so much time reading in that chair over the years that it accepted nobody's contours but his own.

It didn't take me long, comfortable or not, to confirm the flash of insight that had come to me in the bathtub. I looked through the maps twice more, confirming what I thought.

"Of course," I said to no one in particular. I went over to the small copier stashed in the corner of the room and ran off a few duplicates of maps for my own use.

Instead of shelving the book and leaving right away, I went back to the chair and flipped through the book to its vivid picture section. I saw the beauty and majesty of my family's homeland, and blinked back tears over the breathtaking views of prerevolutionary Havana. I could only cry at the waste and destruction of an entire country at the hands of a single egomaniacal old man. I couldn't conceive of how he could live with himself, and I wondered whether he was blind to what he had done or whether he took the path of blaming others for his own misdeeds. Castro liked to say, "History will absolve me." It would be more accurate to say that history will condemn him.

I closed the book, put it back in its place, and went upstairs to my room. Now there were others raping Cuba, I realized, and they were the ones I should be worrying about. This was the last thought that went through my mind as I lay back in my bed and closed my eyes.

It had been a hard week, and it was probably going to get even harder. But in spite of everything that had happened, I slept the sleep of the innocent.

I WAS BACK IN THE OFFICE EARLY THE NEXT MORNING. refreshed after a sound, dreamless sleep and time spent with my family. I bustled around the office, preparing what was sure to be the first of many *café con leches* that day.

Then I went to my desk with the morning edition of the *Miami Herald*, looking for a story on the shooting of Tomás Cardenas. There was nothing there.

"Strange," I whispered to myself. It had been three days since I killed the attorney in self-defense. Cardenas was a prominent, well-known attorney. I wasn't exactly an unknown myself—especially to Miami's crime-beat reporters.

A couple of reasons might have explained the story's absence from the paper. The authorities might have asked the paper to hold the story until they could locate Cardenas's family. Or else Aurora's fine hand was at work—she might not have wanted to contaminate her precious grand jury by having them read about the case in the paper, thus leaving open a possible appeal down the road on grounds of bias. I prayed it was the former rather than the latter, but in either case, three days was a long time to hold back such an explosive story.

I wasn't about to complain. The silence worked to my advantage. If I was on the right track in figuring out this case, it was better that no one associate me with Cardenas's death. If my luck was holding, in fact, word of Cardenas's death might not yet have spread.

Tío Ramón still didn't know about the shooting. He had been the one who put me in contact with Tomás, and he might feel responsible for the entire situation. Until I was sure what role Tío Ramón had played in all this, though, I would keep him in the dark.

It was still early when I finished my first coffee. I opened up the window, listened to the parrots' morning songs and squawks. It was so peaceful that I could almost forget about people trying to kill me, or about how far people were willing to go for a piece of property. I tried to keep that feeling close at hand as I picked up the phone and dialed a familiar number from memory.

"Detective Anderson?" I asked as soon as I heard the distinctive grunt of his answering his cell phone. I had tried to call him at his office, but I had learned that he was out in the field.

There was a lot of static on the line, but I thought I heard a sound like an anguished groan when Detective Anderson realized it was me on the line.

"Lupe, please," he said. "It's too early. Just tell me you haven't come up with another dead body."

"No dead bodies," I said. "But listen. I hear that Aurora is going to the grand jury on the Cardenas shooting on Thursday. So I need to try to wrap up this case—before she has a chance to take me down."

I didn't elaborate on how I came to know this piece of sensitive information, and I knew I didn't have to. Detective Anderson wasn't going to press me for details.

"What do you need, Lupe?"

Bless him, he didn't hesitate a second before offering his assistance. If I had ever doubted for a second that the man was true blue, those thoughts were permanently banished.

Although, I had to keep in mind, Detective Anderson had his own motivations—and they didn't have much to do with affection for me. I knew that Detective Anderson's type of by-the-book, hard-bitten cop had little use for lukewarm careerist prosecutors like Aurora—she was just the kind of prosecutor who put her own needs ahead of a particular case's, and was as likely as not to hang a cop out to dry.

I told Detective Anderson just about everything—my suspicions, and how I hoped to lay a trap for the person I thought was responsible for everything that had happened. He listened without comment—which I took as a good sign, considering that I was proposing navigation through some pretty tricky waters.

"Listen, Lupe," Detective Anderson finally said with a sigh. "You just do what you have to do. And don't give me any more details. I might have to try to stop you if you do."

"But I can count on you?" I asked him.

"I've got your back," Detective Anderson said.

Those four words made me feel immeasurably more safe and secure.

"Thanks," I said. "I owe you."

We hung up. I then picked up the phone and placed a call to an old associate I hadn't talked to in a while. I knew he still had a thriving business practice, though, since I had sent him quite a few referrals. Anyone who ever used him came away very pleased with his work.

Spliceman was half man and half ferret, but he was also the maestro of electronics. My heart started thumping as I spoke to him, making plans to visit his workshop in Little Havana. A second call quickly set up another meeting for early the next morning.

Everything was set in motion. I didn't know if I was doing the right thing, or if this was going to be my biggest mistake yet.

One way or the other, it was all about to be resolved. And not a moment too soon.

39

I WAS AS PREPARED AS I WAS EVER GOING TO BE. I said a quick prayer to the Virgin, asking her for help and placing my faith in her. Ever since the second call I placed, I had been consumed with nerves. It was one thing to plan for laying a trap, another still to execute it. I made one last call to Detective Anderson, bringing him up to date. We kept the conversation very vague and circumspect, each of us knowing we had to be sure not to implicate the other.

Then I got in my car. The morning was hot, steamy, the kind of tropical day that made one want to slow down, maybe lounge beside the water somewhere.

Tomorrow, I said to myself.

I had to wait only about ten minutes outside the First Intercontinental Bank before Carlos Suarez arrived. It had been years since I'd last seen him, but I recognized him instantly.

"Lupe Solano," Carlos said with a smile, kissing me on the cheek. A flash of insecurity showed through his veneer of self-confidence and relaxed ease.

Carlos was just a few inches taller than I was—which made him a very short man indeed. He was slight of build, with longish light brown hair that looked professionally

styled. I couldn't see the precise shade of his eyes, because
he was wearing glasses with light green tinted lenses. He
was dressed in dark gray cotton pants, a light gray Calvin
Klein T-shirt, and scuffed brown leather loafers on his
sockless feet.

"Where's Tomás?" Carlos asked, looking around.

I felt something click into place. When I'd mentioned
Tomás Cardenas might join us, Carlos had sounded curious but had given me no indication that he had learned of
the lawyer's death. Now I knew for sure. As far as Carlos
was concerned, Tomás was still among the living.

"I haven't been able to reach him the last couple days,"
Carlos added. He stood up straight, trying to impose a
height advantage over me. Now I was seeing the real Carlos
Suarez—arrogant, aloof, impatient with me already. "I
only came here because I got a message from him telling
me to meet you if you called."

"How gracious of you," I said, barely containing my
feelings. Carlos made a show of looking at his watch, then
regarding me through his tinted lenses with a little sneer
of contempt.

Oh, he felt something closing in, didn't he? He just
didn't know what it was. Not yet, at least.

I had given Spliceman a very limited time in which to
perform another of his miracles, but he had done his
work perfectly. I gave him a couple of tapes of recordings
from Tomás Cardenas still stored on my office voice
mail, then written out what I wanted recorded in Tomás's
voice. It hadn't been a long message, just the following:
"Lupe Solano's calling you this morning. We should go
and meet her."

And it had worked.

And now here was Carlos, alone with me in front of

the bank. I knew about Cardenas, that's why I was there, and Carlos had to suspect I was on to his scheming as well. And Carlos was alone, without his lawyer to back him up. It was fun to watch him squirm and pass it off as superiority.

A steady stream of people kept passing us on either side. The Miami branch of First Intercontinental Bank wasn't in a big building, but it seemed to be very busy for its size. I wasn't expecting physical trouble, but it was reassuring to have so many people around. Although it had almost healed up, I could still feel the bump and cut on my head.

"It's been a long time since we saw each other, Carlos," I said, seeing if he would take the bait.

Carlos shrugged, as though not interested in small talk. He looked around, up and down the street, expecting to see Tomás Cardenas. Well, he was going to wait awhile on that one.

"Tomás is going to be here, right?" Carlos said.

Now it was my turn to shrug. Carlos glanced around, then back at me, and I could tell he realized all wasn't right in his world. His eyes narrowed behind his tinted lenses, making me glad I had chosen a public place to meet.

"Let's not worry about Tomás," I told him. I reached into my purse and took out the safety deposit key. "But he did give me this, so we can go inside the bank together and take out the documents in the box."

Carlos looked completely puzzled as he eyed the key. "Tomás gave you that?" he asked.

I was so nervous that I was chewing the insides of my mouth, making me taste blood. But I couldn't let Carlos see that I was anxious in any way. My entire plan depended on Carlos believing my story about Tomás giving me the key.

"Yes, I got it from him," I said to Carlos. I was careful not to lie, while not divulging any details.

Carlos frowned, but seemed to relax a little bit. If I was having dealings with Tomás, he seemed to figure, then I must have been all right with their plan.

"But why do you want to see the documents?" Carlos asked. "I'm not sure I understand."

My hand wandered to the strap of my brassiere, where I knew the three medals of the Virgin were pinned. Carlos was tensing up again, and I could sense that I was losing him. He was going to bolt, and I was going to have to deal with Aurora.

"I want to see Tomás," Carlos added.

"We probably won't be able to reach Tomás all day. Look, if we're going to be partners, I have to see for myself what's been going on," I said, not really knowing where the words were coming from.

"Partners!" Carlos exclaimed, making a couple of passersby look at us with curiosity.

"Didn't Tomás tell you?" I asked, feigning surprise. "Tomás offered to cut me in on the deal, once I told him what I had found out about your clever little scheme."

Carlos looked up and down the street, as though seeking help dealing with me. He reached into his pocket, and I instinctively tensed. But it was only a cell phone that he pulled out, not a weapon.

"I'm calling Tomás right now," he said. He punched in numbers with angry stabbing gestures. "I don't believe he'd make a deal like that without talking to me first."

I waited silently while the phone rang. And rang. Finally Carlos reached Tomás's voice mail.

"It's Carlos," he said, more an accusation than a statement. "Call me on my cell phone. Right away. Now."

He switched off his phone.

"Look, Carlos," I told him. Enough was enough. "Tomás isn't going to call you back."

"And why is that?" Carlos turned on the phone, probably about to try another number for the deceased lawyer.

"Because he's dead."

Carlos's jaw dropped at the same moment as his phone. I looked down, and saw that Nokia made a pretty sturdy product—it had landed on concrete, bounced three times, and was still in one piece. I bent down to pick it up, then handed it over to Carlos.

"You're full of shit," Carlos said. "Tomás just left a message on my machine this morning."

"Why did you do it?" I asked in a gentle tone, knowing this worked best. "Why did you kill Alexander? Was he going to back out on the deal? Was he threatening to expose you?"

"What are you talking about?" Carlos started backing away from me. "You're crazy. I'm going to find Tomás and then—"

"I'm not crazy," I said, following him. "And neither are you. It was pretty smart, actually, what you planned. But what happened? Did Alexander get jealous when Tomás came into the picture?"

Carlos stopped moving away from me. His face went slack, and in that moment I knew that I had been right. My speculations had just jelled into fact.

I had never felt right about Carlos. I couldn't swallow the party line the family had given me about the lack of contact between him and Alexander. So I had hired Marisol to follow Carlos and see what he was up to in Miami.

Imagine my surprise when she showed me photographs of Carlos and Tomás walking on the beach by Ocean Drive, hand in hand, then locked in an embrace.

The word shock barely describes the reaction I'd felt. I had been really attracted to Tomás Cardenas. I had never for a second suspected that he was gay, and that he was only playing me along in order to find out what information I might have uncovered. I figured it served me right, since I was entertaining thoughts about being unfaithful to my boyfriend, Alvaro, and my lover, Tommy, at the same time.

It had been during my visit to Tomás Cardenas's office with Detective Anderson that I had snooped through the lawyer's calendar and found the name Alexander Suarez corresponding with a date before Alexander's murder. I couldn't account for Alexander's whereabouts during the entirety of his final trip back to Miami, but I knew he had spent his first afternoon with Tomás Cardenas. So the three were definitely linked together.

Carlos folded his arms and shook his head. "You're delusional," he said. "You don't know who you're fucking with."

Carlos wanted to shut me down, but I wouldn't have it. Visions of Aurora dangling handcuffs danced before me.

"Don't walk away, Carlos," I said. "What's going to happen to the hotels if you walk away?"

Carlos's eyes blazed with rage. All around us people walked past, oblivious to the scene we were enacting. If someone had asked me what we were arguing about, what would I have told them? The legacy of families ruined by politics and greed? The lengths to which men would go for money? Or the nature of the relationship between my two male cousins?

"Shut up," Carlos said, moving closer.

"Stop right there," I ordered him. "I'm talking about the deal you're putting together to build hotels with Hotelcuba, the Spanish corporation represented by de Villegas."

"You're full of shit." Carlos took a step back, then moved closer to me. It was as though he was in my orbit, trying to pull away but attracted by the knowledge I possessed about his misdeeds.

"You knew about the deals in Cuba that were being cut every day because of your position at First Intercontinental," I said to Carlos, lowering my voice so that people walking past wouldn't hear. "It must have been painful to watch all those deals being made, while you weren't getting even a little cut of the action."

Carlos cocked his head, and I could see I'd hit the right notes. "If someone's going to profit from Cuba, it should be a Cuban," he said.

"And all the choice properties are being taken," I agreed. "But you had an edge—your family's history in the sugar business."

For a second Carlos looked at me, really looked at me, as though taking my measure. He took a couple of steps toward the bank building and leaned back against the stone facade.

"Is Tomás really dead?" he asked me.

"I wouldn't lie about something like that," I said. "You know, you and Alexander really came up with a brilliant scheme. You'd persuade the owners of sugar mills in Camagüey or near the ocean to sell the old mills to this Spanish corporation. The properties would be evaluated as mills, with little real value. Of course, once this coastal land was starting to be developed, its cost would go up dramatically. You'd be priced out—even at ten cents on the dollar. You knew who owned the old mills, how to contact them, and which ones would be most amenable to selling. That's why the corporation entertained the deal. How much were you getting, Carlos? A finder's fee? Or a real piece of the action?"

Carlos pursed his lips and looked off into the distance. It was hot, no doubt about it, but that didn't entirely account for the sheen of sweat that had formed on his forehead.

"And since Tomás was involved in the sugar-mill owner's group, he was the perfect person to bring on board," I added. "You tempted the old owners who had no money, offering them a little money to pay for their burial and something to leave their grandchildren. Tomás was like a vulture circling around them, pretending to represent their best interests but really finding a way to get them to sell."

"Enough." Carlos raised his hand to silence me. He took a deep breath, then flashed me an enigmatic smile. "Okay. You have it all figured out. Congratulations. So where do you come in?"

"Alexander and Tomás blindsided you, didn't they?" I pressed on. "They went around you and wrote Tío Ramón a letter offering to buy the two mills your family owned in Camagüey. They got greedy. Those two mills are located in prime real estate, a little cove that's tailor-made for a luxury hotel. You see, my guess is that you wouldn't bring your father into this. He's too resourceful. He might hire someone like me to look into things and see what's really going on."

"You think you know everything," Carlos said. "Now how the hell did you get so deep in my business?"

I thought that dragging Tío Ramón into the discussion

would rattle Carlos, but I was wrong. He was nervous and shaken, but I wasn't about to pierce his defenses entirely. Not yet, at least.

"Well, I couldn't figure out why anyone would be interested in investing in Cuba's sugar business," I said. "It was a losing proposition, between the declining industry and all the bullshit an investor would have to go through in dealing with the government."

So far, I wasn't sure that Carlos had said anything deeply incriminating. That had to change, I realized. Carlos seemed to be regaining some of his old confidence.

"You got that right," he snorted. "The sugar business sucks."

"So I made a list of the mills that had received purchase offers," I continued, "then connected the dots. Turns out the mills are located on, or at least near, the coast. That's when I realized the potential investors weren't interested in sugar at all."

I had to talk a little louder as a bus went by. It was strange and surreal, all this everyday life around us while we were having a conversation that was going to change both our lives forever.

"I asked myself: What is Cuba's cash crop?" I said. "And I realized: tourism. After Castro falls, someone is going to get very rich building hotels and resorts on the coast. And that *was* going to be you."

My emphasis on the word *was* seemed to wake Carlos up.

"You're smart, I have to give you that." Carlos flashed a distinctly creepy smile as he adjusted his sunglasses. "But you've just given me a bunch of bullshit speculation. You haven't explained how Alexander died, you haven't explained anything. Now you say Tomás is dead. Maybe he is, maybe he isn't."

Carlos spoke in such a cavalier manner about the dead, I resolved in that moment that I was going to get him. He forgot to add China and de Villegas to the list, but they were going to be avenged as well—if I had anything to do with it.

"Your father killed Alexander," I said. "But not because he was in the business of stealing from his fellow Cubans."

Carlos blinked. "Shut up," he said.

"Your father killed Alexander because he couldn't hide from the truth anymore," I added. "He knew that his son and his brother's son were lovers."

The look of astonishment on Carlos's face spoke volumes.

"My father didn't kill Alexander," he said, moving close, his voice dropping to a whisper. "Tomás did it."

"No, your father did," I said. "Your family has to have been suspicious about you and Alexander for a while—they barely want to speak about either of you. That's why your father lured Alexander to the Ecstasy—to tell him to stay away, or to be done with him once and for all. It wasn't as Tío Ramón claimed, that Alexander had been the one to set up the meeting."

It pained me to say all this, to make these connections, and I couldn't even consider what this was going to do to Papi. For the moment, I just wanted to get through this nightmare and come out on the other side.

Carlos sagged against the wall. He looked at me, suddenly like my cousin and not my enemy.

"I thought for sure Tomás did it," he said. "I was sure my father was innocent, just like he said."

"Tomás got Alexander in touch with your father, Carlos. They were cutting a side deal without you." I was tempted to touch Carlos's arm, to comfort him, but then remembered myself. "So your father requested a meeting at the hotel. I think he was going to try to pin the murder on Tomás—Alexander's business partner—except for the fact that the hooker witnessed the aftermath. That's when your dad really got into a complicated situation."

Something changed in Carlos, some shift that I had seen before, and I knew what it meant: he had accepted his situation. Whatever I was going to ask of him, I was probably going to get. For the moment, though, what I wanted was for him to listen.

"China had been a client of Tomás's," I told Carlos. "He had represented her in a legal problem a few years back, before Tomás made partner at his firm."

It was amazing what one could find with unrestricted access to a suspect's office. I had Detective Anderson to thank.

"China owed Tomás," I said. "So when he needed her services, she was glad to help. Tomás must not have trusted your father, so he brought China to the Ecstasy for backup— it was more her kind of place than Tomás's. The murder meant that the deal with Tío Ramón had fallen through, but at least Tomás had gotten rid of one of his business partners. And then, after your father was convicted of the crime, the Suarez family properties would be yours to dispense with—as the designated family trustee, no one was going to challenge you. China probably tried to get some money out of the situation and that was what got her killed. She didn't realize what coldhearted bastards she was dealing with."

I felt a pang of responsibility for China's death. After I had gone to see her, she had realized that she was sitting on potentially valuable testimony. She must have contacted Tío Ramón and told him that she was going to reveal the truth about what she had seen at the Ecstasy: that Alexander had been alive when Tío Ramón entered Room 7.

"And you were the one who killed China, Carlos," I said, eliciting no immediate reaction. "She told Tomás that I had been to see her, that she knew what was going on. But she made a mistake. She thought she could play each side against the other."

"She was a whore," Carlos whispered, looking down at the pavement. "She shouldn't have . . ."

His voice trailed off.

"You killed her to protect your father," I said. "She was threatening to testify against him. You say you thought that Tomás had killed Alexander—well, I can see that. Alexander was excitable, maybe he was going to tell your father more about the mills than Tomás wanted him to know. But your father didn't care about that. What disgusted him was the fact that Alexander was having an affair with his son."

Carlos looked away.

"When Alexander and your father fought a few months ago at your family house, it wasn't about money. Was it?"

Carlos shook his head. "No," he whispered.

"Your father knew," I said. "He told Alexander to stay away from you. He threatened his life."

Carlos's lips moved, but no sounds came out.

"And Tomás killed de Villegas," I added. "As American citizens, you couldn't invest in Cuba because it would be a violation of the Helms-Burton Bill. You could establish an offshore corporation, but as soon as it was known that Cuban-Americans were behind it, the whole thing would fall apart. I figure de Villegas must have come to tell you that he and his firm didn't want to be your point men anymore. He probably even said he was going to report the plan to the U.S. government. That was enough to get him knocked off."

Time was up. I wanted Carlos to answer more questions for me, but the day was waning. I needed to get to Detective Anderson. Carlos hadn't said much that was particularly incriminating, but it would have to do.

"I was too close to the truth," I said. "And that's why Tomás decided I had to be killed."

Carlos straightened up and looked around.

"Actually, that's not entirely true," he said.

"What do you mean?"

With that, he reached around behind him and pulled out a small handgun from the waistband of his pants. I had no time to do anything as he looked me in the eye, pointed the gun at me, and shot me.

40

IF I LAY VERY STILL. NOT BREATHING AND NOT moving and concentrating very intently, I was able to hear what was going on around me. I tried to open my eyes but couldn't coordinate the muscles I needed to do so. I could identify the voices of my family someplace nearby, especially that of my sister Lourdes leading them in prayer. I must have been hallucinating, though, because I was able to pick out Mami's voice saying the rosary. It made no sense. I remembered that she was dead. Now that I thought about it, none of this made any sense at all.

I was numb, no sensation in my body. It was then that I got really frightened for the first time. I mustered all my willpower to conquer a rising tide of panic. I told myself this was all temporary and that I would soon be my old self again. Still I heard my family praying for me, instilling more worry than comfort.

I tried desperately again to open my eyes and look around. I needed to figure out what had happened to me, but it was too difficult. I could think, I knew who I was, but my senses slipped away the harder I tried to grasp them. It was all too exhausting, I thought. And that was all for a while. Some time passed, though I was unaware of it.

WHEN I OPENED MY EYES. EVERYTHING AROUND ME WAS WHITE. I thought I had died and gone to heaven, but that didn't seem too likely—not with my recent track record on Earth. The pain I felt all over clinched it. I knew heaven wasn't supposed to hurt.

Keeping my eyes open required too much effort, so I closed them again and drifted off. I was never too comfortable with white, anyway.

I heard swooshing and beeping sounds that I eventually realized were machines and indistinct voices in the background. It seemed I was lying immobile in a hospital bed. Fine, I thought. No need to go anywhere. Or do anything. Like Leonardo's spa idea, although I was pretty sure he wouldn't want to join me.

I WOKE UP AGAIN. MY MEMORY WAS WORKING A LITTLE BETTER: I started to recall talking with Carlos Suarez, and all the accusations I had made. I remembered him shooting me. It had felt like a giant fist punching me right in the chest.

After I fell to the ground, chaos had broken out. I blacked out, then looked up to see a face bending over me, blocking out the sun.

"Detective Anderson," I had said. "The tape. Get the tape."

I wanted to make sure that the wires Spliceman had attached to my body were intact. Carlos hadn't made a complete confession, but I knew there was enough to have him arrested—for shooting me, if nothing else.

"We got it," Detective Anderson had said as he felt for the wire. "It's here."

I had passed out with visions of Aurora dancing in my eyes again. This time, I was laughing at her. She wasn't going to get me. Not this time.

I DON'T KNOW HOW MUCH MORE TIME PASSED BEFORE I regained consciousness. I opened up my eyes and tried to focus on the hospital room. I saw a table, a chair. And a man sitting in it.

"Lupe, you're awake," Detective Anderson said with obvious relief.

"Hi," I answered. I turned my head a couple of inches. "What's going on?"

"You got shot, but the doctors say you're going to be okay. You're going to need some time to recuperate, but there's no permanent damage." His eyes bored into mine. "Your family just left. They were here—all of them—for two days and two nights without leaving your side. The doctor finally sent them home to sleep, after about an hour of convincing them you were going to be all right. I told them I'd stay in case you woke up."

"And they obeyed?" It seemed so out of character.

"They didn't want to, actually, so I told them I'd arrest them and throw them in jail if they didn't." Detective Anderson paused and allowed himself the shadow of a grin.

"Thanks. Otherwise they never would have left," I told him. And then I thought about what he'd said. Two days! I had no memory of all that time passing.

I lay back and thought about my last recollection— Carlos Suarez shooting me.

"What about the Suarez case?" I asked. In spite of my state, I needed to know. Tommy had once called me relentless. I had been a little offended at the time, but there was an element of truth in what he had said.

"Ramón and Carlos are in custody, charged with multiple counts of murder." Detective Anderson folded his arms and leaned forward a little. In the harsh fluorescent hospital light he looked more haggard and rumpled than ever.

"And Aurora?" I dreaded even saying her name. I heard the heart monitor in the corner pick up its rhythm.

"She isn't going to be a problem. I took care of her," said Detective Anderson. I must have looked skeptical, because he added, "A couple of years ago Aurora screwed up big-time on a major case and I saved her ass. She owes me, and I called in the favor."

As soon as I registered what Detective Anderson had said, the beeping heart monitor returned to normal. Talking so much was more effort than I had realized, and I felt my eyes close involuntarily. I opened them again and saw Detective Anderson staring at me.

"No more bodies, huh?" I whispered to him. "This one is still alive."

"Don't joke like that," Detective Anderson said. He sat on the bed next to me and took my hand. "You almost died."

"So that would have bothered you so much?" I said, my voice feeling a little stronger. "Too much paperwork?"

Detective Anderson shifted on the bed so his face was close to mine. His hand held mine tighter.

"Don't say that," he said. "I would have been . . . I would have been devastated if anything happened to you."

Through the fog, I repeated what he had said in my head. I was stunned.

"You care?" I asked. "So it's not just about the body count?"

"I care a lot," Detective Anderson said. He leaned close and lightly kissed my lips. "When you're out of here, I hope you'll let me show you how I feel. Life is too short. I've learned that."

Dios mío. I drifted off.

When I woke up, he was still there. This time it was I

who reached for the detective's hand and squeezed it. I looked into his eyes, saw the affection there that I had never noticed before.

"Detective Anderson," I said in a dreamy voice. "So what's your first name, anyway?"

"It's Maxwell, Lupe," he replied. "Maxwell."

And he gave me a smile that I had never seen cross his face before. I decided that he was going to have to get rid of all those old khaki suits, if there was ever going to be any hope for us. Then I drifted off again.